I0593192

A Wild Ride To Love

Deep in the heart of the tropics, paradise is not what it seems.

Brenda May

COPYRIGHT

C opyright © 2021 Brenda May
     The rights of Brenda May to be identified as the author of this work has been asserted by her in accordance with the Copyrights, Designs and Patents Act of 1988.

All rights reserved. No portion of this book may be reproduced in any form without written permission from the author, except as permitted by Australian copyright law.

A record of this title is held at the National Library of Australia (Ebook) and the State Library of Queensland (Print and Ebook)

Disclaimer:

This book is a work of fiction. While the place names are real, the characters, events and specific homes are invented by the author and any resemblance to reality is purely coincidental.

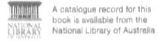 A catalogue record for this book is available from the National Library of Australia

DEDICATION

Dedicated to Vanessa Taylor, lifelong friend and recently departed from this plane of existence. A lover of the written word and forever in my heart. Safe journey my friend.

I also dedicate this book to my daughters Jenna and Caitlin. Many times they waited patiently in the growing dark for their dinner. "Just one more paragraph girls"...wink.

CHAPTER 1

"I'm looking for Joe."

Blocked from view by the milling crowd, Jo smiled. Sometimes it paid to be small.

The raucous male voice continued to probe the spectators. "Heard he thinks he's the best on the track." The arrogant tone held the impression of someone ripe and ready for battle.

Jo leaned comfortably against her trail bike waiting for the right time to make her presence known. This was her racetrack, her turf, and she wasn't going to let some idiot from an invading bikie gang spoil what had been a day of exhilarating competitive fun.

"Where the hell are ya' Joe; man up." Annoyance laced with sarcasm dominated the challenge. It was followed by a loud tinny whine, and by the dust rising into the clear blue sky, she figured he was doing donuts.

With an un-ladylike snort Jo stood, facing the direction of the commotion. Enough with the foul language and childish antics. Time to meet her foe, and time for her foe to be floored by the fact he was going to have to race a woman.

"If you want to race the best, you'll be racing me." The authority in her voice rose above the excited chatter of the growing crowd and settled on her intended target. Adrenalin spiked and an air of unusual reservation ricocheted through her body as the rebel turned and made eye contact. He radiated pure power that seemed to grow as he advanced with slow purpose toward her. Like the Red Sea the spectators parted, and a hushed murmur fell in his wake.

Jo barely felt the supportive claps on her shoulders. She stood her ground, determined not to be intimidated by the six foot plus overdose of testosterone. Hell, she'd grown up with five older brothers, military style.

His, "who in the fuck are you?" stirred her up even more.

Flicking back long fiery hair, purposely left untied for dramatic effect, she tilted her head, squinting against the hot tropical sun. She stood unyielding, hands on hips and feet apart. "I'm Jo. You want to race the top rider?" She did her best impression of being taller than her five-foot three frame. "Well, that's me. I'm Jo. And I am the best." She finished the statement with a tightening of lips and a stubborn lift to her chin as she glared up at him.

A cold expressionless mask stared back. Intense arctic eyes chewed into her resolve and she fought the urge not to be the first to turn away. Unable to detect any reaction to the fact a female stood before him instead of the expected male, not only pissed her off, but unnerved her as well.

She almost sighed with relief when the intensity of the contact altered. Her reprieve was short lived as his mouth lifted in one corner, producing a mischievous smile with the hint of the devil dancing in his blue eyes.

"I'm sure you are the best, darlin'."

His deliberate low smoky tone rippled over her nerve endings. Her retort to the degenerative endearment died on her lips as feather light sensations pricked at her skin in the wake of his wandering gaze. His unhurried journey seemed to scrutinise every minute detail of her body, annoying her even more.

She always dressed for practical comfortable. Well-worn faded jeans tucked into her boots, plain t-shirt and leather jacket. Standard racetrack attire before the protective gear was added, and if he didn't drag his eyes back up to her face quick smart, she would slog him one.

Her fists clenched.

His nose flared and his eyes widened as they lingered on her chest. She cursed as her nipples puckered with betrayal and hoped to hell they were covered enough by her jacket that he wouldn't notice. She certainly wasn't going to embarrass herself by checking. Jo gritted her teeth trying her best to ignore the growing fire in her cheeks and the awareness his scrutiny stirred. She drew on her preferred companion. Anger.

How dare he! First, he and his idiot friends invade the fun filled, trouble free trail bike championships, creating noise and havoc as they showed off their 'supposedly' superior skills in the dusty car park. Now, this hulking giant, who she presumed was the leader, was arrogantly demanding to pit himself against the best. Well, that was her, Josephine Brennan, and if he didn't like it, he could back right off.

She toughened her stance, only to find her face burning hotter as he mixed honey into his smoky tone.

"Do you ride as good as you look?" He moved closer, towering over her until he blocked the mid-afternoon sun from her view.

Not one to back down, she saw no alternative but to play the game he'd set. She breathed calmly and relaxed her shoulders, flicked at an inconsequential piece of dust on the leg of her jeans. "You have the finesse of a flea and are as subtle as a pair of hessian underpants," she countered in an exaggerated bored monotone. "Are we going to race, or what?"

A laugh burst from his rugged features completely changing his harsh lines and she had the feeling he hadn't laughed in a long time.

"For now." The coldness crept back into his voice as he said, "I think we'll race."

Jo knew she had the crowd's excitement behind her as the rebel arched his dusty leg over an even dirtier bike. His smile echoed the chill in his eyes as he removed his leather jacket and tossed it aside to reveal a skintight t-shirt, emblazoned with the words 'Born to Ride' on the back.

She almost forgot to breathe. What she had thought was the bulk of his clothes turned out to be solid muscle, well-toned and clearly defined. Her brothers were just as tall and muscular, but the Kilimanjaro's on this bad boy positively called out for attention. Tattoos branded his bare arms, bold and confident, enhancing his stance as a force to be reckoned with. She shut her mouth and swallowed, remembering at last to take a breath, angry at herself for the mocking knowledge glinting in his eyes.

Tying back her hair with a green silk scarf, she gave the aggressive stranger sitting astride his bike a harsh stare. He was as dangerous and as tough as the trail and a surge of adrenaline flared to meet his challenge.

Her face burned with anticipation and excitement as she discarded her leather jacket and secured her helmet, imitating his expression. She threw caution to the wind, knowing it was madness to race without full protective clothing, but his defiance had to be met and his attitude rekindled the wild streak she always had growing up.

Jo adjusted her goggles, pulling the thick elastic strap over the back of the helmet to keep them in place and straddled her bike.

"Go Phantom," one of his mates yelled, "She's just a fuckin' girl."

She rolled her eyes at his name, but the 'just a girl' remark fuelled the fire in her belly. "At least wear your goggles.' Cause you'll be eating my dust." The words were almost lost in spin of her back wheel as a cloud of dry dirt billowed up behind her.

Jo shot a quick glance in his direction as he drew level at the start line and revved her engine back at him, more determined than ever to wipe the sardonic smile off his face. There was no time for further thought as the sudden bang of the starter's gun combined with the noise of the motors drowned out her shout of exhilaration as the contest began.

The Townsville racetrack was one of the best in Australia, the toughest in Queensland. Set on the outskirts of town, the course wound precariously up the steep sides of a tree studded, rock strewn hill. Its valleys and gullies crisscrossed with creeks and streams made for a tough and diverse terrain. In the wet season the track was used for mud racing, to see who could get the furthermost without collapsing in the glutinous slosh. These races were fun, drawing huge crowds of both participants and observers. It usually ended up with plenty of laughter and everyone covered in slimy red from head to toe. Late in the season, this was the last organised race before the heavy summer rains came. Now, the track was sun baked dry and as dusty as hell.

Jo led through the sand drift and the first two creek crossings; her opponent tucked in close for the third. With an inborn awareness she sensed his next move just a fraction before it happened and mentally kicked herself for thinking this beginning circuit would take a moderate pace. Already committed to the crossing, she went down the incline and into the shallows of the firm bottomed creek, water spraying up high behind her and as she emerged and started to climb the bank at the other side, she saw him shoot past in a blaze of speed. He had taken the fools folly, a thin bridge which spanned the creek and left no room for error.

The overpass, although narrow didn't create the problem, the exit did as the wooden planks ended just short of the track. Executing the jump to perfection, he slid around the corner with his body in ideal balance, low to the ground. The sand mound, which often collected many riders, was safely behind him as he sped off a good few meters in front of her.

With a scowl of self-disgust, all Jo could do was sit behind him, cursing under her breath, weaving back and forth between the huge boulders as they took the slow climb up the steep path to the top of the hill. The race was not over yet, they still had a long way to go and there was no way she would give him an inch. His determination, visible in the set of his broad shoulders, and his large body handling the exertion of twisting his heavier bike this way and that with ease pissed her off, so she applied more pressure, sticking so close behind their wheels were almost touching.

Beginning the downhill descent was slow going and treacherous, requiring skill and daring to gain any speed at all. Rear wheels spun out sideways on the steep grade, and they hugged the wall of the hill as the tree filled gully fell sharply away at the tracks edge. Just before the track widened and as they manoeuvred their machines around the bend towards the fourth creek crossing, Jo swung to the outside edge, forcing him to stay on her right giving her the advantage she sought. Phantom had no choice but to continue along the easier, well-worn trail through the creek bed, while she took the quicker but harder track straight ahead to the jump ramp, enabling her to cross the wide part of the creek in a flying leap giving her the lead once again. Sailing through the air, body down low against the bike she landed clean on the other side, stabilising herself with an outstretched foot as she swung back on to the track, just seconds ahead of him.

A smile of triumph crossed her face as she heard the commentators' voice over the loudspeaker system, the words were all jumbled together but she knew they would be cheering her on against the challenging bikie. The track was fast again now, the decline gradual as they raced, leaping with controlled grace as they sped over the rolling jump mounds and around the last corner to the home stretch. A third of the race was over as they roared past the start line.

Phantom's bike, obviously more powerful on the straight, drew easily ahead and the crowd cheering in flashes of colour and noise urged them on. His huge machine, almost too fast and bulky for track racing, needed all his skill and strength to control it as he spun around the first corner in front of her, she stuck close to his heels, quick and deft, her small frame matching the light weight agility of her bike.

It wasn't just her competitive spirit that sent the blood running through her veins; it was the knowledge that she would have to draw on all her racing skills to match his raw dynamic power.

He's playing games, she thought with astonishment as she was handed the lead with blatant ease, the notion of it sending a strong wave of apprehension all the way down her spine. Having surprised her on the first round by choosing the fools folly, she had expected him to do it again, but this time he had taken the creek, and left her to make the jump and take the lead. She could hear the crowd going wild with excitement.

"He is playing games with me," she muttered, unsure of whether to be angry or amused. It wasn't as if he wasn't competing, far from it, this was the fastest and hardest she had ever ridden, but he seemed to be taking it all in his stride as if he didn't really care about the outcome. *Well I do!* Then she smiled as realisation ricocheted through her. Knowing the real contest wouldn't begin until the final round, she relaxed, not realising how tense she had been and enjoyed the feeling of abandonment as she accepted the unspoken conditions he set.

"So, you want to play?" She yelled over her shoulder. Without losing speed she veered down to the creek, allowing him to take the jump ramp, his laugh of pleasure teased her emotions as he flew past. They played it that way to the end of the second circuit, never relenting in speed or intensity, but allowing each other to pass like a couple of kids enjoying a game of tag. They finished the second round as they had begun... Even.

CHAPTER 2

J o knew the crowd would be listening to the loudspeakers as the commentators reported the race's progress. It was impossible for everyone to see the whole race. Observation bays had been constructed at the most thrilling jumps and turns and from the open veranda of the club rooms, huge screens adorned each end, providing coverage for spectators who preferred cool, clean comfort. She heard their roar as they raced neck and neck down the home straight.

Just as she began to wonder why he didn't pass, Phantom opened up the throttle and leapt ahead as they began the circuit for the final time. Jo knew the track like the back of her hand but racing against him elevated it to a whole new level. With five older brothers and belonging to an extremely competitive family, Jo always strived a little harder to keep up with their father's expectations. Although she was as rough and as tough as her siblings, she was always being told she held a little bit back in reserve. Not today. She could feel the fire in her veins and the determination to make not just her father, but herself proud. She had to win against the intruder at all cost.

More familiar now with the layout, Phantom stretched his skills to the max, using brake and throttle to perfection. Itching to pass him, Jo stuck so close, you wouldn't be able to put a pin head between them. The fools' folly loomed ahead. She wasn't surprised when he took the quicker track over the bridge, this round was all or nothing. Committed to the win, she stuck like an angry hornet behind him. No way would she take the slower route.

Wheels clunked over the wooden planks, went silent as she was in the air, and for a moment when landing, there was the thought she would be able to take him as they slid around the corner. He retained his lead and she stayed hot on his heels.

The track narrowed, winding as they climbed the hillside. Once around the hairpin bend, she twisted and turned into the next few corners, trying to nudge through on the inside. He hugged close to the hillside blocking her attempts. Her mind raced ahead and as they approached the last corner before the straight and the ramp to the flying fox, she dropped back a gear, swung precariously close to the steep drop off on the outside edge, twisted the throttle and leapt forward drawing level with him.

Bits of dirt and rubble tumbled over the edge as she pushed her bike to the limit. Once they hit the straight he used the raw power of his machine, but instead of roaring ahead, he cut across in front and slowed slightly. Jo swore out loud, having no choice but to move back towards the safety of the hillside. Instead of sitting snug behind him, she took advantage of his slowed speed, zooming ahead and slipped back in front and to the outer edge as the track widened, giving her the advantage to take the Flying Fox.

He drew level refusing to give ground as they hit the ramp together. Jo could see him out the corner of her eye as they became airborne, then lost sight of him as she landed, spinning a flurry of dust in his direction as the track turned sharp left. Having the inside edge put her ahead in the lead up to the rolling jump mounds.

Jo had never in her entire life been on such a high. Adrenaline was running triple time. The desire to win so strong it blocked all other thought. She couldn't conceal her wild excitement as she shot a glance at the devil racing beside her.

Their eyes met for barely a second and his were as wild as hers felt and for a moment frozen in time they were as one, united with the wind, running wild and free defying death and re-grasping life all in one fluent rolling motion. Then they were apart again, and his laugh sounded loud and genuine as they rounded the last corner to the home straight.

To the cheers of the frenzied crowd they sped towards the finish post.

Jo knew he was going to win. His bike had the power to outrun hers on the straight. She felt no disappointment, only a strange unity with the man riding behind her and an overwhelming sense of satisfaction for pushing herself to the limit. Adrenalin was still running rampant and she braced herself for his roar of triumph as he speed past.

It didn't happen.

He hung half a bike length behind and off a little to the right, avoiding the bulk of the dust billowing behind her. He grinned as she glanced backwards, his teeth white and even flashed against the dirt brown that covered his face.

He was letting her win.

The realisation was like crashing into a solid brick wall at high speed, and for a split-second shock made her slow to react.

"No!" she screamed, anger making the move dangerous and aggressive as the hard pressure on the brakes and the simultaneous releasing of the throttle threw her into a tailspin, almost collecting the still grinning rider as he veered sharply out of harm's way. The rear of her bike spun around in a one-hundred-and-eighty-degree slide, spraying fine red dust in a billowing cloud towards the crowd, effectively blocking them from view. As her bike came to a standstill facing the direction they had just come, she knew it had been too late. They had already passed the finishing post and she had won.

Disregarding her bike and helmet Jo let them fall to the ground, her body still pumping with adrenaline, seethed with anger and disappointment. A whirlwind of conflicting emotions surfaced then dived again before she could get a grasp on what they were. Through a haze of confusion she watched him dismount, heave his bike onto its stand, hang his helmet on the handlebar, then lean with easy comfort against the seat, legs outstretched and arms crossed over his broad chest.

She felt betrayed but couldn't work out why, almost understanding what he had done but not quite able to put her finger on it. Anger surfaced again, and this time Jo grasped at it like a lifeline, reeling it in until it fuelled her body into action.

Five foot three inches of stomping fury arrived at his feet as he rose effortlessly, standing tall and undaunted. Green eyes flashed a warning of what was to come as she clenched her fists tight at her side and looked up to stare him directly in the eyes. The fact that he towered over her didn't register. She was used to dealing with tall, hulky men, all of her brothers and her father hit the six foot plus and topped the muscle-bound scale and it simply didn't occur to her to be intimidated by his size.

"That was the best race of my life and you go and destroy it with a blatant act of outdated chauvinism, you...you inconsiderate, feeble excuse of a pig-headed male." Jo's voice rode fire, her fingers dug into the palms of her hands. "How dare you let me win."

Her words seemed to fly over the top of his head as he looked down at her, his body language oozed amusement, and the slow sexy smile that crept to his lips was too much for her to handle. With a speed born from years of diligent practice, her right arm flew towards his chin, body tensed for impact as she threw all of her fifty-five kilos behind the swing. His throaty chuckle did nothing to stem her fury as he side stepped the move with equal speed causing her to fall unbalanced against his chest. He reacted just as quickly as she tried to thrust her knee up between his legs.

"Hey Wildcat, that's playing dirty." He whispered as he drew her body so close to his it was impossible to move.

Momentarily stunned, Jo couldn't believe she had missed. She was fast and accurate but certainly hadn't counted on being beaten the first time she attempted to use it.

Groaning in sheer frustration as his grip tightened to counter her struggle, she froze. Confusion reigned, every nerve ending went on red alert as his arms shifted to hold her in a possessive circle. Her head came under his chin. One large hand slid sensually over her buttocks pulling her lower torso into binding contact with his, showing her in no uncertain terms his desire to have no barrier at all between them.

His other arm firm against her back pinned her to his chest, his hand nestling up under the hairline at the base of her neck.

"Who's playing dirty now?" Her words were muffled against his heart, which beat in fast unison with hers. Instead of answering he ever so slightly ground his hips in a firm rotation causing her to gasp as flames of pleasure shot high up the length of her spine, only to contract again into a ball of white heat as the hand at her nape grasped a handful of hair, pulling her head back.

"Just say the word Wildcat and I will let you go."

His words washed over her, and sensations ran wild as his mouth lowered towards her. Panic set in as she fought for a rational emotion. Controlled anger came to her rescue as the pressure on her back eased, allowing some movement of her arms. Actions spoke louder than words, she brought her hand up under his shirt in what she hoped was a seductive movement to the sensitive area just under his arm. His low growl of delight turned to a yelp of pain as her fingernails sank into the tender flesh.

"Fuck," he bellowed, pulling back to clench the offending hand in a blood cutting grip. Expecting to feel the full force of his aggression, Jo closed her eyes already regretting the separating of their bodies. She waited for retaliation, preferring passing pain to the alien emotions he was evoking.

Nothing happened.

Jo felt her hair being released in a lingering caress. The gentle pressure of strong fingers opening her still clenched fist and the sensual smoky tone of his voice compelled her to open her eyes.

"Lucky for you, this is the wrong time and place." His words held a hint of a promise of things still to come. For a moment Jo thought she saw deep regret in his eyes before a shutter was drawn and she was left on the outside, cold and alone. An odd sensation flickered through her body.

It was with a strange detachment, she watched him lower his mouth towards the open palm of her imprisoned hand. She saw rather than felt the warmth of his breath as he kissed the indentations her fingernails had made. He raised her hand to place it on top of the area she had pinched. His heart pounded a strong, steady rhythm beneath her fingers. Sensations overloaded, the intimacy of his actions ignited a flame of panic causing her to rip her hand out of his grasp and step back a pace.

"After today, I don't expect to see you again, so you can cut out the pathetic 'wrong time and place' crap and go back to whatever hell-hole you crawled out of." Jo glared with all the hatred she could muster.

"I guess 'or what' is out of the question then?" The smile accompanying his suggestive words didn't reach his eyes and he was back to the arrogant male he had been before the race.

Jo felt the strength of her own personal space returning. Ignoring the fire in her cheeks she said, "All I ask for is honesty, I won't accept winning the race." She adorned a glacial look that most men backed down from. Her fierce eyes never left his as she unpinned the track badge from her dust encrusted shirt.

Their eyes locked in a duel surpassing anything she had ever encountered, and a slight smile lifted the corners of her mouth. Jo knew she had great inner strength, once her wall of defence was up, not even a bulldozer could knock it down. Phantom's eyes widened, and then accepted her challenge with a grin that matched her own.

Although he didn't step any closer, Jo felt as though she were being smothered.

Sensations alien to her sky-rocketed, instead of confusion and anger, this time Jo recognised the feeling for what it was... desire. Everywhere his eyes went the sensations followed, devouring every part of her body in a way so intimate, it was as though he was touching her. It left her defenceless. This man had found the one element where she was way out of her depth and she faltered not knowing how to respond. Not knowing if she really wanted to. For the first time in her adult life a man had the upper edge, and with it the power to make her conform to his will and it scared her.

Jo went on the defensive.

"This belongs to you." She threw the track record badge directly at him. It bounced against his chest before settling in a puff of dust at his feet. His grin widened, turning him devastatingly handsome and she knew that he had sensed her fear and it excited him. Abruptly the spell between them broke as Phantom's line of vision shifted over her shoulder to the approaching crowd.

"Party's over for now," his whisper carried clearly across the small distance between them. "Meet me tonight and we can put our thoughts into action."

"Go to hell..." She spoke through gritted teeth as she turned her back on him to greet the enthusiastic crowd.

"Been there, didn't like it."

Jo gasped as his hand threaded through her hair. She stiffened half turning towards him, her mouth wide open ready to protest. Too late she saw the mocking humour in his eyes as his deft hands undid the ribbon releasing her hair to cascade down her back.

"The colour will remind me of your eyes Wildcat, when they are begging for what you so obviously want." Phantom pushed her gently towards the approaching crowd. "Ask Kevin where to find me if you want it back."

CHAPTER 3

Scanning the spectators looking for Kevin, Jo could feel Phantom walking close behind cramping her personal space. She stomped a little faster, dodging in and out of the congratulating crowd, stepping on elongated shadows as the late afternoon sun broke through a dip in the distant hills.

Phantoms', 'ask Kevin where to find me,' stewed in her mind. How in the hell did he know her brother? Kevin certainly hadn't let on when he had encouraged her to race this man, laughed and joked about how cool it would be, like old times, if the idiot didn't know he was racing a woman. She smelt a rat, and she intended to put a stop to whatever game he was playing.

"You seen Kevin?" She asked a familiar face as he clapped her on the back telling her it was an awesome race; then walked on when he shook his head.

"Great race..."

"Haven't seen you on the track for a while..."

"You still got it girlfriend..." Jo acknowledged them all with a wave of her hand and a fake smile. She was fuming and cursed being small. Couldn't see a damn thing in this crowd.

Maybe he was hiding in the club rooms. Now she was on the move, her anger began to disperse. Holly shoot that had been a race and a half, adrenaline continued to roar though her body, and she had to admit it had felt good giving the track everything she had, despite the ending. Racing up the steps she stopped almost at the top and turned to scan the crowd. Even from this height advantage she couldn't see Kevin.

The Phantom however was a beacon. His gang were laughing and goofing around, but he stood apart, arms folded, leaning back against his bike as if nothing in the world bothered him. She felt a bit silly; he hadn't even followed her as she thought. As if he could feel her eyes upon him, he turned giving her a mock salute.

Did he know she came from a military background? She glared at him a little longer, before shrugging it off, no way he could know. It wasn't common knowledge. Not with the field of work her father was in. Everything was hush hush, something to do with national security. All her older brothers except Kevin were involved in either the military or some government business.

Jo had never wanted any part of it. Not that there was a lot of choice growing up. The strict military schools, the training camps, designed to make boys into men. The fact her father's sixth child happened to be a girl made no difference.

A twinge of nostalgia flicked over her heart as she kept scanning the crowd for Kevin. What if she had grown up with a mother instead of in a house full of testosterone? She tried to push the yearning away, knowing it would lead to a more recent tragedy. The thoughts persisted and she resigned to let them run their course so she could release them and move forward. She had, at least, learned that much over the last few months.

Her mother at eight months pregnant, had been killed in a car accident. Well protected inside the womb, she had survived. Her father named her Josephine in his wife's memory. Then, nicknaming her Jo, proceeded to treat her as he had all his other sons, disregarding her sex as an unimportant obstacle that simply wasn't worth worrying about.

As she grew, her eleven-year-old brother Robert Jnr., would tell beautiful stories of the memories he had. Stephen only a year younger would often interrupt with a tale of his own. The twins Matthew and Patrick...and there it was.

She sucked in a breath.

Patrick. A spear of sorrow stabbed her heart and she sat on the step waiting for it to flow through and out of her body.

It had been just over a year since he had lost his life. Five years her senior, full of fun and laughter, snuffed out in a boating accident. She missed him, and knew she wasn't the only one, her whole family had been rocked to the core, each dealing with the loss of a sibling in their own way. Twenty-eight was too young to die.

Breathing deep, she embraced the here and now, thinking of the positive things in her life. She adored her family above all else and looking back, she had thrived on the physical side her upbringing provided. The last few years as a personal trainer had been rewarding mentally and physically. There was nothing she liked better than helping others achieve health and fitness. Patrick and her mother would be proud.

She stood, looked up into the darkening sky for a moment before scanning the dispersing crowd one last time, turning she went up the last few steps, hopefully Kevin was inside.

The welcoming embrace of cold air danced over the sweat on her skin giving her instant relief. It might be getting dark, but it was still as hot as blazes outside. Covered from head to toe in dust, sweat and dirt she desperately needed a shower.

"G'day Mac." Jo waved in the direction of the barman. A few others milled around the club room setting up for the race presentations and the all-night dance party that would follow. "Seen Kevin?"

"He's upstairs; great race, we watched from the screens." Mac flicked his head towards the large TV set into a wooden wall off to one side of the bar. "Man, that was some race. What happened at the end? The cameras were covered by dust. You were both winners, smashed the track times, calling it a draw. Bit of a gentleman letting you greet the crown first."

Jo snorted, "He's not a gentleman..." her words faded away as she remembered his slow sexy smile, "definitely not." She pulled herself together, unclipped the rope barrier and made her way up the curved dark wood staircase leading to the VIP lounges. Kevin stood with his back to her looking out one of the windows that framed the race grounds.

Out of the blue she realised how distant she'd become. How little she had seen of her family as she was too caught up in her own self-absorbed grief. Encouraged back to the racetrack by Kevin a few weeks ago, she knew now, she not only missed the thrill of the race, but the companionship of her closest brother and the loving bond with her family. Looking at Kevin as he turned towards her, she was no longer angry and slipped into the role of annoyed best friend.

"So where and how do you know Phantom?"

At least he had the grace to look contrite, he might be older by eleven months but the closeness they had growing up always saw her take the lead, even if it was into mischief. They always bailed each other out. She saw a difference in him now. He pulled up tall and straight, looked her in the eye and said the last thing she expected to hear.

"Straight to the chase as always hey Jo. Dads in VIP 1. He wants to see you after you have cleaned up."

"Dads here? Why? Is everything ok?" Jo caught her breath and squeezed his arm. "You look pale, what's happened?"

"Jo, nothing's wrong, the family's fine. Promise. Just get cleaned up." There was a slight hitch in his voice as he said. "Dad just wants to see you about something."

She immediately felt relieved, then smelt that rat. Too much of a coincidence him being here today of all days and Kevin knowing Phantom. "Why don't you just tell me how you know that idiot biker?"

"Come on Jo. Don't be stubborn. Dads waiting."

"Stubborn!" Her temper flared. "I'll show you stubborn." She stormed to the door of the VIP room totally convinced her father was behind this shenanigan and wanted to get to the bottom of it.

"Jo don't..."

She stopped with her hand on the door handle. There was something in his voice that made her turn and look back.

"Just get cleaned up and listen to what he has to say. Please."

It wasn't so much the plea in his voice, but the fact there was something obviously happening, and it was upsetting him. He was totally on edge. "Fine, but you're coming with me, I have a few questions that need answers." She walked off expecting him to follow.

Kevin opened the door to the small two bedroom self-contained unit, various members of the family used when they were in town. Jo turned on him as soon as they were inside. "Phantom, is that really his name?" She didn't bother waiting for an answer, "he called you by name and said you'd know where to find him later."

"Let it rest Jo. Clean clothes are in the bathroom."

"You really are prepared, aren't you, I was going to go home after the race." She plonked herself down on the edge of the bath and took off her boots and socks, careful not to get too much dust on the cream tiles. Despite not being happy with what was happening she trusted her brother and her family completely.

"So, can you tell me anything?"

"Patience never was a strong point with you."

She heard him sigh and waited, knowing victory was close.

"Yes, I know the gang. I have been hanging out with them on and off for a couple of months."

"So that's where you've been disappearing to on the weekends." Jo gave him a big grin. He might annoy the hell out of her, but she could never stay mad at him for long. He might be her brother, but was also her closest friend.

"I've been doing modifications to their bikes."

"And here I was thinking you had a secret girlfriend."

She could hear amusement in Kevin's voice and saw it in the crinkle of his eyes.

"Still playing the field, when I do, you'll be the first to know." He turned away, hesitated and turned back again. "Look, if you don't mind me sitting in the doorway, I'll tell you about the gang while you shower. It will save time; you know how dad hates to be kept waiting." His eyes sparkled with mischief. "And I know how long it takes you to shower."

Jo laughed along with him. Growing up in a moderate size house on the base with only one bathroom, had not promoted lengthy showers. Get in, get the job done, and get out. It wasn't until her rebellious teens when she started to grow her hair long in a defiant act against the desired military cut that she started to take her time on hair wash days.

She looked at Kevin's mop and said, "You'll be taking longer than me the rate you're going."

Kevin shrugged, sat on the floor in the doorway and ran his fingers through sun-bleached sandy waves. "It fits for me right now."

"Actually, it suits you." Jo stepped into the shower recess. It was well designed, made to handle the grime from the track. The tilled wall ran almost the full length of the bathroom, giving ample room to disrobe, and leave your clothes on the bench, before stepping into the open shower. It didn't occur to be concerned about her brothers' proximity; they couldn't see each other but she could still hear him.

They had shared a room together as kids and learned to respect each other's privacy in an extremely small space. In fact, when she had moved into her own flat a few years ago, she enjoyed the space and freedom but missed him terribly at the same time.

"Speak up," Jo raised her voice as she soaped up her hair. "I'll be finished before you begin."

"Ok. You were right, I know the Range Riders. I've been working on their bikes from the Innisfail shop, been on a few of their runs and out to their house a couple of times. We've had them under surveillance for a while. They live approximately thirty km's south of Innisfail, and inland by about ten klicks, nestled in the foothills of a valley the locals call, the range."

Jo didn't miss the 'we' or the 'surveillance' but let it ride. If they thought she was going to have anything to do with whatever 'they' were involved in, they had another thing coming. Better to let him talk so she could gather as much ammunition as she could. She had an idea, if her father was here, she was going to need it.

"Can you hear me ok? You're awfully quiet?"

Jo rinsed the last of the shampoo out of her hair and applied a liberal amount of conditioner. "Of course I can hear you, just hurrying that's all. So, what else do you know about them?"

"The gang have been living in that area for a number of years, the owner died, and the property was inherited by the son. Access to the valley is by a narrow dirt road winding between low lying hills. When you are through, the valley opens up and it's a straight run past sugar cane fields and half a dozen farmhouses before it winds up in what is nothing more than a track to the foothills.

These hills join the larger Bellenden Ker Range. At the end of the track there is a shed where they keep the road vehicles. Access beyond that is a bike only river crossing, and a private property gate. They have a house in the rainforest. Police raids in the past have turned up nothing. Occasional local pub brawls and speeding through the country roads has so far been their biggest crime, on the surface they are a remarkably trouble-free gang."

Jo poked her head around the wall, she stared at him for a long second, then asked for her clothes. Stepping out moments later dressed in denim jeans, a plain black t-shirt and towelling dry her hair. "So why the interest in a nondescript gang?"

"Your hair stuff's in your duffel bag."

"My duffel bag?" The glare accompanying the words stopped Kevin in his tracks.

He made his way across to the kitchenette keeping a distance between them. "I have a key, remember. I didn't break in, and I locked up when I left."

Jo unclenched her fist, in a bid to keep a check on her anger, no doubt he was following fathers' orders, who, in full bellow was a hard man to ignore. Standing in front of such a formidable force was no easy feat and many an opponent had buckled under such an authoritative boom. Not her, she had stood up to him all her life. From the moment she could talk, she had felt like she was in opposition to him. Oppose him as she did, she also loved and respected his loyalty to his country and family.

No point pushing Kevin for any further information. She finished brushing her hair and tied it into a long braid that hug down her back. Let it dry in its own time.

"Let's get this over with so I can take my 'duffel bag' and go home." Jo flung the door wide and stormed off in the direction of the VIP lounge.

CHAPTER 4

Kevin raced ahead and barred her entry. With his longer hair and the stubble on his chin he didn't look like the clean cut man she knew and his eyes held an expression she found hard to define. Almost like encouragement but laced with worry. She didn't have time for this, she just wanted to get it over with and go home.

"What are you up to now? Going to give me a pep talk, well it's a little late for that." She made a grab for the door handle.

He hid it with his body and held up his hand in a stop sign. Paused, then smiled. The kind of cheeky, 'I'm with you' smile he used to give her when she was in trouble and angry at school. She hadn't seen that expression for a long time and her eyes immediately flew to his fingers to catch the old familiar message she knew would tap out. *There was a little girl, and she had a little curl right in the middle of her forehead.*

It took her back to the days when life had been easy and full of mischievous fun. Their four older brothers passed through military school with flying colours. 'A' class role models. When it came their turn to make their peers proud, the school and family had been in for a huge shock. Born close together, their father opted to have them in the same grade. Perhaps it was the lack of a mother's stabilizing influence during their first few years that made them more reckless, and although they excelled at the academic side, their joint flair for adventure created havoc with the strict discipline of the private military school.

Jo touched the will 'o' wisp curl that flicked near her eyes, running it through her fingers in quick salute. The complex codes she and Kevin had created during their childhood came flooding back. It felt like it was only yesterday and the fun of using them again snapped the band of tension building up at the base of her neck, and she knew whatever happened next, her brother had her back.

With a reminiscent smile, she completed the verse, her finger movement as slight as his had been, *'and when she was good she was very, very good, and when she was bad she was horrid.'*

His fist tightened in the old sign for *'chin up, things aren't that bad.'*

Reaching out she gave him a quick hug, smiling her appreciation at him. With a twinkle of mischief in her eyes she said, "Grab my stuff, this won't take long." She opened the door and with a flounce went through, closing it softly behind her.

The dark wood interior permeated a clean freshness that embraced the spirit. It embodied everything that was her father. Subtle lighting produced mysterious corners and where the lamps shone brightest, the strength and durability of the hard wood furniture stood solid and unyielding. He was alone and rose as she entered the room, six foot six and cutting a fine figure of a man, strong and formidable at the age of sixty eight.

"Great race Jo." He stepped forward before she could open her mouth to say hello, clapping her on the back like she was one of the boys. "Drink."

It wasn't a question; it never was with him. Jo watched his confident manner as he moved towards the compact bar nestled discreetly off to one corner. She knew from long years of experience, that whatever plan he'd concocted, he expected to win. Damn it, she wasn't going to make it easy. An idea of what she was going to be asked to do had been mulling around her head, she wasn't stupid by any means.

Being manipulated didn't help her temperament, so she gave him her best scowl of disapproval as he handed her a large glass of Glenlivet. Matching his assessing stare, she decided to try and throw him off balance by stepping outside the square and speaking first.

"I know about the connection with Kevin and the Range Riders. He tells me he's been fixing their bikes and I gather he knew they were coming here today." She forced her hand to relax as it clenched tight around the chilled glass. "Why he encouraged me to race beats me, but if it's to get me interested in the gang for some reason, you can forget it. I don't like being set up. I just want to go home."

Jo saw the tell-tale tick by his left eye, and braced herself for the army officer bellow.

"It's time you realised not everything in life is going to go your way." Sir Roberts' voice boomed and echoed around the room. "Kevin has worked long and hard to get a foot in the door of this gang. We need you to back him up on this assignment, I don't want him going in alone. The gang is called the 'Range Riders' for a reason." His expression demanded no defiance. "The hills that surround their property are criss-crossed with tracks and trails, many of them dangerous, most of them dead ends. Plane surveillance is useless as they change the trails regularly and the forest is so thick, we can't even pick them out.

A second group, the Hell Raisers live on the other side of the mountains, approx. thirty-five klicks as the crow flies, in the foothills of Queensland's highest town. We believe the two gangs are connected by these trails, using them as smuggling routes. So far we have been unable to pinpoint locations."

"But Dad..."

He held up his hand cutting her off as he continued. "We know all this from information we've gathered. You and Kevin are being sent in on reconnaissance only. After your exhilarating performance today, we hope you will have access to those trails for race training."

"But..."

"That's where Axel Stone, or Phantom as they call him, comes in. To the best of our knowledge he is their leader. After today you're going to be their top racer. The fact that you are a woman just makes the game more exciting to them."

Jo breathed deeply for control, casually moving over to the comfortable deep burgundy leather armchair, placing her untouched drink on the coaster sitting protectively on the antique oak table, before settling herself down into the chair's engulfing folds, very much aware of the watchful eyes of her father now she had stopped trying to interrupt.

Time for a different tactic. Looking up with calculated vulnerability into his eyes, she questioned, in a voice laced with softness. "Are you sure that's what Kevin wants, he has done his military time, over four years just to please you. All he wants to do is run the workshop in town, I'm sure he wants nothing to do with your covert operations."

"You have no idea what Kevin wants, he might want to run the shop, but only as a cover, the last few months we have had some enlightening chats about his future and believe me this is a thing he wants to do."

Watching him approach she looked up, sinking deeper into the folds of the chair making herself seem fragile and vulnerable. He towered over her, and by the scowl on his face, she could see he didn't like it one bit. Usually forthright and standing her ground, Jo hope this reverse psychology would show her father how strongly she felt. It might be underhanded, but all's fair when you are at war.

A slight shake of his head and a fleeting look of regret was replaced with grim resolve as he pushed his point home with a vengeance.

"You won that race today against the toughest adversary you are ever likely to come across..."

"Damn it! You saw what happened out there." Her fists clenched. She almost rose from the chair trying to take control of her temper. "He let me win and you know it."

"It couldn't have worked out better if we had planned it that way. It didn't matter who won Jo, it was how he reacted to you that was important."

The impact of what he said sat heavy in her heart. Relentlessly he continued, "We had already decided that it was the wisest move to have both you and Kevin working together. You make a great team. He needs someone he can trust, someone who can help secure a position close to the important members of the gang, take advantage of their friendship and gain valuable information."

"What you are really saying is you think I can get close to the 'dynamic Phantom' just because of his foolish notion to throw the race this afternoon. Well, what happens if I don't want to get close to that son of a..."

"JO!" The suppressed anger sent a thread of cold dread down to the base of her spine. "Like it or not, Axel Stone is the member we have to target. He is one of the leaders and if we can get a line to him, we are one step closer to getting the bastards behind bars."

Jo jumped to her feet in frustrated anger, the vulnerable act over. It had been after Patrick's funeral when he had last used that tone with her. Well she would walk out this time as well if he tried to intimidate her again.

"What do you require me to do... play the hussy... sleep with him? Learn all his secrets then pass them on to Kevin like a good little spy." She placed the palms of her hands on the curve of her hips and wiggled them with sarcastic provocation.

The shock registering on his face made her attempt to control her rising anger. "Dad, I have never slept with a man in my life...it's...it's...it's just not something I can do without the right kind of feeling..."

The look of hurt on her father's face caused her words to drift away. After a moment he continued in a quieter tone. "You both have something this gang wants, Kevin for his genius with bike repairs and modifications and you for your skills on the trail bike track. He modified Axels' bike for this race so it had a faster edge. The group survives on all members pooling their money, they often race to procure funds, after today I don't think they will be able to resist wanting you to join them, you rode against their best. It was your ability and courage they were testing. The winning wasn't important. Kevin has been waiting for this opportunity for months."

The fight physically drained from her body.

"You must help map the trails between the two groups. We can't get close to the other gang, for reasons I can't tell you, but what they are up to is criminal and a lot of innocent people will be hurt if we don't stop them. The only way is to send in two unknowns to the smaller group. You are not expected to do anything other than report back with what you discover about the trails, anything else will be covered by back up. We will have a highly trained team standing by ready for immediate action. You and Kevin will be extracted the moment they are mobilised."

He paused, then continued, a rare teasing tone gracing his voice. "As for sleeping with anyone, that has always been entirely up to you, although for your added protection, Kevin is to play the role of your boyfriend. We have left nothing to chance. You both should be free to investigate the tracks and trails of the Range Riders while having the security of a mock relationship with each other. You really will be quite safe."

Staring thoughtfully at the silver haired man, Jo acknowledged how well her father had judged her. Knowing he had said the last few words to perk her up her spirit, she couldn't help but comply.

Turning away she moved to stand in front of the thick security window that looked down on the clubroom below. The presentations were in full swing but she hardly registered a thing. All this manipulating was driving her crazy. Deep in her heart she realised that things would not have worked out the same if she had known the plan right from the start. For one, she would never have reacted to Axel Stone and the race with such hot-headed hostility.

Jo clenched her fists. Even the thought of him stirred up feelings she had no intention of acknowledging.

She turned back to her father, perching her bottom on the thin window ledge, and gave him an almost imperceptible nod of her head.

"I take it that's your way of saying yes." his concern for her evident in his tone.

Jo looked at her father and suddenly was extremely tired. The emotional strain of the day had finally claimed its toll. "Yes, Sir," she said, her voice quiet and resigned. "I will help just this once, and support Kevin in mapping the trails. I know there is a lot you are probably not telling me. I can only imagine national security is involved. As long as you realise I am not interested in becoming an active member of MICI or whatever it's called."

"MICO. Military Intelligence Covert Operations. And there are a few other things I can tell you."

The furrow between her eyes deepened and she wished he would put his arms around her for once in his life and give her some of the comfort she had always wanted. Shoving the thoughts away, she sighed deep and long. "Fine. I've already said, I'll do what you're asking."

"What I am about to tell you is classified information." The solemn edge and serious tone made her body tense in anticipation.

"Evidence has come to light that their connections with a second bike group, The Hell Raisers have deepened. Over the last few years, various government agencies have lost three agents who were working undercover in connection with this second group. Although we have tried, we haven't been able to get close enough to the higher members of the gang. One agent was killed, very professionally made to look like an accident."

Jo's hairs stood on end, she had a horrible premonition she wouldn't like where this was going. She shook her head as he paused, seeming to gather strength before continuing in a painful tone. "The other two were blown beyond recognition in a 'boating accident'."

Patrick's name hung unspoken in the air between them.

The grandfather clock against the far wall chimed the seventh hour, and a slight thud, thud, thud drifted up from clubrooms as the band began to play.

Grief and disbelief chased each other through her system. Her father continued as if trying to leave the sorrowful part about Patrick's murder behind.

"The rest of your brothers are aware of this. Right or wrong, we agreed as a family to let you think it was an accident."

Jo shut her open mouth and clenched her teeth together, realising deep down she had never believed Patrick's death was an accident. It had just been easier to accept at the time. She had no time to dwell on what had been said as the voice of steel continued.

"Do I have your attention, Jo?"

"Yes, sir."

"This is for your ears only. Kevin is too deeply involved, and another reason we need your help. We cannot afford to drive a wedge between the friendships he has formed with Axel and the gang. We are letting you know, so you realise just how important it is for the trails to be mapped, your eyes will be in places we have never been able to get close to. Once we secure the connection between the groups, we can make the next move."

He paused and she nodded at him to continue.

"We believe Axel Stone's connection to the Hell Raisers is deeper than it seems on the surface. He is very good at keeping his smaller group clean and above the law, but we think he was directly involved with the death of Patrick." Jo felt the blood drain from her face, she felt dizzy and his next words had her gasping for breath. "The...the boat they were on was his."

Her father took a step forward, arm outstretched as she pushed away from the ledge, staggered a few steps before spinning maladroitly and falling back into the chair, downing her untouched scotch without a flinch.

Leaning forward she placed her hands over her face for what seemed like an eternity, grateful her father left her to come to terms with it in her own time. When she raised her eyes, she could feel the fire in them. "I'll bust his ass, if I can't do that...I'll kill him," she swore. "Dead or alive he, will, pay."

"JO! This is *NOT* a vengeance mission! That's why I told you everything else before this. There is more at stake here than this one man, and yes, if you can bring him to his knees in the process all's well and good, but the mission of mapping the trails must come first. We will get him and everyone else involved, but we must cast the net so we can catch them all."

He leant forward and placed both his arms on the chair and stared down at her. "Do you understand me? I want the whole *fucking* lot bought down."

The venomous use of his hated swear-word drilled his point home. She looked up into eyes reflecting the bitter anger she felt and for the first time in her life she felt a union with him that went soul deep. Whether or not he had manipulated her to this point was irrelevant, that they were in agreement for the first time in her life connected something between them that had been missing since her birth.

Finally, she understood her father's commitment to duty, the ability to depersonalise and see things as the bigger picture. "I am with you one hundred percent, and I will do whatever it takes. I promise you."

She stared at him long and hard before continuing. "But you must understand. I still don't want to be involved in any part of MICO, other than bringing these bastards to justice. For the record, I resent being manipulated, yet see the necessity of it and it scares the hell out of me."

She ran a hand over her forehead pushing the curl out of her eyes. "You think I'm cut out for this kind of work. No matter what you say, I don't. Rest assured, I shall give it my all and I *will* have Kevin's back, I can't bear the thought of him going in alone. You've pushed me dad, but maybe, just maybe one day you will let me be me, but for now I concur. I will help bring the whole damn group down and Patrick's killer to justice."

Despite what she said, she had the unnerving feeling that she had slotted perfectly into the prefabricated mould her life ordained. She couldn't stop it; her mind raced a mile a minute, organising thoughts and plans on what still need to be addressed and done.

It was a long speech and her father had remained impassive. She swiped away the tears that hung just beneath the surface and looked at him with a newfound understanding. Tough and as abrupt as her father she stated. "We need Kevin, there are plans to make."

CHAPTER 5

What Kevin expected when he came back in and what he found were in direct contrast to each other. As they sat around the table, he watched spellbound as Jo and their father, Sir Robert, animatedly created plans, scenarios and back up plans for the back up plans. Looking so much like the photos of their mother, he could see now she was her father's daughter through and through. Ideas bounced off each other like super balls being thrown full pelt in a squash court. They were so attuned; heaven help anyone who crossed their paths.

Finally they were satisfied.

Sir Robert was the first to stand. "Kevin knows where they are camping for the night. Under my orders he took the liberty of arranging for some of your personal belongings to be brought from your unit. The rest we purchased. You should find the new clothing appropriate."

He reached out and shook his hand, then surprising him even more by leaning forward and embracing Jo in a lingering bear hug before hastily stepping back.

"There's one last thing." He motioned them closer dropping his voice to a whisper. "This is on the quiet, family only. If you hear the names Brodie or Willow, I want you contact me asap. Not through the regular channels, but on my private number."

Kevin raised his eyebrows and nodded, glancing at Jo. She seemed as confused as him, but there was no time for questions as their father waved a dismissal for them to leave. When they were at the door he called out, giving them a long hard stare.

"Josephine, Kevin Watch each other's backs and...and come home safe." With those parting words he turned and walked over to the bar.

As they left, Kevin turned to his sister wide mouthed in bewilderment, *"Josephine."* He has never called...Ow!.. "What the..."

"Don't think you can call me Josephine...and *that* was for lying to me."

"Ouch." He yelped again rubbing and flexing his arm at the same time. "What was that for?"

"For being right about lying to me. If you had told me the truth I never would have raced and that my dear brother would have been a very bad thing."

Kevin stopped walking and faced his sister, suddenly sober and sincere. "I am glad you're with me Jo. This is my first assignment and it feels good knowing you have my back. To tell you the truth, I didn't want to go in on my own. Ever since Patrick... you know died, I've been restless, wanting to do something."

Jo surprised him by reaching out and giving him a comforting hug. It was so out of her character he hesitated at first, then swallowed her small fame within his beefy arms, pulling her close. She only came up to his chest and although she felt small and fragile, he knew her body was strong and physically fit. He hadn't been kidding when she punched his arm, it still hurt.

"I know Patrick's death wasn't an accident." She stepped back and looked up at him, determination etched in her expression, eyes flashing courage. "I am ok with not being told the truth."

Kevin sighed with relief. He hated her not knowing. Over the long sad months, it had driven a wedge between them. She'd turned away and consumed with his own grief, he had let her go. He went to say he was glad she knew, but she got in first.

"I think finding out now is perfect timing. I can put it all into perspective. I needed the time to come to terms with losing him." Her voice cracked. "I still miss him so much." Kevin pulled her back into his arms as her soft words called out to his own heart.

"Me too Jo. Me too." He squeezed tight before he released her. Not wanting to dwell on the sadness. "Come on sis, let's kick ass and bring the fuckers down."

He grinned at Jo's expression, knowing she hated swearing. "Get use to the foul language, honey."

"You are NOT calling me honey."

"Darling? Sweetheart?...Schnookums?" He almost cracked up at the horrified look on her face and it warmed his heart to see her focus shift away from sadness.

Finally, she chuckled. "You're an idiot. I'm Jo, as usual. I'll flatten you if you call me anything else." He took a playful step back as she shook her fist under his nose, sticking up his hands in mock surrender. "Ok, ok, Jo it is."

"What's our next step? Whatever it is I hope there's food involved. I am starving."

The gang's taking advantage of the free camping, over by Sandy Creek. If we get a move on there might be some dinner left, but there are a couple of things before we go. One, we missed presentations, but we can pick up your winnings at the bar. Errr...You must give it to Phantom. As a member of the gang, all race wins go in the kitty."

He didn't like the way Jo was looking at him and knew she would kick up a fuss at what he said next. "Two, you can ride pillion on my bike."

"Like hell I will," she spluttered. "He can have the race winnings, I don't care, didn't deserve it anyway. But I'm taking my Ducati."

"Don't sell yourself short Jo, that race was something else."

She crossed her arms over her chest, wearing her stubborn streak like a badge.

"I am the messenger here, want to go back and take it up with dad?" He watched as Jo's anger dispersed as she thought things over.

"I think it would be more convincing if I rode my own, but whatever you say."

Kevin decided to drop it for now, aware she gave in way too easily. Lightening the mood he joked. "Just remember to act like you love me once in a while."

"Never doubt that for a minute bro. I understand what's required and I'll play my part don't worry."

Kevin hoisted her duffel bag onto his shoulder. He had it retrieved from the room whilst she was in discussion with 'Sir Robert.' and wondered, not for the first time, if she realised how important their father and his organisation was.

"Come on Jo, let's get this show on the road."

CHAPTER 6

The first thing Jo noticed as they strolled into camp was the mouth-watering aroma of the barbecue. Meat sizzled on the open grill and someone had thrown small foil wrapped parcels into the permanent stone circled cooking pit and they were just checking to see if they were ready. Steamy tendrils of garlic, carrot and sweet potato blended with steak and sausages and Jo felt like she had died and gone to heaven. Her stomach announced their arrival with a loud rumble.

A petite blonde saw them and jumped up from a wooden log seat, rushing over to give Kevin a hug. "Kev, great to see ya. I looked before the race but couldn't find ya."

Jo was taken back as she turned and threw her arms around her as well.

"That race was epic. Phantom's been teaching me to ride, but I'm not real good yet. Maybe you can teach me too. How long did it take ya ta get that good? Never mind you can tell me later. Come and meet everyone; and ya just in time for dinner." She grabbed them both by the arms and dragged them into the circle of fire light. "Hey everyone meet Jo." She threw her arm in a circle pointing at various people. "That's Spike, Stretch and Grub, Freckles' cookin', she does awesome meals. Over there is Al, Jeckle and Phantom's around somewhere, have you met him yet, oh 'course you did, you raced him." She slapped her hand on her forehead. "Those four hanging out at the back are, Beth..."

"Shut the fuck up Babs." Jeckle rose and ambled over to where they stood. He and Kevin bumped fists together in greeting. "Great work on Phantom's bike, fuck load of power on the straight."

He totally ignored Jo which suited her fine. She was hungry, tired and just wanted to eat and sleep in that order. She was not in this to make friends, although the young blonde certainly had a lot of charisma.

"By the way my names Babbles, Babs for short. We all got nick names, I wonder what yours will be, unless ya got one already?" Her grin was contagious as she grabbed her by the arm and pulled her off to the side. Kevin wandered off without a backward glance, talking bikes with Jeckle. Jo figured she was on her own for now and wasn't really happy about it.

"We're just about to eat, so ya come at the best time, but I s'pose ya better see Phantom first, ya part of our group now aint ya?"

Jo was finally able to get a word in as Babs quizzically tilted her head and waited for an answer. "I don't know really. Kevin implied that I was. Is there something I am meant to do?"

"You can hand over the race winnings." The sexy rumble of Phantoms voice floated over her shoulder causing the hairs on the back of her neck to stand on end. She jumped, spun around and took a step back. All three movements blended into one quick motion.

Seeing him up close and personal set her teeth on edge. All she could think about was he killed her brother and for a short moment doubt flooded her ability to respond. She let her anger sit just below the surface ready in case she needed it.

"It's yours anyway." Jo dug in her pockets then realised Kevin had put it in his.

"Kevin's got it." She shrugged nonchalantly standing her ground as he stepped closer.

The only light came from the cooking pit and a couple of small lanterns on a nearby table and towering above her, his eyes took on the appearance of being on fire.

"Do you often pretend to be a man, Jo? I don't particularly like being conned."

Jo was just about to remark about not having a sense of humour when Kevin slid up beside her and confessed.

"It was me mate. I kinda talked her into it, she actually had no idea what was going down today." He slapped the winnings into Phantom's hand. "I thought it would be funny. We good?"

Void of expression Phantom stared at her. Jo held her ground, she didn't back down when she was racing, and she wasn't about to start now.

Slight amusement crept into his eyes and she felt her heart skip a beat as his features softened. Then kicked herself when she realised it wasn't aimed at her. He turned saying. "Heya Babs, grab me some food."

"Sure Phantom." She bounced willingly off towards the barbecue.

Phantom tucked the envelope into his back pocket, clapped Kevin on the shoulder and said, "We're good, get yourself some grub."

Kevin was gone before she could blink. She caught up with him at the barbecue, he looked up at her and winked, a laden plate of food in his hand, "I'm going to sit with the boys." He ambled off leaving her to get her own food and mingle with the female members of the group.

Grumbling under her breath at this typical Australian scenario, she rejected the idea of forcing her way onto the boys table before it grabbed hold. Already she could feel the need to adopt a calmer attitude. Damn it she never had been good at being patient.

The food tasted as delicious as it smelt. Sitting at the woman's table, was better as it was set away from the heat of the fire, she tucked into her meal with gusto. Immediately she felt better with something solid in her stomach. Looking up she saw the women watching her with curious looks on their faces.

Babs broke the silence. "Wow, you eat as fast as ya ride."

Jo laughed along with them and it set the tone for a surprisingly pleasant evening. They were quite a mixture of characters most of them younger than she originally thought. Spike was bizarre with her hair every colour of the rainbow and arising into a rigid peak from her forehead to her neck. Jo was most intrigued to see how she would put her helmet on for the trip back.

It was midnight before they turned in. Some had tents set up, the rest like her and Kevin had swags thrown on the ground. Glad she had taken the initiative and placed hers a short distance away from the group, Kevin had no choice but to follow.

She nestled into the comfort of her swag. After the jungle training which had been part of her military upbringing, something to sleep on was luxury. Raising her arms, she tucked them behind her head and started counting stars. Sleep still refused to come. To her left Kevin lay snoring as if trying to compete with the cicadas buzzing in the trees. The moon hadn't yet risen, it was waxing so when it did it wouldn't give off a great deal of light.

She had to concede the night had been relaxed and fun, instead of the drunken hooliganism she had envisioned it to be, it was more like a gathering of happy friends, talking, laughing, and sharing a few beers.

The men had joined them, except for Phantom and Jeckle who stay at the table paying them no interest. Soft spoken Freckles was coaxed into strumming a few tunes on her guitar and Spike surprised her with a bright, lively timbre to her voice, quite the contrast to her wistful exterior. Stretch upturned his tin plate and beat out a pleasant accompanying rhythm and she had the feeling they had many nights like this.

Jo made sure she sat with her back to Phantom and Jeckle finding it easier on her temperament if she didn't see them. Not once did they join in, nor were they asked to participate. When she finally decided to go to bed they were nowhere in sight. Her eyelids slowly started to close as she relaxed deeper into her swag.

CHAPTER 7

S he listened.

In the small hours of the night the camp was as it should be. Muted moonlight played in the overhead branches, forming inscrutable patterns around the edges of the leaves. High in the trees the continual high-pitched buzz of hundreds of cicadas ceased in unison, leaving her ears ringing in the eerie quiet. Propping herself on her elbows, she probed for any noise within the camp. Kevin and his bitch had swags further away from the rest of the camp, it was hard to tell if they were sleeping, she watched for a while, they stayed still and silent. Except for the odd grunt or snore all was peaceful.

Although she preferred a tent, tonight she opted for the convenience of a swag. She stood and paused before slipping into her jeans. The lazy thud, thud, thud of a foraging wallaby and the hoot of a distant owl was perfect cover as she picked her foot placement carefully and silently left the camp.

He would be waiting for her call. This had been her first opportunity. Not really, but she would glean a small amount of pleasure letting him think that. Heading in the direction of the toilet block, she half expected someone to call out so they could accompany her. To her relief the camp stayed ignorant.

A few other campsites sat as silent ghosts. None had ventured close to the rowdy group of bikers as they kicked up a storm on the dusty grounds and raced in the riverbed. On runs like this it was always their intention, once other campers had settled their spots away from the group, they had relaxed, having the whole back area to themselves.

Halfway across the open ground she veered to the right, she was too far away from the camp now for anyone to notice her change of direction. Once under cover of the trees, the moonlight was not enough. She flicked on her phone torch locating the spot she had chosen earlier that day, knowing no-one from the camping ground could see her as she settled cross legged in the loose sandy bottom of the dry riverbed. Away from the trees and the undergrowth she felt safer from snakes. A slippery reptile crawling over her legs was not on her bucket list.

Ever cautious, she waited a moment listening to the natural sounds of the night. Satisfied, she called the number she had memorised years ago, despising the man who made her dance like a puppet to his bidding. Although they had never met, they had been partners for a long time. Without him she probably would have been dead by now, although she wouldn't put it past him to have set her up right from the beginning. A teenage prostitute, beaten, abused and discarded like a dirty rag, she had managed get back to her squat to find a large envelope containing a phone, money and instructions tucked into her meagre belongings.

With nothing to lose she had obeyed, and her life had changed forever. After each phone call and completion of the task she had grown richer, stronger, confident. She had done disgusting sexual things, killed for him, played whatever role he demanded of her. At the same time, she used her brain by saving most of her money. Investing wisely creating a nest egg big enough to retire and live in luxury for the rest of her life, but for now she had to be careful, not let him hear her revulsion as she spoke.

He answered immediately and she gleaned a small amount of pleasure as his raspy voice complained about the late hour of her call. Waiting patiently for him to finish whining and demand her report.

"It's just as you predicted." She spoke softly, hating the fact his fingers were in some very important pies. "Jo rides like the devil and is now a member of the gang along with that brother of hers." She wondered, not for the first time, how he had known MICO were going to infiltrate them again. He had to have a mole in the organisation. "Yes, I'm listening." She detested the demeaning authority in his voice and held the phone away from her ear as a hacking cough racked his chest, she waited for the inevitable hawk and spit that would follow before she put it back to her ear. Disgusting man, he needed to give up smoking. Even now she could hear him lighting up another and drawing in a deep wheezy breath as he told her what she must do next.

After hanging up she sat for a while, absently rubbing her fingers through the dirt in small thoughtful circles, the familiar action soothing to her troubled mind. She didn't like the fact the agents were on their trail again, she wished she could get rid of them now, take off and begin her new life. Greed kicked in, just a little while longer. This job was paying big money, she should see it through, and her boss was right, as far as the agents were concerned, better the devil you know.

She stood dusted off her jeans and made her way back to camp. It would be daybreak in an hour or so, she settled into her swag curling on her side in foetal position. Sleep evaded her, but she closed her eyes anyway, concentrating her thoughts on the new life that waited her.

Chapter 8

Jo woke to cackling laugh of Kookaburras announcing the arrival of the day's dawn. Each tried to outdo the other as they broadcasted their territorial ownership to the trees around the camp.

She lay back in relaxed comfort enjoying the sound, and for a moment, the cool the day would bring. Townsville had been uncharacteristically humid as well as hot this year and by the look of the lightening sky, today would be no different. Beside her Kevin stirred, pulling his pillow over his head in protest. Unable to resist she reached out and clobbered him with her pillow. "Rise and shine lazy bones."

"Go away." He pulled the pillow tighter, as if trying to block out her laugh as well as the growing light. He never had been a good morning person. She sat up stretching the kinks out of her back by raising her arms up and over her shoulders, then bending to grab hold of her toes and putting her head on her knees.

A few of the group were up and about and Jo contemplated going for a morning run as was her usual routine, deciding against it as she watched Phantom, restart the fire and put a pot on to boil. She didn't want to draw any attention to herself.

"Morning." Babs, up and dressed was as bubbly as the night before. "I've been up for ages, I just love camping, does you good to get away from the everyday routine of home life don't you reckon?"

"Fucking shut up."

Jeckle evidently was not. He grumbled out of his tent, scratched his groin and ambled sleepily over to the ablutions block. Spike and Freckles climbed out of their swags at the same time, both looking as though they could do with a few more hours sleep, their hair wild and messy, as they grabbed towels and clothes before heading in the same direction.

"Morning Babs." Jo said as she reached for her bag. She liked the way the woman was unaffected by the rudeness that seemed to constantly sprout out of Jeckle's mouth. She must be very secure with who she was. Now she was humming softly as she packed her swag away.

Rummaging through her duffel for clean clothes she asked. "What time do we leave?"

"Thirty minutes. Those who aren't ready get left behind." Jo jumped and her heart skipped a beat. Phantom was fully dressed in his riding gear and holding a cup of steaming hot liquid. Her nose twitched and she couldn't help but lick her lips. She'd die for a cup of strong black coffee.

Nudging Kevin none too gently with his boot he said, "Up and at em, Rev, you can help us secure the trail bikes onto the truck." He turned, took a noisy slurp of his coffee, stared blankly at her for a short moment then ambled away.

She couldn't help but admire the cut of his jeans and how snug they sat. Her attention was drawn to a flash of green sticking out of his back pocket and her temper flared when she realised he was goading her with her scarf. Memories of his closeness after the race turned the heat up on her anger and in a flash she knew what she had to do. Bugger not drawing attention to herself. She raced hard and tough yesterday and that got her into the gang. Why stop now.

"Kevin, roll up my swag, I'll be back." Not waiting for an answer she bundled up her clothes and took off at a jog. There wasn't much time.

It took precious minutes to get to her destination. Throwing the door open at the top of the steps, Jo raced into the bar area of the club. After the late after party, the cleaning staff were still working and someone would remain on duty until the last of the campers left. She recognised the man stacking the clean glasses away. "Hi Pete, in a hurry, need to wash and change, can you grab my keys from the back room, I'll be back in five."

Ten minutes later she called thanks over her shoulder as she dashed out and down the steps. Flinging open the shed door, Jo was relieved to see her bike was where she left it. For a dreadful moment she thought her father might have had it moved and she would have to sprint back to the camp. Now she had a bit of time.

Running her hands over the polished to perfection yellow body of her Ducati Scrambler Icon she knew Kevin and her father would be angry. She dismissed a twinge of guilt. They wanted her help, they got it, but she wasn't going to change who she was in the process. She didn't ride pillion.

Her stomach rumbled and she hoped they were going to stop somewhere for breakfast. It was a good three hour run to Innisfail. Kevin must have her helmet, it wasn't sitting on the seat where she had left it. Kicking the bike into gear she roared out of the shed and across the camping ground, muttering an unheard sorry to the other campers as she kicked up clouds of dust.

Kevin's annoyance was visible before she pulled up. He stood hands on hips, feet apart and glared as she eased to a halt in a small puff of dirt.

"You got my helmet?" She asked sweetly, keeping the engine idling. She had timed it to perfection, everyone was ready to pull out. She looked anywhere but at Kevin's face. Spike was behind the wheel in the small truck, a grin plastered across her face, she gave Jo a short nod. Al, sitting next to her stared at his phone. Babs was mounting up behind Grub, and Freckles was already snug behind

Stretch. One of the other girls, Beth was riding her own bike, she flashed Jo a wide toothed grin giving her the thumbs up. The other three she hadn't got to know had bikes of their own.

Bypassing Jeckle was a petty payback point, she could ignore people too. Finally, she rested her eyes on Phantom, he had his helmet on with dark sunglasses. He mounted his bike, staring straight at her, pulled his bandanna up over his nose before he kicked his bike into gear.

Jo fumed. Her scarf was being used as a bandanna. She clenched her teeth and turned to Kevin, whose eyes flashed warning signs.

She swallowed her temper and tried to pacify Kevin with an attempt at humour, "Want to bet my Ducati is faster than his Harley?"

Kevin's voice matched the annoyance in his eyes. "Not testing it. There are riding rules."

"You got to be kidding."

"Jeckle's on point, you don't pass him. Phantom's at the rear, in case of any mishaps. Behind him will be Spike and Al in the truck."

Jo opened her mouth to protest. Kevin did a great imitation of their father by holding up his hand for silence and continued.

"We stick to the speed limits, ride no more than two abreast, allow room in-between so cars can pass. In about three hours, we fuel up at the servo where we turn off the highway."

He tossed her helmet, secured his own, mounted his bike and kicked it into life, moving in line as they started to rumble. By the time Jo fastened her helmet and slipped on her gloves the group were at the camping ground exit, with the exception of Phantom and the truck. Just as she was ready to move, he took off at a leisurely pace as if he was leaving her behind. She kicked it into gear, opened the throttle and roared past him realising she was stirring up dust and not caring. Let the bastard choke.

The riders headed north. Jo thought once they reached the open highway Jeckle would kick it up a gear and speed. She was relieved he didn't, as much as she loved riding fast, there was a time and place for it. But she wished with all her impatience he would sit just above the hundred not below. It was bad enough being near the rear of the group, she felt boxed in and longed to fly to the front to see the open road spread out before her, instead of staring at the backs of the other riders. She could see Kevin behind Jeckle, contemplated overtaking and pulling in next to him, then thought better of it, she had already upset him enough today. Settling down to her position in the pack, Jo relaxed and enjoyed the ride.

Jo sighed with relief when they finally pulled up at the designated service station, she was tired and hungry and hoping to grab something to eat or a least a drink, but no-one even bothered to take off their helmets. In turn they fuelled up, passing the hose to the next person and moving away. Jo switched off her engine, stretching the kinks out of her body waiting for her turn. Phantom doing the same on the other side on the other side of the pump leaned across and spoke, "Spike pays."

Although she had ridden this way many times, she hadn't paid much attention to the small towns leading off the highway. Riding inland from here meant they must be getting close to their destination and by the way her stomach was feeling she couldn't determine if it was nerves or hunger.

This time when they continued, the pace was slow through the small township. Jeckle sat on fifty-five, keeping a steady speed past the police station, a newsagent, the pub, an oval and a small country school. House were dotted in-between with glorious views of the distant rainforest clad hills across the recently harvested sugar cane paddocks.

As they approached a T intersection, Phantom pulled out, passed the group and tucked in on Jeckle's left. Side by side they drew to a halt, looked across at each other, revved their engines and sped off. Phantom to the left, Jeckle to the right. It all happened in a split second. At the rear Jo watched each individual react and make a decision. Kevin chose right, sticking close behind Jeckle, most of the others followed, Beth and another rider swung left. Jo didn't stop to think, she should have followed Kevin. All she saw was the open speed limit sign, the straight stretch of road, Phantom getting ahead of her, and the freedom to let fly.

She passed the first two riders with ease, pumping through the gears to get maximum acceleration, her eye on the leader some distance ahead. Farms and house flashed by. The road was straight and clear of traffic. Far ahead she could see the hills it must lead to.

Gaining on Phantom she felt exuberant, the pace, the freedom, the feeling of being in control. The road required her attention, the surface was in typical country condition, rough and badly repaired. One moment she was playing catch up the next she was so close she realised he must have slowed without brakes. She applied hers, but it was too late to follow, he swung around the sweeping curve to the right, his bike and knee riding low to the ground.

"Shit, shit, shit!" She hit the brakes harder as the road turned to dirt. The bastard hadn't indicated either. Her braking system was one of the many features that had drawn her to the Ducati scrambler, the wheels didn't lock and it allowed her to retain traction so she could stick out a steadying foot, spin on a pivot, reapply the throttle and take off in hot pursuit. First down, then up and over the small embankment on the side of the road she raced down the short tough grass of the headland, picking out the best course to ride, all the while cursing under her breath. There was a long triangular piece of no man's land between the junction of the two roads and the cane fields. The short cut was rough, but it took off the wide sweep of the corner.

Another reason to love her bike, it handled well both on and off road. Sticking to the headlands wasn't quite as fast but it saved her precious seconds. Scanning ahead for an exit point proved almost impossible as she could only concentrate on a few feet ahead at a time. Phantom was pulling away and the other two riders were almost level with her on the road to her right.

Trusting her instincts she applied more speed, spied a possible exit just before the headland petered off and judged her entry back onto the road. The drainage dip although wide, was tough on her and the bike. She took it at a longer angle, gritting her teeth as the undercarriage scraped against something hard and had to use all her strength to regain control. Losing traction and using her foot as a push off, she dropped back a gear, then gave a burst of speed jumping out onto the road surface a mere bikes length in front of the two riders. All she had to do now was catch and pass Phantom. The desire to beat him consumed all else.

It proved an impossible task. The road narrowed even more and wound through tight hairpin corners as it climbed and dipped through small rainforest clad hills giving no opportunity for overtaking. She stuck as close as safety allowed, trying to keep the pressure on for him to maintain speed. Whether he did it to annoy her, or what, she didn't know, but he slowed his pace, turning the ride into a graceful swing from side to side as they followed the curves.

This time he braked and indicated well in advance. As they stopped at the intersection, Jo could hear the rumble of the others off to the right and realised it must be a loop road. Tapping her fingers impatiently on the grip, she felt her throat close over in frustration, why in the hell didn't he go, there was plenty of time. She glared at his back, hating his casual manner, and the fact she could do nothing about it.

He moved forward slightly and turned his wheel. For a moment the sun glinted off his left side mirror drawing her attention. As the others came into view he leapt in action roaring off in front of them pushing his bike to the max. Adrenaline prickled Jo's skin, she almost went to follow him, before realising there was no time to execute the same move.

With no choice but to wait, Jo and the two riders fell in behind the group. Kevin was still up front behind Jeckle and Jo half wished he would drop back and ride with her. Irritated she added a scowl to her pursed lips. If this was what gang life was going to be like she didn't know if she could do it and keep her sanity.

Slowing, she allowed the last two riders to overtake her. Beth drew along side, gave her a thick gloved ok signal and dropped back behind her. Jo raised her hand in understanding and applied a little more speed and fell in line with the others. She couldn't even be last if she wanted to.

They turned directly towards the hills. Jo zoned out, concentrating on the scenery around her. They took the road at a sedate pace, it was only wide enough for one car, so if someone came from the opposite direction one or both parties had to pull off to the side.

Banana and papaya farms littered the landscape. Once the forest started the road turned to dirt and the rainforest closed around them. Tall trees overhead formed an interlocking canopy and it was like driving through a shadowy green tunnel alive with sparkling splashes of sunlight and Jo felt herself relax under the splendour around her.

They crested the hill and started on the downward trek, loose gravel flicking up from under her wheels. Breaking out of the cover of the forest, the valley was revealed in all its glory. Surrounded by lush rainforest hills, the brilliant contrast of the rich blue sky and the farmland on the flat, spread out before her, painting a picture postcard.

Sunlight glinted off the river as it ambled behind the farms to the right, over the other side of the bank the hills rose to an impressive height. They crossed a number of sturdy wooden bridges as smaller creeks wandered across the scenery to merge with the river. The road ran straight and true through the middle of the valley, until the hills closed around them. The forest was thick, and Jo felt immediate relief from the growing heat of the day. Just off to one side was an aluminium shed that Jo remembered housed the road vehicles. Butterflies danced in her stomach. It was evident they had arrived.

Phantom pulled into a small clearing, turned off his motor indicating for Jo and Kevin to join him. The others continued down the single bike track, across the creek and disappeared into the undergrowth beyond. She could hear the bikes for quite a distance as they went deeper into the forest.

"This is the beginning of the property of the 'Range Riders'," Phantom said, sitting astride his bike. He removed his helmet and clipped it over the handle bars. "Once you cross the creek, there's no going back. Is that clear?"

He looked to Kevin for confirmation as if Jo didn't exist. Grinning Kevin took off his own helmet and nodded his acceptance.

"Our place becomes yours, just as you become part of the group. Loyalty is the key word. We work together for each other, for the good of the gang. This is your last chance, if you can't cut it, I suggest you fuck off right now." His face was a cold mask, and his tone void of expression.

"No worries, mate." Kevin grinned, warm and friendly.

Annoyed at being ignored, Jo dismounted, placed her helmet on her bike seat and walked a short distance, admiring the crystal clear creek that ran under the causeway.

"This includes you, *Jo*," he called out. "It might do you good to pay attention, don't want you going the wrong way."

Silently she seethed, biting back retaliating words. She knew what he was getting at and she refused to bite. She raised her hand in acknowledgement but kept her back to him and looking down at the flowing water.

"Just to clarify things." He walked to where she stood. "When you join the gang, you belong to us body and soul." The last words were designed for her ears only and the low smoky timbre dancing in his voice caused her to glance sideways to catch the glint in his eyes daring her to challenge his last statement.

She decided not to disappoint him.

"My body," her voice matching his in quietness only, "does and always will, belong only to me."

"It was meant as a figure of speech, not an actual reality." He let out a low chuckle. "But remember, you're in my territory, and I swear one day I'll make you retract those words."

Kevin sauntered over, placing his arm possessively around her shoulder and drawing her closer to him. "We know and understand the rules and will abide by them." He drew himself up to his full impressive height. "This is one possession I won't be sharing." He hugged Jo closer to his body.

Phantom's smile didn't reach his eyes as he studied them shrewdly. "In this group it's up to the individual who they fuck. If she wants to fuck you, fine, but there's no harm in trying." His face became relaxed as he slapped Kevin on the back, his laugh of friendship echoing around them, inviting them to join in with his humour.

Kevin complied, turning to Jo as he laughed, giving her a wink that she supposed was meant to be reassuring. She gave him a half smile, as they turned back to their bikes.

Phantom held out her helmet. "Welcome to my territory." Jo jumped, as the softness of his words coincided with a pleasant tingling when their fingers accidentally touched. She knew he felt it too. For an ever so slight moment, he let down his guard, his eyes filled with a desire that almost shocked her to the bone, as quick as it came it vanished, along with a none too silent oath as he mounted his own bike and led the way to the house.

CHAPTER 9

Jo ended her early morning run in the grassy clearing at the back of the house. Three glorious days since they arrived in the valley where the Range Riders had their home and it was hard not to get complacent. The surroundings were incredible, even for someone brought up in North Queensland and used to seeing the lush jungle greens of the tropical rainforest. Late November humidity and the pre wet build up already teased the temperature to the twenty nine degrees Celsius mark, even though the sun had only just begun to create its dabbled pattern through the trees.

Breathing heavily, she dropped to the grass in push up position, enjoying the fire in her muscles and the refreshing bursts of clean cut grass each time she almost touched her nose to the earth.

After a short pause, she flipped onto her back, finishing her daily exercise routine with thirty quick crunches. Puffing she lay back looking up at the trees, needing some time to regain her breath before starting cool down stretches.

There was something invigorating about a workout in the fresh country air and she was glad to be keeping to her practice of rising at the crack of dawn. Now, an hour and a half into the day the open sky was a vibrant blue. The leaves of the bordering trees danced slightly in the morning breeze moving in time to the wind chimes on the veranda as they added their musical notes to the chorus of bird song.

Jo closed her eyes letting the serenity calm her ever racing mind.

"Day dreaming about me, are you?"

She hadn't seen him in the three days since they arrived. Jumping instinctively to her feet, she completely underestimated the way his physical presence impacted her equilibrium. A warm ball of pleasure glowed annoyingly into life, as it had every time she tried to analyse what she knew about him.

As long as he kept his distance and Kevin was close by Jo knew she was safe, so she shrugged dismissively. "Just watching and enjoying the sound of the birds." She smiled, determined to give him nothing to pick on. Women weren't treated that great around this place. So far, her ability on the race track had earned her a small grain of respect and with the protective presence of Kevin she had been left pretty much to her own devices.

"A rather energetic way to watch birds," he drawled, dropping his backpack on the ground to lean back in a relaxed manner against the trunk of a large mango tree.

An instant burning awareness crept up her neck and flooded her cheeks. She thought she had this under control. No way could she be attracted to a man who had something to do with the death of Patrick. So why is it that this tall dark handsome...she laughed silently, trying unsuccessfully to hide a smile of amusement. *Tall, dark and handsome, well that's a cliché if I ever heard one,* she thought. *But it's true'* her rebellious inner voice argued. He was tall, towering over her by at least a foot and he was dark, his skin tanned to the colour of smooth bronze, highlighting his impressive array of tattoos.

The day old stubble on his angular face enhanced, rather than diminished his proud features and with certain expressions you could see a throwback to a New Zealand heritage. Hair as black as midnight on a moonless night waved in a short unruly order, seemingly to stick out at all angles but giving the impression it had been styled that way by a master hairdresser. Although Jo couldn't see it while he faced towards her, she knew that a single, long piece of braided hair, thinner than her little finger, hung down past his broad shoulders, almost to the small of his back, like a tiny piece of memorabilia left over from his rebellious youth.

Handsome...oh my god yes... he was handsome alright, resembling a Maori Warrior and she was sure that many women had been impaled by those sexy eyes, never to quite recover from their impact. She had to mentally stop herself from reaching out and giving a gentle tug on the small gold cross dangling from his left ear.

Carried away in her assessment, Jo dissected his muscular frame, centimetre by centimetre. Every muscle and bulge were scrutinised then digested by her senses. A lot of his body was exposed, his t-shirt only half sleeved and slanting off his shoulders amplified the tattoos on his bulky biceps, while the tight body hugging fit of his shirt emphasised the hidden power of his chest. She could see small, tight nipples outlined against the fabric, hardened by her survey.

A slow ripple started at his shoulder, working its way past his chest and across his stomach, her eyes following its passage in fascination as it waved and rolled over every muscle on its journey downwards. It stopped and seemed to grow at the junction where his thighs met his torso, and the thin fabric of his running shorts were no protection at all in hiding the desire awakening in him.

Transfixed she stared until she noticed him taking a step towards her. Her attention was switched to the movement of his legs as they edged forward again, his sandshoes, dirt stained and well worn, kicked against a mango which had fallen to the ground.

He stopped and stood still. Her eyes flew to his face, her body responding instantly to the hunger that flared in his eyes. No-one had ever made her feel this way before and he hadn't even touched her, deep down she knew this was the man she wanted to take her through her first rites into womanhood. With all his worldly wisdom her father had said she would know when the right man came along and he wasn't wrong, no other person had ever even remotely made her feel like this.

Horrified she couldn't stop the feeling, her body giving her no choice but to savour the sensations and to let them grow until they radiated out of her, surrounding them both in a web of desire that was almost tangible. His eyes deepened to a smoulder, the space between them dissolved and it was as though he reached out and caressed her skin and like a magnet, she was drawn towards him.

With the first move of her body, the tensions changed dramatically. His warmth turned to ice and the door slammed in her face, she reacted instantly, separating them like two positive magnets forced apart on contact.

Warily they watched each other, both still slightly dazed. Jo raised her eyebrows and tilted her head trying to work out what had just happened.

Slowly the outside sounds filtered into her senses. The Eastern Whip Bird whistled its distinctive note, the sharp crack like sound at the end of the call making her jump and blink in response. Other birds joined the morning chorus, sweetening the atmosphere with their songs.

Sunbirds, the male in full splendour with its iridescent blue throat feasted on the nectar of flowering Grevilleas and Banksias that surrounded the lawns. A juvenile Butcher Bird snapped his large grey beak at an insect on the grass, before it hopped lazily away to search the ground under the umbrella tree at the far side of the garden. Normality returned to the world.

In an alcove close to the mango tree was a bird feeding platform with a flat piece of wood nailed to a round pole stuck in the ground.

Axel seemed to be the first to recover. He glared at her with distrust and annoyance. She stared back transfixed on his expression as he reached down, fumbled in his backpack and pulled out a plastic bag filled with bananas and papaya, not noticing as something small dropped onto the ground by his feet.

It lay, a bright pink temptation just on the edge of her peripheral vision and she fought the urge to look down to see what it was. The colour teased to life a long forgotten memory and suddenly it was Christmas when she had been four or five and amongst all the presents under the tree, a hot pink bunny had sat. She remembered panicking as all her brothers chose a gift, passing up the bunny and opting for cars, trucks or toy guns instead, and when her turn came to pick, the rabbit had been hers and for years it had been her treasured companion.

A loud harsh bird call finally snapped their staring match and Axel turned away as he tipped the fruit onto the feeding platform, allowing her to steal a quick glance at what he had dropped. Her heart skipped a beat, it was a small pink teddy bear, not a rabbit, but that didn't alleviate the urge to walk over pick it up and give it a comforting cuddle.

"Is that fruit for the Magnificent Rifle bird?" Jo questioned, picking up her towel and moving slightly away wiping down her arms, holding it like a protective shield in front of her body.

"That's very specific." Following her lead, he put even more distance between them stooping to pick up a fallen mango which was ripe and ready to eat, at the same time seeing what he had dropped and hastily shoving it back into his pack, glancing up to see if she had noticed.

"I heard him call." Jo convincingly scanned the trees as if searching for the bird, not wanting to confront him about the teddy, but filing the toy into her growing list of confusion about the man. She felt a silent sigh of relief when he didn't mention it either.

Taking a pen knife out of his pocket, he sliced off the skin to the juicy orange flesh inside, popping a piece of fruit into his mouth.

Her tongue darted out moistening her lips as she watched the chewing motion. Jo stepped back even further as he took up his position once again leaning against the mango tree...'De Ja Vu'... they were back to when he had first spoken a few moments ago as if he was trying to wipe out what had happened in-between.

Jo knew there was every reason to hate him. This man was most likely a killer, yet she had felt more without even touching him, than she had ever felt for any man before and she wasn't sure how to deal with it.

Watching him lean easily against the tree trunk, munching away on the mango, he seemed harmless enough. There wasn't much she couldn't handle in life; she was tough and knew it. Whatever this was between them, was something she didn't want to explore, it made her feel strange and vulnerable.

Stay with the plan and stick with Kevin until they could bring him, and the rest of the gang down seemed to be the most sensible thing to do. With a smile born out of false security, Jo took herself back to his original question. *Daydreaming about me are you?'* Well damn him, you couldn't go back, you may want to, but you couldn't. You could only try to forget and correct.

Feeling confident, she tossed him a cheeky grin as she turned away, throwing sweetly over her shoulder, "Daydreaming yes, but not about you."

"Josephine!" The sharp full use of her name stopped her dead in her tracks. Angrily she spun to face him.

"Catch." The words were out before she had turned completely around, and automatically she stuck up her hand and neatly caught the mango he had thrown.

"Maybe lover boy would like it for breakfast?" Pushing off the tree he started walking towards her.

Wanting to flee from the sound of his mocking laugh, Jo forced herself to walk calmly towards the house. Closing the back door as she went through was a bit futile as she felt him directly behind her, so close she could almost sense his warm breath on her neck. Turning sharp left away from the living area and down towards her bedroom and the safety of Kevin, she shut the door behind her with a hurried click.

Of course, there was no lock and there was no Kevin. The bed she had slept in was a crumpled mess, but at least he had thrown the blankets he used to sleep on the floor, on top so it held up the cover of them being a couple. As far as she was concerned Kevin could stay on the floor. Her original intention was to take it in turns, but her anger needed an outlet, he helped get her into this mess, he could damn well sleep on the floor period.

CHAPTER 10

Jo opened the small wardrobe with the intention of adding the
contents to the mess Kevin had left on the bedroom floor.
Hesitating, she sat on the end of the bed. This room reflected the
whole house, messy and in need of a good clean. Why be like them?
She had always followed her own heart and not buckled to the
pressures of other people. So what if she was clean and tidy, maybe
it would rub off on some of the others.

Feeling a little less on edge, she took off her runners and socks,
wiggling her toes in freedom wondering what today would bring.
On the day they arrived, it had been all systems go getting the trails
bikes and gear from the truck up to the house. Her trail bike was
taken to the workshop and her road bike along with the others was
locked in the shed with the truck. Since then it had been relaxing,
swimming, chatting and she was getting restless.

Jo found she liked almost everyone and despite the mess she
loved the freedom of the open style plan. It was cleverly designed
and housing at lots of people with apparent ease. People seemed to
come and go. She hadn't seen Beth or Spike since they arrived, and
a few people had turned up last night and slept on the veranda. It
was all very relaxed and civil, not what she thought it would be like
at all.

Due to her racing status and Kevin's prowess in bike modifications they had been allocated a small room. It had been a godsend; she didn't know how she would fare if she had to share like some of the others did. She also liked the shut door policy, you either left it be or knocked if you wanted to speak to who was inside.

In the privacy of their room last night she had discussed with Kevin about opportunities to let MICO know what they had found out so far. Like a lot of outlying areas, they were in a mobile phone black spot. The only option had seemed to be the next time either one of them went into the closest town. Which would probably be Kevin getting bike parts.

Jo took out the small old-fashioned flip phone, her father had given her, from where it was tucked in her sports bra and grinned, looking forward to telling Kevin she had found a better way. This morning, on the off chance, she had composed a message and hit send. As she had been jogging along the valley road, she had felt the phone vibrate as it fell into service for a brief spell. On the way back it had buzzed in the same spot with a reply.

Reading, then deleting the messages as she jogged, she had been elated her hunch had paid off. Now MICO knew that the leader was not Axel as they had thought, but a man named Viper, and more importantly, there was a second house somewhere deeper in the rainforest and up the hillside where the elite part of the gang lived, she figured that was where Spike and Beth had gone. She hadn't seen them since they arrived. Axel was one of three 'lieutenants' who took it in turns staying at the lower house looking after things. He was just the front man for the outside world.

Grabbing the things she needed for a shower, Jo padded barefoot down the corridor. If Axel had turned up it meant goodbye to Jeckle for a while and in a way, she was glad. Jeckle was appropriately named, his moods switching as easily as most people smiled and she had kept out of his way as much as possible. The third lieutenant, they had been told, was an unsavoury soul named Feral.

Shower finished, Jo opened the door that led down the narrow passage to her bedroom and peeked out. Fortunately the hall was empty, so, pulling the towel tighter around her body she made a quick escape back to her room. She hated getting dressed in the damp, mouldy bathroom. At the first opportunity she was going to buy a dressing gown, others may like walking round half-dressed but that didn't mean she had to. And if Kevin called her a prude again she would flatten him.

Jo dressed in a simple light green loose flowing skirt that swished above her knees as she walked, complementing it with a pale green embroidered short sleeved shirt, with tiny buttons up the front. It was an outfit that Kevin had picked, and she had to admit, he had chosen well. Although the top was skimpier than she normally would have worn, stopping a good couple of inches above the waistline of her skirt it showed off her tanned midriff to a great advantage but more importantly it was cool and comfortable.

Slipping on her mother's gold ring and a bracelet to match, pushing the latter up her arm until it was tight against her skin, she quickly pinned her hair behind her ears with a couple of combs, letting the rest hang loose to cascade down her back. Later when it got hotter she would plait and twist it into a bun, but for now she liked the feel of it hanging free.

Taking a few deep breaths, not sure if it was her nerves, or the unwanted excitement of Phantom being back which was sending her stomach into a whirl. She smiled with confidence at the mirror, giving herself the clenched fist signal for ' chin up, things aren't that bad ' before turning to the door to face the outside world, pausing only briefly to pick up the mango on the way out. No point wasting it she thought.

The kitchen was to the right, along the corridor and past the door which led to the back garden. Off to the left, the large living area opened out as she came out of the passage and once again she marvelled at the design of the house. It wasn't large. Whoever had designed it had incorporated full length sliding doors opening onto large verandas, which not only gave you the feeling of open spaces but provided you with an extra living area in the open air, while still protected from the weather. The woodwork of the interior helped it to blend in perfectly with its outside surroundings.

There was no-one in sight, but she could hear the hub of conversation coming from the kitchen, which again was a master craft of design, unique in the fact that it only had one full wall. And that wall served a very logical purpose; it housed all the cupboards and the fridge/freezer. The stove was on an island bench in the middle of the floor and the sink against a half wall that sort of melded together with the laundry as they extended out on to the back patio, which was screened against insects. Opposite the main wall were more sliding doors opening out once again onto the veranda which surrounded the whole house.

Without hesitating Jo walked past the end of the living room and into the kitchen through the large opening which stretched from the main wall to the veranda, a warm smile of good morning on her face. The veranda doors were open wide and she called a general greeting to all and sundry, before opening the cupboard to prepare her breakfast.

The huge polished wood table on the veranda was almost full. It could seat up to a dozen people at a time. Even at the hour of nine am, there was laughter and a high sense of good will amongst the people who sat there. It was an incredible family like atmosphere. Any squabbles were dealt with quickly and efficiently. So far it hadn't happened in the three days they had been here, but they had been told that any problem, gripe, whinge, or whine which couldn't be solved promptly was taken to the lieutenant on duty, where it was swiftly and efficiently dealt with. Phantom and Jeckle, when the latter was in the right mood, were reasonably fair, Babs had informed them. Feral on the other hand was cold and callous, everyone would be on tenterhooks when he's around. Jo was not looking forward to meeting the third lieutenant. He sounded by all accounts rather loathsome and she was glad to hear he didn't come down very often.

"Good morning, you were up early again."

Jo jumped as Kevin came up directly behind her, wrapping his brotherly arms around her waist and dropping a light kiss on her cheek as he leaned over her shoulder.

Not being used to close bodily contact, she let out a little squeal of protest, before remembering where she was and who she was meant to be. Relaxing back against his chest, she tilted her head until she could see her brother's face, giving him a look of mock indignation. "Good morning back to you sleepy head, when are you going to start getting up at a decent hour of the morning?"

He released his embrace and allowed her to turn to face him.

"Give me some space you big lug," she mouthed softly, pushing at him playfully on the shoulder.

Kevin leaned forward and planted a soft kiss on her cheek, lingering close to her ear so he could whisper. "Come on sis, you're doing great, it's just a brotherly hug, we need to be convincing." He chuckled. "Just pretend I am irresistible."

"What makes you think I know how that feels?" she hissed at him remembering to keep her voice low and close to his ear.

A puzzled frown crinkled his brow as he pulled back in surprise, "Oh, Jo," he said softly. "This is not easy for you, is it?"

He laughed as if they had been sharing a joke as someone walked into the kitchen, but Jo saw the gentle concern in his eyes as he scanned her pale face. Sliding his hands to her waist and giving her some space by holding her back at arm's length he said, "So what have you planned for today? I'm going back over to the bike shed, got some adjustments to finish on Vipers' bike. Probably take most the day."

As he was talking, Jo was aware of the unusual feeling of Kevin's warm hands on the bare flesh of her waist. It wasn't offensive, he was her brother, and in their small house they had shared a room from birth right through school until military training. Being close to him was natural, it just felt weird skin touching skin, and she couldn't remember ever having had that kind of contact before, with anyone. She also became aware of a figure resting against the island bar watching them intently. Kevin's back was half turned, so it was Jo's eyes which were caught and held.

Axel leaned against the island bench, legs forward, one crossed over the other, his hands resting on his waist. He had observed the greeting between the two with consuming interest. He wasn't called Phantom for nothing. He silently drew conclusions from people's actions and was invariably right in his assessment. Something about these two didn't click. Body language was wrong; pauses where actions should have been free flowing, feet and head placement opposed to each other.

To most people it would have gone unnoticed. Not him. As a growing boy, his life had depended on perfecting this skill. Character assessment was as natural as breathing. From the moment he first met Kevin, a tiny something niggled in his brain. It had been enough to keep him interested in Kevin's bid to become part of the group. Then 'Jo' had been thrown in his path, the stunning Josephine with more natural spunk than he had anticipated. He wanted the puzzle pieces where he could see them, so he had accepted them into the gang. They proposed an interesting challenge, but it would be only a matter of time until he worked why they wanted to be here.

One eyebrow raised, he glanced down to where Kevin's hands rested loosely on Jo's waist then back up to her face. It was almost as if she objected to his hands being there. No, objected was the wrong term, he couldn't really pinpoint it and it annoyed the crap out of him. She was comfortable, but she should have been more, he knew how *his* woman would feel and react if *he* held her in such a possessive embrace.

She would lift her arms around his neck and run fingers through the hair on his nape in an effort to draw their bodies closer together, instead of loosely against the chest as she was doing now. He would smile his need of her, hands following the line of her spine to the firm round contours of her rear letting her know just how much he wanted her. Instead of pulling her close into contact with his body, he would run a teasing trail up over the curves of her waist, dipping hands under the hem of her shirt to trace an enticing path to the silky skin beneath her breasts. He would coax them into life by running tantalising lines below and to the sides of them, lifting his thumb in fleeting contact as the peaks became ridged, throbbing for the feeling only his hands could give. Then he would kiss her hello. A kiss full of passion and promise as he pulled her into an embrace of protection letting her draw strength in the knowledge of his...

Babbles burst into the room. "Heya guys, looks like we are in for another scorcher. So hot already my clothes feel all wet...an...clamm...y." the last words trailed off as she looked from Axel to the couple by the bench. She grabbed the milk out of the fridge and fled muttering her apologies for interrupting.

Chapter 11

Jo was hypnotised by the expression on Axel's face and aware that her body was responding to his visual onslaught. It wasn't until Kevin placed himself in the direct line of her vision, forcing her to break eye contact with the man behind him, that she realised something was amiss. He smiled down at her as if nothing had happened, and said, "Hey, come talk to me while I change. Not exactly dressed for working on bikes, am I?"

Her eyes unfocused and re-focused as his words sank in. She saw the concern on his face even though he was trying hard to hide it. What on earth was happening to her, she was here to do a job, not to fall for a man who was most likely involved in not just criminal activities, but the death of her brother and the other agent.

The thought hit her hard. Her head started to spin as the blood drained from her face. The fact he was high up in the group made it more than likely and all she had done in the last couple of days was relax in paradise.

No wonder things had been strained between her and Kevin, they weren't working together as a team. She knew he was her sole source of protection and their father had entrusted them to have each other's backs. It was time to kick into gear, accept the fact she found Axel's sexual attraction alluring, ignore it and get down to the reason why they were here. Jo didn't delude herself, she realised there was a very bright spark between them which certainly wouldn't take much to fan into a full roaring flame. It was up to her to keep it surrounded in ice, to quell any flicker before it had the chance to spread and run rampant. At the same time, they couldn't afford to break contact with him. She wasn't stupid, she knew there was more to her assignment than her father let on. And not for the first time she wished she knew more about the business her family was involved in.

At last she remembered she wasn't alone. Her brother was here, and he could handle the likes of Phantom. All she had to do was stay calm and out of the way, report any finding whilst she was jogging and concentrate on getting to know the bike trails. The sooner the job is done the sooner life could get back into its normal pattern.

The worry and concern etched into Kevin's features drove the point home of how foolish she'd been. Leaning forward she gave him a peck on the cheek, concentrating on showing him how strong, competent and resilient she could be through her expression. She banished any trace of vulnerability and replaced it with calculating control, and when she deepened her grin, she confirmed to him the demons she had been battling with since they arrived had vanished and his resourceful, strong willed sister had returned and with a vengeance.

Jo relaxed as Kevin pulled her into a hug of pure love and adoration and whispered in her ear, "Well done beautiful."

Pushing away to an arm's length she acknowledged him with a simple smile. "After you get changed, come back here and I'll walk over with you. I haven't had breakfast and I am starving. I think I have a mango somewhere."

Giving Kevin a wink of confidence, Jo stepped out from his protective embrace. She had to face Axel sometime, no use putting it off.

It was like being hit by a steamroller. He hadn't turned off the charm, if anything he seemed to have increased it and for a slight moment Jo was almost lost again. Instinctively she knew she couldn't connect with his eyes. Picking his chin as a focal point, she spoke to it rather than to him, deciding on a direct action instead of pussy footing around.

"Do you want something? Or do you just get your kicks out of watching other people say good morning?"

Axel's eyes narrowed. "I can show you how I get my kicks, but three's a crowd."

Fire grew in her cheeks as a silence stretched between them. His smile had her wishing she knew what was going on inside his head, but she kept fixed on his chin and wasn't going to risk even a small peek as to what was in his eyes, she wasn't stupid. All she wanted to do was put enough distance between them.

With great deliberation, Axel brought one finger up to scratch the tip of his chin. Jo immediately lowered her eyes to the base of his neck only to find that his hand dropped to scratch there as well. She looked away, only to find that at his next words, her eyes flew straight up to clash with his.

"Be ready in a couple of hours, today we go and ride the range."

If you think I am going up there alone with you. You've got rocks in your head. Out aloud she said. "Great, who else is coming?"

"There will be a few of us." His eyes shone with amusement. "In fact, if you can spare a couple of hours Rev, it would be good if you checked the track over too. It might help you understand why those modifications we were talking about are so important."

"Sure, I'd like to try out what I've already done to Viper's bike."

"Well, now that's settled, I'll go and have my breakfast." Jo leant forward and gave Kevin a light peck on the cheek. "See you soon." She winked and with a smile designed to dazzle the darkest night, she walked out of the kitchen with a very provocative and sexy roll to her hips.

Jo's exit left Kevin open-mouthed in surprise. When his sister decides to get her act together, she goes all the way and he noticed that it didn't just take his breath away.

Axel was following her progress to the table on the veranda with an almost animal hunger. It made Kevin very aware that his dear sister was treading on very thin ice. Recalling Axel's words from the first day they arrived he threw them back at him now.

"As long as she chooses me, she's mine. Won't forget that will you?" Kevin rose to his full height drawing almost dead level with the towering Phantom. The two men faced each other, tough and unrelenting.

"If she chooses you, you have nothing to worry about do you?" said Axel, placing his hands aggressively on his hips.

Kevin copied the move. "Providing she's left to decide for herself, no I haven't"

"Nothing wrong with trying to influence somebody's decision is there?" This time Axel made a threatening step forward as he spoke, a light sneer on his lips.

Kevin stood his ground, if it came to a fight, he could hold his own. "As long as it's her choice in the long run...mate."

"That's the rule...*mate*."

Kevin pressed home his point.

"Do we have a pact? Whoever she chooses, the other accepts it and leaves her alone."

"We have a pact; the choice is hers." Axel relaxed his stance extending his hand to seal his words and when Kevin didn't take up the offer he added, "...and the other must back off."

Kevin reached out and two strong sun-browned hands clasped together in agreement. The way Axel had said the last few words stuck in his mind. It was almost as if they had been said to him instead of the other way around. He had no further time to dwell on the matter as the other mechanic, Fast Eddie, stuck his head around the far wall calling out for him to join him in the workshop.

Chapter 12

J o found the morning not as stressful as she had expected. After
breakfast she helped Freckles do a rough job on the kitchen.
Naturally the women were left to clean up the mess. While Jo
washed the dishes the willowy redhead with a quiet, but friendly
nature came and dried up.

The grime around the sink from last night's effort left them both
feeling quite ill. Housework was done in a very haphazard way. If
you felt like cooking, you cooked, usually enough to feed yourself
and a few others. There were always things left over in the fridge for
those who couldn't be bothered. You only cleaned if you felt like
it and on the first day Jo had to suppress the urge not to sterilise
the place from top to bottom, silently vowing not to let it get her
down. With a bit of luck, they would be out of here in no time at
all.

"Thanks for the hand, you coming for a swim" Freckles asked,
hanging the tea towel over the oven door to dry.

"Maybe later, going to 'ride the range' this morning."

"Rather you than me."

"Ever been tempted to go through the 'forbidden gate' and up to
the range?" Jo finished wiping the sink, leaned back and looked at
Freckles questioningly.

She scrunched up her face and shook her head. "Told you when you first came, never been to the range, never want to. I have been up to the upper house though, for a couple of parties, but not the range."

Jo liked Freckles, she had been one of the people who had been assigned to orientate them to their surroundings, explain the rules and most importantly show them where they were not allowed to go. The point emphasised very strongly about what would happen if you went beyond the boundaries, and into the forbidden areas. Formalities done they had spent most of the hot days in the cooling waters of the crystal-clear creek and the nights were filled with fun and laughter as they were introduced to the rest of the gang. Over the last few days an easy friendship had developed between the two women. Jo liked her personality, she defiantly knew how to hold her own amongst the single males, fobbing off their advances with a firm easy humour.

Freckles studied Jo for a moment then leaned close and dropped her voice low, "I shouldn't be telling you this, but you've been good to me since you come, just like Phantom, an' I don't want you to get hurt." She looked sideways to make sure no one was around, her voice hitting a bare whisper. "The range is dangerous, Feral's up there, and...and sometimes people don't come back. They say they left the gang, maybe they did, I don't know?"

Jo was taken back. "Are you sure? Have you said anything?" She took a gamble. "What about Phantom? You said he's been good to you, can you ask him?"

Freckles shook her head. "No one would listen to me; besides I like it here. I was living on the street and Phantom got me a room here, he's been kind, didn't pressure me to go back to my folks, not that they cared anyway, taught me to stick up for myself with the boys. I was in a real bad place, been here two years now, I owe him."

"You said he was kind, can you tell him?" Jo pushed, "Do you trust him?"

Freaking a little at the intensity of the questions, Freckles back away, "I shouldn't have said nothing, just wanted you to be careful."

As she turned to leave, Jo's 'thank you' made her hesitate and when Jo put a hand on her shoulder she looked back.

"Sorry I didn't mean to offend you and I meant it when I said thanks, and I will be careful."

The young woman matched her smile. "As I said he's been good to me, I owe him, he said he's been where I was." Her smile faded. "But he lives in the upper circle and Feral's his friend. You do the math."

She watched Freckles walk away and mulled over the new information. A pink fluffy toy, and now kindness, it just didn't gel with the arrogant killer she thought him to be. Deciding not to mention it to Kevin yet, wanting him to draw his own conclusions and see if they match hers. Something about Phantom just didn't sit right and it intrigued her.

Chapter 13

Jo looked at her watch as she leaned comfortably against the smooth trunk of the ancient tree that provided a wealth of shade from the otherwise scorching tropical sun. The others should be here soon. Axel had changed his plan and told those who were going up to the track to be at the repair shed after lunch as a few problems to Vipers' bike had held things up.

Already having eaten, Jo explained to Kevin that she wanted to get out in the fresh air for a while. She had enjoyed the time on her own and had arrived a little early at the meeting point, found a nice shady spot a short distance from the shed and settled down to wait. It was now just after noon and she smiled to herself as she switched her phone to music and adjusted the ear buds. With a bit of luck, she should have about half an hour before the others came.

To hear the soul soothing sounds of her favourite music was sanity to her ears. For the last couple of days, the thump thump of rock, punk, and heavy metal...whatever they had on, was full blast and the noise had been permanently imprinted in her brain. Not that she disliked all the music. She enjoyed a variety of beats for different occasions, it just was too much and too loud. Eyes closed she let the calming sounds of the saxophone wash in waves over her body sending her into a state of total relaxation as she absorbed the fluent flowing notes, feet gently tapping and head slightly nodding to the passionate rhythm.

Something soft landed in her lap and she let out a startled cry that echoed back through her earphones. A mottled long-sleeved camouflage shirt spilled from her lap onto the ground. She looked up into the piercing blue eyes she had avoided all morning, instantly steeling herself for the onslaught of emotion which was sure to surface.

He reached down and pulled out her ear plugs and put one to his ear. At the same time she pulled the cord out of her phone, glaring her disapproval at his actions. Laughing he snatched the phone out of her hands and held it out of her reach as she scrambled to her feet.

For an instant they both stared at each other. The one thing she didn't want was to be sprung listening to what would be no doubt classed as old-fashioned sentimental music.

"May I have that back please?"

"Well, aren't we polite all of a sudden?"

Jo had forgotten that well-spoken polite attitudes weren't really the norm around here, so she with added sarcasm. "It's mine, fucking give it back." She immediately regretted lowering herself to his standards as she registered the hint of battle in his eyes. *Keep your cool, Kevin can't be far behind.*

What made him relent she didn't know, but she wasn't taking any chances as she backed away from him and put the phone away in her knapsack. Giving him a sideways glance, she felt a little better now there was some distance between them.

After brushing the dirt off her favourite riding jeans, she held up the shirt he had thrown on her lap, striving to keep her voice normal she said, "What's this for?"

Phantom cocked his head in her direction.

"Does that mean you want me to wear this?" She dangled it loosely on two fingers.

"Yes." He gave her an all-powerful smirk, designed to raise her hackles. It was as if for some inexplicable reason he wanted to see her lose control, who was she to disappoint, her eyes flashed as she snapped back;

"Why should I?"

"One thing you had better learn, whatever I say goes... Got that?"

Jo tried unsuccessfully to swallow her anger.

"Your shirt's no good," he continued. "Too bright. Dull greens only on the track, no-one rides the range unless I am happy with what they wear."

Jo bit back a smart remark. Damn him, he was so easily able to provoke any emotion he chose out of her. The tightening of his jaw, the narrowing of his eyes and the deep blue vein that was pulsing wildly at his left temple showed her he was not as unaffected as he would like to make out. But she wanted to rock his superior cool. Calling him Axel to his face should do it.

A quick glance at her watch, a gamble that the others would be on time and she threw herself into an action that even shocked herself.

"And why is it you came early, Axel?" she said huskily, undoing the top two buttons to her shirt. "Had you planned to help me get changed?"

From the corner of her eye she saw him move too fast for her to react. She gasped for breath as he pushed her backwards into the tree trunk, pinning her arms behind her as his body enveloped hers.

The firm taut muscles of his shoulders and chest dwarfed her. It was hard for her to breathe as his hands grabbed a handful of her hair.

Shocked, Jo tried to struggle, but his fully aroused manhood pressed into her lower abdomen, forcing her hands even harder into the trunk of the tree. Her head was tilted back as far as it would go, and she was completely cocooned by him. His lips quivered a hairs breath away from hers as he spoke low and threatening.

"Is this what you were asking for?" His tongue flicked out and lightly touched her dry, tightly closed lips, its soft moist tip sending a shock wave of sensation plummeting through her system.

Jo fought back with her only means of defence – attack.

"Yes." But instead of shutting down, his eyes deepened to a royal blue and his tongue moistened his mouth as if he was preparing for a feast.

She fought back the desire to moisten her own lips in answer to him. A ball of white heat inside her simmered and she was barely able to contain it from running rampant. She wanted so much to give in to these wonderful alien sensations but knew if she did, she would be lost.

She needed a focal point. It was a trick she had learnt as a young girl when her brothers had cornered her. Not that this was any comparison, but the principle should still work. Forcing herself to concentrate on the pain where his hands pulled tight on her hair brought her back to reality.

"Yes," she repeated, her eyes narrowing slightly. "I wanted to see you lose control."

His reaction was everything she desired. He took a sharp breath and relaxed his hold as he stepped back a fraction. The slight withdrawal was enough for Jo to half slide her arm out from behind her, but then he pushed her up tighter against the tree. The bone on her wrist caught against a knot which was sticking out of the trunk and she stifled a cry as she felt the soft skin tear.

"Liar," he mocked, back in full control, his eyes holding an almost amused admiration before the cold callous animal reappeared. His hands released her hair and he slid them behind her ears to the crown of her skull where he slowly began to massage the scalp.

Pain was replaced with pleasure as his fingers moved firm and sure, his thumb catching the sensitive area just behind her ears.

"I...we...don't." For the first time in her life Jo was speechless as sensations shot from the tip of her head making her breasts tingle against the firmness of his muscles. She tried to pull her hand free, feeling the skin rip even more, but the pain was smothered as his chest answered her hardened nipples with ripples of delight and Jo knew she was lost as his mouth came crashing down towards hers.

The kiss was as strong as the man, the pressure of his lips firm and unrelenting as he tried to gain access inside her mouth, but her tightly clenched teeth barred his way. His deep growl of displeasure brought an uncontrollable smile to Jo's mouth and his lips stopped against hers.

Stillness overcame them. Two unmoving figures huddled against a tree at the edge of a forest. The sounds of activity outside drifted through Jo's senses. Rainbow Lorikeets in the over-head trees chattered and twittered playfully as they competed for the small berries that grew in clustered bunches high in the branches above. And in the distance a door slammed, and people's voices could be heard. She looked into his eyes, green, mocking blue. She revelled in the challenge of driving him to lose control, bringing his emotions to the surface so he would have to face himself as well as her.

Her aggression matched his, with all the years of her military upbringing coming to the surface, stopped her from feeling any form of compassion towards the man. The years of suppressed violence bubbled through her veins and although she hated it, she knew it was the only way to keep an emotional distance from what was happening.

Dominating blue drank in the essence of defiant green. In the silence and stillness that was between them, the rules of the game were discarded. A challenge was acknowledged and dismissed. In the flick of an instance and a new demand was issued.

Remain impassive to this, if you can.

His lips, still locked with hers, stiffened in a cold smile. Slowly he released his right hand, his left still clenched tight in her hair. His tongue sent light flickering messages to the moist skin on the inside of her lips, tracing her teeth and the pattern of her gums in the softest of caresses, probing gently with silky movements designed to melt the toughest opponent.

Suppressed anger battled with pleasure. She almost went to bite his tongue but stopped realising it would give him the opening he required. He sighed long and deep against her teeth, the action sending waves of pleasure rocketing in every direction as she tasted his fresh mango breath. She tried to close her lips against him, but he chuckled deeply, his words muffled as he teased, "prepare to lose Josephine."

Jo mocked him with her stare, they were worthy opponents. He would not gain access by making her talk. She almost gasped as his free hand slid in a slow caress down the length of her neck, resting on the sensitive pulse at its base. Her eyes widened in protest as he popped the last small button to her blouse, creeping his fingers inside, walking them sensuously towards their goal.

"Just say the word and I'll stop," Axel mumbled against her teeth.

It was hard to concentrate as his fingers slipped over the fine lace of her bra, tracing the outline of her nipple as it flared to life under his caress. His touch, so unlike the man, was sweet and delicate, it sent veins of fire racing through her body.

Alien sensations threatened to override all else as a moan of delight tried to escape her throat. Soft fingers lifted her bra, catching a firm ripe breast as it spilled over into his palm. Jo's eyes misted over as he squeezed and moulded the firm flesh as if it was a piece of warm putty in need of reshaping.

He released her breast, letting it bounce freely in the hot afternoon air, trailing his fingers around the nipple before tracing a feathery path up to the soft skin around her neck. His lips were insistent against hers.

Jo, floundering in a sea of sensation, tried to arch her body against, but he was unrelenting. His size hid her from the outside world and his eyes shone with devilment. Resting his hand in the dip of her shoulder he caressed it lightly as he mumbled something crude against her clenched teeth.

Her anger, bubbling beneath the surface, rose to shine through her eyes, piercing him with their intensity, like green daggers trying to cut him down to size.

"That's it my little kitten," he chuckled. "Let me feed your anger." With those words he pinched her on the sensitive skin of her neck, twisting the soft flesh until she cried out in exquisite pain.

The advantage was his. As her mouth flew open in surprise he plunged his tongue deep into her warm depths, discovering every crevice with swift controlled thrusts, tantalising her into joining the duel with her own tongue.

To Jo it was the final release, all the pent up emotion and tension from the last few days finally had an outlet. With her anger blown to a full and fiery pitch, she liberated its hostility in the form of passion, matching his hunger with warfare of her own. Anger was an emotion she knew. Even in the form of passion she was able to control it, analyse and isolate the feelings, savouring each one, unwilling to let it go until the next burst of pleasure demanded similar attention.

She felt Axel try to control the kiss, taking her lips within his, moving them in gentle rotation, letting their warmth and moisture slide together to create sensations of a softer, more sensual nature, using pure passion to calm the duelling tongues. Jo was not to be denied her wrath, she had his measure now, and she would make him pay for the unwanted emotions he was provoking.

Without realising it, she trusted him to call a halt before things escalated out of control. Although aware of her surroundings, her thoughts were not quite as rational as they should have been, she should have learnt by now anger was never a reliable emotion to act upon.

As she struggled against her trapped position Axel relented, stepping back slightly and slowly relinquishing his hold. He placed his hands on either side of the trunk just above her shoulders giving her the freedom to move. Draping her hands around his shoulders, she felt his muscles ripple and shudder as she twined his long thin plait around her fingers, twisting none too gently in her desire to have him increase the pressure on her mouth.

As she leant forward, Axel pulled back with teasing resistance, his tongue slipping out of her mouth to trace delicate patterns on her demanding lips, the movement giving her total freedom from her enclosed prison.

The effect was explosive for them both. Jo drew his tongue back into her mouth, sucking on it in an instinctive primitive rhythm designed to send the blood rushing to Axels' head and overpowering the need to cool the passion between them. He slid his hands down to her buttocks pulling her close against his torso, so she could feel the hardened desire she aroused in him. At the same time, he swung her around so that he was up against the tree and she was pressing forward towards him.

The sensation of now being the aggressor sent Jo's passion into overdrive. Free to move, she flaunted her womanhood, kissing him back with a fever she had never known was in her, exploring the mysteries of his mouth with hungry thrusts of her tongue. Rubbing and arching her body in provocative gestures against his, her hands roamed with free will over the tight t-shirt which covered the bronzed muscles of his broad chest and shoulders.

*Stop me...*her mind screamed...*This has gone far enough.*

Instead of stopping her, Axel encouraged her with a reckless passion of his own. Edging her into unchartered depths of desire as he tore his mouth away, to suck, bite and feast with greedy hunger at the smooth line of her neck. He left a trail of raw sensitive nerve ends as he suckled the responsive hollow at its base with a fiery intensity.

Following the graceful curve to the right, he lightly sank his teeth into the delicate flesh of her shoulder, releasing an animal growl of pleasure at her unbridled response as she twisted her neck to the side to allow him greater access. The movement enabled him to bring his hand up to her now exposed breast, enclosing its firm roundness in the warmth of his hand.

A strangled sob caught in her throat as she felt herself spiral on the edge of reality, trying desperately to find the truth of the situation. His breath harsh and rasping in her ear brought her back to earth with a bang. "Unless you want me to fuck you right here in full view of my friends walking up the road, I suggest we save it for a more appropriate time."

The degrading term turned Jo's passion back into pure explosive anger at his derogative interpretations of her newly found sexuality. It didn't register that she had provoked the unwanted situation in the first place. She knew later she would be mortified at what she had done, at what she had allowed to happen, but now all she could think about was salvaging what little of her self-respect she had left.

Jo felt vulnerable, hurt and angry. Axel was looking at her in confusion. All she could think about was regaining control and not letting him see how defenceless she felt. He was so busy watching her face, he didn't see her clenched fist fly towards his jaw until it was almost too late. Even though it knocked them both slightly off balance as he turned his head to ride with the impact, it stung her knuckles. Reaching out he grabbed the loose folds of her shirt as if he thought she was going to flee. Jo had no intention of doing any such thing. She had never run from anybody in her life and she wasn't about to start now.

They faced each other an arm's length away. For a moment Jo thought he was going to hit her back, but instead of his fists he used words, cruel hurting words that tore into her heart.

"I had you figured for a slut, but not a tease." The pure disgust in his voice was a perfect match to the expression in his eyes." This time I have no choice but to let you go, but I tell you now," he leaned close, pulling her slightly towards him, running his fingers down the length of her open shirt, catching her breasts in a light caress. "Don't ever let me get you alone, because I won't let your fucking teasing stand in the way of what I will do to you." Then he proceeded to graphically inform her in non-polite terms exactly what it was he would do.

Anger flared as if the brutality he offered was an appeasement to her guilty soul. Then slowly the shame of what had transpired between them hit her full force and she was horrified at the repercussions that were bound to occur. Anger faded and she felt the blood drain from her face in disgrace. Tugging against his grip on her shirt, she looked down at her swollen breasts, still throbbing from his touch, watching in horror as the taut rosy nipple sprung into new life as he touched a finger against it as she pulled away.

Adjusting her wayward bra with shaking fingers, she pulled her shirt tight across her chest as she looked back up at him, unable yet to tackle the buttons. He gestured with his arm for to take the khaki shirt from his outstretched hand, but all she saw was his expression glorifying in her humiliation.

Jo shut her eyes, swallowing her pride and trying to gain back some self-esteem. For a couple of long minutes she breathed deep and relaxing in the closed blackness of her mind, controlling and rearranging her thoughts. When she opened them again the brilliant green of her eyes was as cold and hard as the granite wall she had erected around her heart. How she could have let him affect her in any way was beyond her comprehension, he was no doubt up to his neck in the criminal activities they were trying to uncover, responsible for Patricks death, and she all she could think about now, was how she would enjoy helping to put him behind bars where he belonged.

Almost ripping the shirt out of his fingers, she shoved her arms into the sleeves and buttoned up both shirts. Her "Go to hell you immoral bastard," only enhanced the coldness in his face.

"Wrong word choice...a bastard has a mother." With that he walked away.

Luckily, she had her back to the approaching group and by the time she turned to greet them she was fully composed. At least on the exterior.

Chapter 14

Axel's anger and aggression disbursed in the wake of her erect frame. Moving his jaw from side to side to ease the ache her fist had left, he kept his face impassive as he watched her smooth interaction with the new arrivals, noticing how she kept herself at Kevin's protective side. He had never been so confused about a woman in all his twenty-seven years. Everybody he had known fell into a category he could catalogue and file.

Not Josephine, there was more to her than met the eye. Every time he thought he had her figured, she did a one hundred and eighty degree turn in the other direction. She inflamed a desire in him to push her to her limits just to find out if they were as obscure as his.

And she was dangerous. This hot-headed, passionate woman was playing him along, why or for what purpose, he didn't know.

This morning in the kitchen, he had watched the flush rise to stain her cheeks, and had smiled at her discomfort, not sorry that he had caused it. She unsettled him in a way he couldn't explain. If she wanted to push his buttons, be it on her head, it might just help him understand what game they were they were up to.

There was enough on his plate right now, more than enough, and it wasn't going to get any better. Things were escalating fast and he wanted all the players where he could see them. Timing was everything. The delectable Jo and her lover boy with their off-kilter body language was a complication he didn't need, but on the other hand couldn't be ignored.

He smiled as he walked over to the group, a cold cynical smile he knew would make his face look sinister in the dim light of the forest. Dangerous games were right up his alley, he had been playing them all his life and this one was proving to be the most interesting of all. Watching her now added another piece to his puzzle. She was an impressive actress, portraying a cool confidence he knew was contradictory to what she was feeling. Why? It was a good question. It was also one he couldn't answer...yet.

"Let's go," Phantom ordered as Jeckle appeared on the track behind the gate. "Kev you double with me, Jo with Jeckle. Al, Grub and Stretch you're on your own, straight to the range. Beth will be waiting at the shed. She knows what tracks we will be riding today. I'll see you up there later."

"Why double, you've seen us ride?" Kevin's voice held a note of confusion.

"Newbies who haven't yet been initiated into the group not only have to double up, they also have to be blindfolded." Axel stared at them arrogantly, dangling his baited hook.

Jo was the first to bite, jumping in with sarcasm of her own, before Kevin had the chance to even open his mouth. "Don't you think that's over reacting and childish? It's only a racetrack after all."

Although his face remained unemotionally detached, Axel internally smiled, she hadn't disappointed him. They were good adversaries. She was also going to push him to his limits. Well, this little wildcat had met her match in him. It was time she learnt a lesson in control. He was second in charge of this group and he couldn't afford to have a new comer challenging his authority.

"You forget you are runts here. You've already been told that past this gate is a no-go zone. So far you are only on the outer edge of the group. Up there." He pointed in the direction of the steep hill with his outstretched hand, "up there is the heart of the group and we don't just allow anyone into our domain...until we trust them."

He leaned forward so his face was only an inch from hers. "We don't trust you, either of you." Axel shot a look over at Kevin who was glaring at Jo. "Trust is earned, and so far, you're not doing too well."

"How do we know we can trust you?"

Jo's question was quick and off the mark and said with an impassive expression as if she was trying to impersonate his cool control. It made Axel raise his eyebrows in interest. Kevin wasn't hiding his annoyance; he was staring hard at Jo, blatantly not impressed with her stance at all.

Axel stared her down, he was sure she was trying hard to make him lose his cool. He gritted his teeth feeling the tightness all the way to his temple, determined to stay in control. Hell, all he wanted to do was kiss her again. A slight smile escaped her lips as she closed off her expression and let her eyes glaze over so they stared through him as if he didn't exist. She infuriated him.

Enough was enough, he pulled a blindfold out of his back pocket, held it up in front of her face, and with great deliberation drawled. "I'll have to find another for your mouth."

He took great pleasure in seeing her cheek fire up as she snatched the dangling blindfold out of his grasp and stomped over towards Jeckle's bike, ignoring the rest of the gangs, including Kevin's, explosions of laughter.

CHAPTER 15

For Jo there hadn't been much time after that for thought, as they were introduced to one of the most invigorating and challenging experiences she had ever had. Once they arrived at another small shed, they had been allowed to take off their blindfolds and were given their own bikes. Jo was pleased to find her own trail bike ready and waiting even if she wasn't impressed to find it had been repainted into dull greens and browns, no shiny chrome, just flat lifeless paint. From then onwards there had been no time to talk to Kevin or feel any antagonism towards Axel as she was thrown full force into the vigour of the track.

Her father hadn't been wrong when he had said the hills were criss-crossed with trails, even with her mapping skills she was having a hard time orientating herself. She couldn't even tell in which direction the lower house was, except it had to be down. Of the upper house there was no sign.

The trails themselves were narrow, just enough room for a bike to fit. Too often she had been caught with her arms wide and had been scraped or snagged by sticking out branches and she was begrudgingly grateful for the long sleeved shirt. In many places the trees and undergrowth grew over the track so low that you had to flatten yourself against the bike or you would have been knocked off.

Jo tried to maintain speed. An impossible task unless you knew the trails well and even then, you would have to be constantly alert. The dips, curves and corners were sharp and dangerous. Twice, when Axel had given her the lead, she had almost fallen off as the track veered sharply away, just managing to hold her own as he sat hot on her heels.

The last time she had zig-zagged up a steep hill, Axel had applied more pressure, urging her to ride faster. As she mounted the crest the trail disappeared and she had ended up flat on her bottom bruised and sore, her bike with a busted throttle and a buckled wheel. As Axel had come up behind her, she had seen him take the well hidden path to the left just before the crest and she had almost cried with frustration and exhaustion. He hadn't even bothered to wait. In the end she had to extract her bike from the undergrowth and follow him limping.

She hadn't seen Kevin since they had arrived at the small shed, as he had gone off with Jeckle and Grub to another part of the track. Al and Stretch had been with her and Axel and she was impressed with the two younger members. Their riding skills were advanced and their devotion to Axel bordered on the edge of hero worship. As much as she didn't like to admit it, Axel was good with them too, treating them with just the right amount of toughness for them to want to do their best.

Now she didn't know where any of them were, although the bikes were surprisingly quiet, she could hear the rise and fall buzz in the distance, but it was hard to know what direction they came from. All she could do was follow the trail that he had taken and hope to meet up with the others. Not that she minded. As far as she was concerned, they could take their time, there was no way they would leave her in their elite Upper Circle area on her own, and the peace and solitude, even for a short while was welcome.

She may as well use the time to recharge her batteries and take in as much as she could of her surroundings. Instead, as she battled with her busted bike along the narrow track, she found her thoughts drifting into unwanted avenues without realising she was doing it.

His eyes, alive with burning heat as his head lifted from that devastating kiss was permanently imprinted in her mind, keeping her body flush with awareness. In all honesty Jo had to admit she liked being possessed by him, enjoyed the feeling of being powerless in his arms, revelled in goading and encouraging him to act the way he did, and he hadn't disappointed her. It had made her feel powerful in return, she even knew why she did it and here on her own it was easy to admit it.

Josephine Brennan had finally met a man who could not only chip away at her defences but leap right over them as if they didn't exist and, in the process, making her see the sensual man behind his own wall. She had felt his control, felt him soften the aggression she fed him and that had made her want to push him even further, not wanting to acknowledge the man he offered with his softness.

Jo shook her head in denial. What in the hell was she thinking? Having sex with him was *not* an option. She had always thought love and sexual desire would come together, while every inch of her body might desire him, there was no way she loved him.

Her father had always told her not to be afraid of her sexuality but to listen to it. Telling her in his bold straight forward way, 'you will know in your heart when it is right, when it is the man you want to spend the rest of your life with. When that happens just relax and let love take its course.' The words had been good advice then, but in real life things just didn't click into place with such easy logic. She wanted Axel as she had never wanted any man in her life before. He made her feel things she never knew she could feel, but it wasn't right, it couldn't be. Not with him.

Never in her previous experience with men had she felt even a twinkle of desire. None had made her feel the explosions of longing that Axel had just by giving her a smouldering look. Most men couldn't get past her tough exterior for a kiss let alone to the passionate woman she protected inside. In fact, Axel had been the first man to really kiss her. She felt a slight blush creep into her cheeks as she remembered, acknowledging at the same time the tug of a deep internal craving.

It wasn't as if she was not used to masculine company. On the contrary, in the training camps she had been on she had met many men of the strong forceful kind. In such camps women were few, with both sexes sharing the same conditions and living quarters.

She had learnt how to hold the opposite sex at bay with a cold chilling expression. Only a few had dared to try to break down the icy barrier which surrounded her, to find that dry ice not only burns, but leaves painful scars. Friendship she had been free and easy with, holding a confident rapport with both sexes, but if anyone stepped over the line they met with a fierce resistance, an impregnable force they were unable to get past. Most of the men she knew stayed in the friend category, accompanying her on dates to the usual places with other friends but since Patricks' death, she had been quieter and more reserved, enjoying less the frivolous side of life.

Sweat formed on her brow and she stopped, wiping it off with the back of her sleeve as the hot oppressive rainforest closed around her. She was heading slightly downhill now, her ankle throbbed, and the weight of the bike dragged against her shoulders. The air was so thick and humid she could almost eat it, but she resisted the urge to break the rules and unbutton the thick shirt. Instead she splashed a little water from her bottle over her face. It was warm but she didn't care, it was wet and refreshing. She took a mouthful, sucked up the pain and limped on. "For Patrick," she whispered the words reinforcing the reason to remain strong.

Life hadn't been the same without Patrick. Even now just over a year later she had trouble believing he was not coming back. That she would never see the boyish grin he always wore, eyes alight with fun and mischief. She remembered the happy him, not the closed distant man he had developed into the deeper he became involved in the undercover work that would eventually lead to his death. Here she was now in his world, and it was time to take this clandestine role more seriously. Even if she had been manipulated into it by her father and brother, she had a strong resolve to complete the mission, to make them proud. A tingle of excitement crept into her mind as she ducked under a lower lying branch. To be truthful she had never felt more alive than she did right now.

Jo looked at her watch. She was at a junction in the paths and didn't know which way to go. Well, she had two choices, she could sit here and wait for Axel to come back to her or go ahead on her own. What was expected of her? Was this some kind of test?

Maybe it was and Jo intended to do everything right from now on. No more antagonism towards Axel. No more confrontations like this morning, she didn't want to feel the things he made her feel. From now on, if he told her to do something, she would do it without batting an eyelid. Yes! That's it, a challenge, she would see it all as a challenge. Once she set her mind on a goal nothing would stop her from doing her level best to achieve it.

Jo discarded her bike, sat on the ground and leaned back against a tree. She checked her mobile phone, as expected no service. It wasn't important but she did like to test it at every opportunity. You just never knew.

She tucked her phone away and relaxed, as much as she wanted to explore, she would be expected to wait, so that's just what she would do. It was time to formulate a plan. Contrary to what her father thought she and Kevin weren't working well together, she was waiting for him to lead and show her what to do. Smiling ruefully to herself she thought about her brother, what was she waiting for? Where she was concerned, she had always led and Kevin had always followed, getting her out of the trouble she always ended up in. Well they weren't kids any more and this wasn't some school prank.

Jo rubbed her open palms over her face, things had to be set right, she had to get rid of all the tension and aggression and stop waiting for Kevin to get her out of this situation she found herself in.

First, she had to set the stage. Axel was too damn smart for his own good. She would have to throw him off balance. The only way she could think of doing that was to offer him an apology about the way she behaved this morning, that would really confuse him and confusion was a good way to keep him unaware of how she really felt, then, if she kept a low profile and accepted his leadership without any resistance, surely he would relax and treat her just like the rest of the gang. She had been too aggressive right from the start. If she apologised and admitted she was wrong he wouldn't take much notice of her character change, he would just think he had won the power battle between them. Surely, that shouldn't be hard to do, should it?

'Ok, this is it, you can do it,' she thought giving herself mental boost as the sound of an approaching trail bike grew louder. She was looking forward to beating him at his own power game. Jo sucked in a deep breath as she stood to meet him, shoulders slightly slumped in a position of reluctant surrender.

The momentary flash of apprehension that flew across her face wasn't noticed by Kevin as he climbed off the back of the bike greeting her with a concerned frown. "You ok?" She barely heard him as Axel stared back at her from over the handlebars, his cool blue eyes boring into hers with a cynical glint telling her he had seen her uneasiness and found some form of amusement from it.

"I'm perfectly fine, thanks," Jo said, deciding not to mention her ankle, not wanting Axel's attention anywhere near her legs. A night's rest and it was sure to be fine. "It's not the first time I've come off and I doubt it will be the last if this track is anything to go by." She laughed a little higher pitched than usual and she inwardly kicked herself.

Refusing to look at Axel, she concentrated on Kevin and his inspection of the twisted wheel stating the obvious. "Bike's a bit busted though."

"You did extremely well considering you were riding one of our toughest tracks." Both Kevin and Jo looked in surprise at Phantom in all his arrogance, still sitting astride the bike.

Putting her arm on her brother's to stop the question which sprung to his lips, she smiled and said simply and sweetly. "Thanks.

Toughest track hey, no wonder I fell off." Mentally giving herself a point as she saw the suspicious twinkle in the mighty Phantoms' eye, she may as well start now how she intended to play this task...respectful and defeated. What a sham!

"One day you may just be good enough on this track to' ride the range'."

Jo figured he had thrown out those words to spark a reaction. She had seen Kevin stiffen slightly and knew she had as well. What the hell had he meant by that? They were riding the range now, weren't they? Should they question him on it?

Kevin was quick, covering the need to do anything by drawing their attention to her bike. "Won't be riding anywhere on this for a while, wheels buckled, gunna need a new one."

"Fine, Rev, we'll send Al back with a spare wheel, while you start on the throttle. When you've finished, we will meet you back at the bottom shed, you can double with Al and don't forget your blindfold." Axel's voice lacked the usual challenging note and by the way he relaxed on his bike his next words were almost a welcoming invitation. "Jo, you come with me."

Without hesitation, she answered with a light-hearted, "Sure."

Kevin gave her a quick questioning look, using their private signals for, 'Are you ok?' Jo leant over and gave him a quick hug and a kiss on his cheek, whispering in his ear at the same time, "Just being good, but we need to talk."

"See you later," smiled Jo, overdoing it a bit with a cheeky puckering of her lips and a smoochy kissing sound before she turned, trying her best to disguise the discomfort of her painful ankle as she climbed on behind Axel.

The half hour ride back to the small shed was over before Jo could recover from the shock of sitting so close to Axel. By placing her hands on her knees and not around his waist she had been able to keep some sort of distance between them, but there was nothing she could do about his delicious musky scent and the contact of her legs and inner thighs as they moulded against him.

Like a coiled spring Jo went to leap off the moment he pulled into the shed, only to be stopped by the pressure of a strong sun-browned hand clasping just above her knee. Axel issued quick orders to the eager youth before turning his head towards her, his sharp blue eyes compelling her to stay put as he spoke. "That ankle needs ice. I'm taking you back to the house."

Jo opened her mouth and then shut it; did nothing get past him. Momentarily taken back by his concern, she shook off the unwanted warm feeling that it gave her. Calling on her self-imposed demure. "Thanks," she finally replied. "With a bit of rest, it'll be fine."

"Al. Blindfold." Axel raised one eyebrow, eyes twinkling with provocation. "I still don't trust her."

He surprised her once again by unceremoniously carrying her into the house, dropping her like a piece of scalding iron onto the couch, snapping orders to Freckles and Babs to see to her ankle. Before she could open her mouth to state that it was only a light sprain and she would be fine, he was roaring off again muttering under his breath about her bike.

CHAPTER 16

Jo sat alone on an upturned crate at the shed. The early morning breeze flicked a few flyaway strands of her braided hair against the side of her face. Annoyed she brushed them back behind her ears and scratched where they tickled.

Jeckle had dropped her up on the tracks ten minutes ago, blindfolded as usual. Stating he had something important to do on the trails, he had told her to wait for either Phantom or Feral. One of them was coming from the upper circle, so with a 'stay put' he had taken off.

She swung the blindfold in her fingers before stuffing it in her back pocket. Once again she failed to recognise the connecting pattern between the house and the shed, she had tried to anticipate the twists and turns but each day it had been different. With her foot she traced the pattern in the loose dirt, she wasn't sure; it was more a hopeful thought, but she had the notion the path they took today was familiar. Maybe after eight days they had run out of different routes to use.

Frustration rose to the surface and she let it feed her impatience. Undercover work was far too slow for her liking. She just wanted to gain results, bring the bastards to justice and get the hell out of here. It was like living in a time warp, one day evolving into the next just to be repeated over again. Eight stir crazy days and she wanted action.

Axel coasted down the hillside track from the upper circles house using his brakes just enough to keep the bike at a slow and steady speed. Soft dirt spun up from his wheels and the light whooshing they made as he free-wheeled blended with the sounds of the forest. The interlocked trees not only provided shelter and food for the native birds and wildlife, but it also hid the track from the outside world.

Honeyeaters and fantails chirped and flittered amongst the lower foliage and the soft thud thud of a wallaby bouncing away kept him alert to the track ahead. Too many times he had been surprised by wildlife using the narrow open space, wild pigs, wallabies, bandicoots and once a full-grown cassowary with its vibrant blue colouring and deadly looking black helmet. He had stopped to let the imposing flightless bird pass, holding his breath as its curious eyes looked deep into his as if acknowledging another solitary soul. The encounter had genuinely moved him, and he never stopped hoping for another glimpse of the elusive endangered bird.

He came to a rolling stop next to the shed, his arrival silent. Not that a quiet arrival was intended. It was usual practice when leaving the private dwelling, no noise, no location. Going back up was different of course, but they always waited until there was no one on the tracks relying on the sound to be disbursed in all direction through the surrounding hills.

Automatically he scanned the area above and around the shed, satisfied all was as it should be. The camouflage netting that sheltered the open area was secure. The netting, well below the canopy height, had trees protruding through wherever possible to break the flat surface from plane surveillance.

Axel was about to call out, wondering where everyone was when he saw movement in the shed through the open window. His eyebrows rose with interest as he watched Jo trace something in the dirt floor, her frown intense and body language in sync with the dual furrows on her forehead as she vigorously rubbed it out with her boot as she stood. The dust flurries danced around her legs as she restlessly paced the shed and he was intrigued to see what she would do next.

The last eight days hadn't exactly been easy. Every waking moment she was in his thoughts and it didn't stop there, his nights were filled with hot sexy dreams. Dreams, that in the reality of the light of day, he was able to shove back to a manageable level. It hadn't helped that she had been so amiable since the first day up on the trails when he had watched Jo give Kevin a short but meaningful look. It was ever so brief, but it confirmed to him they were not what they seemed. The question in his mind was could he use them, could he apply Jo's skills at riding to help his own agenda. He had decided to back off, letting them relax and see what grew.

He knew what Jo was doing was an act, he just didn't know why, so he pushed her to her limits with his wants and demands, but little did she know he was being pushed to his own boundaries in the same process.

Axel couldn't help but continue to watch Jo. He had never felt like this before. Innocence was a long forgotten thing and there had been a fair share of women who had embraced what he had to offer. Casual, with no commitment, he made sure it was known right from the start.

Leaning forward on the windowsill he rested his chin in his hand. This woman was so different from any he had ever known. Her back was to him and her sexy round butt swung temptingly as she paced. Khaki trousers were riding low and she had taken off her thick shirt, slinging it loosely over her shoulder. The black tank top she wore clung to her skin emphasising her muscle tone and fitness.

She obviously enjoyed keeping her body in peak physical condition and after only one day resting her foot, she was back out jogging. Usually he had to motivate his charges to get up and get moving. Not Josephine, she hadn't liked it when he suggested him and a few others joining their morning run. She had smiled sweetly, but her powerful legs had matched his and pressed him to run harder.

Looking at her now, she painted a stunning picture and he wondered, not for the first time, if he could trust her enough to incorporate her into his plans. Both she and Kevin were different from the usual group members, a little too nice. It reminded him of Paddy, who on the surface had seemed as rough and as tough as the rest. But a quality of character lay underneath. People saw only what they wanted to see, often looking without really seeing. Paddy had been just as controlled as Jo and Kevin and come to think of it, himself. He had never considered himself like that before. Limited booze and no drugs and totally in control, it was who he had always been.

Any minute now Jo's inquisitive fingers were going to find the terrain traversers used to 'Ride the Range.' He almost wanted her to find them, to see what she would do. Wondering if she would recognise them for what they were, instead she spun around and caught sight of him in the window.

She had a small tattoo on the left side of her chest, half hidden by the cut of the tank top. He had noticed it before when she was swimming but hadn't been able to work out what it was without getting too close. He watched her tongue moisten her lips as they quivered slightly. Mutual attraction shimmered, weaving a natural feel to the air around them.

It was the same every time they crossed paths. This past week of non-aggression towards each other had done nothing to dampen the fire. If anything, it had added enough fuel to burst into a blazing inferno. It wasn't that he wanted her just physically. The emotional element that kicked him in the gut and made him want more was so foreign that it had him on edge.

He knew she felt the same, he could feel it radiating from her, read the denial and indecision in every move she made. Calm logic told him she was someone he could rely on; his gut instinct was rarely wrong. She could be trusted to do the right thing, she was rather moralistic, she might damn him in the process, destroy him even, but the ultimate outcome was the most important factor. If things went wrong again this time he would disappear. He had done it at the age of fifteen. He could do it again, he was older, wiser and this time they wouldn't find him, but he would make sure the child was safe first.

Maybe he would never discover who Josephine really was, why she was here. Mutual attraction aside he had no doubt she was here to do a job. Private investigator? That could explain the stilted relationship with Kevin. Maybe they were partners. They certainly didn't behave like lovers. His thoughts had been stewing ever since she had casually thrown out a very disturbing question.

It had been the day after her ankle had been hurt. Jo had been ordered to rest. After arriving back from the tracks in the early afternoon, he discovered she had hitched a ride on the back of the four-wheeler to the swimming hole. Wanting to work off his frustration he had jogged down. She had been sitting with one of the girls on the rocks besides the cool flowing creek, obviously fresh from a swim as her hair hung in unruly wet locks down her back. She had reached and gathered the strands together, draping them over her shoulder before twisting them to get rid of excess water. True to his phantom nature he had come up behind them unnoticed, only to nearly choke when he heard her casually ask. "Ever had a member called Brodie? I heard some stuff about him and wondered if it was true?"

For the first time his composure completely shattered. Unable to trust his own reaction he hid it by diving into the crystal waters. Where in the hell had she got that name from? A name from his past, a name he never wanted or expected to hear again.

For the next five days while he had been in charge of the house, he had kept her under close surveillance, accepting the submissive role she played and dishing it up right back, politely pushing her hard. Instead of making matters worse, it had surprisingly added a new element of non-aggression to their communication. Being pleasant to each other brought on a whole new dimension.

It had been forty-eight hours since he had seen her, the last two days he had been called back to the upper circle to finalise the plans. One week, that's all he had left. Looking at her now he made a snap decision, he would still wait for Willow's call, but he needed a backup plan, it was time to begin to take control.

Resting both arms on the windowsill he leaned further into the shed, softened his features and his voice, "How brave are you Josephine?"

CHAPTER 17

Jo fought the urge to lick her dry lips. He had been starring at her for a long time and she had to remind herself to remain cool and demure as her voice responded to his soft tones with a huskiness that bordered on the verge of sensual.

"No braver than the next person." Drawing in a deep breath, she broke contact with him, shoved her arms into her shirt and buttoned it up. *As brave as I must be to get out of all this in one piece and with my heart still intact.*

"Oh, I think you under-estimate yourself." He let that hang as if it didn't require an answer and walked around to the shed door.

Jo stayed silent preferring to see where his next move would take them. His facial expression softened even more to what she could only describe as a friendly overture and her heart skipped a beat.

His smile made her blood sing.

"There is something I want to show you...are you game?"

Squashing the urge to turn and run, she slowed her breathing and acted out her role of the demure damsel. "Sure, why not?" She gave a shrug to show how little she really cared then immediately regretted the impulse as he sauntered purposefully towards her.

"I...err..." she stammered. The apprehension and uncertainty that flared was instantly quelled as Axel reached out beside her to the drawer she had been about to open, taking out two identical objects, a gentle, "trust me," sliding from his lips.

Those simple words settled in her heart... Curse him, she did, somehow it went against all she knew, if he was a killer it was so well hidden she just couldn't see it, she didn't want to trust him, what if she was wrong, maybe it was herself she couldn't trust.

Outside in the mottled sunlight he attached what looked like a large watch to his wrist, fiddled with the dial then held his hand out for her arm. "This one belongs to Mouse. It should fit. She's hardly used it, too timid."

Who in the hell was Mouse? Jo wondered if he was attempting a joke. Doing her best to ignore the tingling sensations as Axel secured it to her wrist, she filed the name away. Mouse, no doubt upper circle, and another appropriate nickname, maybe she was Willow?

There was no time for further thought as Axel demanded her attention.

Strength and coldness had crept back into his tone. "Know what this is?" He tapped the watch.

"No idea." Of course she knew what it was, she had used a GPS tracker many times. This one was just a little different.

She turned her wrist back and forth hoping he couldn't pick up her lie. "What is it?" she finally questioned, still looking at the watch instead of him.

"We call it a TT, a Terrain Traverser." He put his wrist next to hers. "Adjust it to the same co-ordinate as mine...here... this button...turn it."

"Ok, done." *A Terrain Traverser, now that was new, she hadn't heard of one of these.*

"Remember the co-ordinates in case you need to reset it, if you can't remember it then write them down."

"I'll remember," she shot back. "What do we do with it? Play hide and seek?"

His smile was chilling. "Oh, that game's way too simple. Today I teach you to know what it is to 'Ride the Range,' and believe me you will need all the courage you possess...and then some."

Excitement and fear twisted together into one. The furrow between her eyes deepened and her head tilted to the side, not for the first time her analytical expression reminded him of someone. He still couldn't place who.

"The choice is yours," Axel added as the silence stretched. "No drama if you don't, just thought you'd like the challenge."

"Tell me," she finally quizzed. "What do we do?"

Axel couldn't help but to burst out in a smile, not realising he had been holding his breath, waiting for her answer. She was going to do it, he knew she could handle it and that would take the pressure off Mouse, who was not confident at all. If it all worked ok today, he could well have his backup plan.

"It's like Google maps, a GPS tracker and a compass rolled into one. Once the coordinates are set the traverser's arrow will keep pointing in that direction." He tapped hers and she could see the arrow pointing off at about 1400hrs. He turned her 90 degrees to the left, the arrow swung to 1700hrs, he turned her again to the right, so she was directly in line with the arrow.

"We go off track, make our own way through the hilly terrain, going off course when things get too rough, it's up to the rider to re-adjust, and to redirect back onto course when conditions permit. This button here will read the lay of the land ahead and show you an optional route around any impassable areas you get caught in. It takes a while and slows you down, so only use it if you get absolutely stuck. The goal is to get to the coordinates ASAP."

"Where are we going?"

Axel pointed in the direction of the arrow. "That way."

Jo almost laughed, saying, "I'm game."

His grin must have been contagious, his heart upped a pace as she grinned back. And he knew in that instant he was making the right decision. "Don't just follow me. When you need to, pick your own path. If you stack your bike, you walk."

He showed her another concealed button. "If you get hurt and can't continue press the emergency signal, I'll come and find you."

He mounted his bike and took off at a neck-breaking speed, yelling over his shoulder, "Don't forget to duck, you'll be left behind."

CHAPTER 18

She hesitated briefly as he took off, she had no idea which way was even back to the house and she didn't think he was taking her there. She remembered Freckles' words... *The range is dangerous, Feral's up there and...and sometimes people don't come back.*

Who was Feral? His name sent a shiver down her spine.

Straight away she dismissed the feeling. Throwing herself in the path of this challenge might just give her some answers. Kevin would be furious, but she saw it as an opportunity not to be missed.

She took off hot on his heels, and after that there was no time for rational thought as the exhilarating sensation of flying through the jungle without a track enhanced her other senses to a point of sharpness she had never experienced before. Many times she had to throw herself flat against her bike, lying low as branches snapped only inches from her head.

For a while she followed him, until she realised he knew where he was going and was purposely leading her into some hairy situations. He ducked when there was no branch and she saw the Golden Orb Spider, which grew to the size of a grown man's hand, a fraction too late. Its gigantic web now in a tattered mess had been strung out between two trees. The golden sticky strands clung to her skin. She slowed but didn't stop as she pulled some cobweb from her face. With her military training in the wilderness of Cape York, they had come across these gentle giants many times. They still sent a shiver down her spine and she hoped to hell one wasn't clinging to her back.

From that point on she blazed her own trail. Sometimes she caught a glimpse of him ahead or heard him coming up behind, but she pushed on at her own pace, forging her own path. Some areas she had to go slow in order to climb a particularly steep hill or avoid huge boulders, other spots she had to back track to find a way over a small creek that sprang up out of nowhere. She became so aware of her environment she felt almost one with the forest and she relaxed into the sensation of the moment, taking each twist and turn as it came, always scanning ahead and constantly re-adjusting her course.

The arrow spun 180degrees behind her. She turned and rode back a short distance watching her direction. It spun again back the way she had come. Still astride her bike she stopped, turned off the motor, and scanned the environment, knowing she was high and almost out of the forest as it fell away at the base of a huge rocky outcrop. She could see blue sky. If she moved the needle spun, she was at the right spot, so, where was he?

Dismounting she looked around, turning a full 360 degrees. He had to be here already. She couldn't hear his motor and a thrill went through her at the thought he might be watching her. She searched again, this time letting her eyes look for a pattern that blended too well.

"I'm impressed," he stated simply when she found him squatting against a tree that grew up alongside one of the large boulders.

For a moment she was worried as he sounded suspicious, maybe she shouldn't have found him so fast, but she was not here to play games. He seemed to let it pass as he called. "We walk from here."

He held his arm out for her to proceed in front of him. As she started to climb the first rock she looked at him. "There's not a huge spider on my back is there?" His grin nearly made her heart miss a beat.

Conscious of him watching her climb she slung over her shoulder, "Don't have to follow me you know; you can find your own path."

His laugh bounced around the rocks as he climbed past to the left. Like a rock wallaby he leapt from boulder to boulder, not slowing down until he was high above her.

By the time she reached the plateau her legs were on fire, this was definitely not for the faint hearted. She ignored his offered hand for the last step, pulled herself up, leaned forward hands on her knees catching her breath. A cooling breeze kissed her cheeks and she straightened wanting to look at the stunning view.

"Not yet, just a little bit further." He tucked a wayward strand of hair behind her ear.

"Trust me, it's worth it, and we'll be out of the sun."

This time when he held out his hand she took it and he led her across the other side of the huge flattened area to what looked like a dead end. A squeeze between two rocks revealed a dirt path. It wound downwards for a few metres, spiralled around and ended under a small overhang that was almost cave like. Relief was immediate once they were out of the midday sun.

Tiredness fled before the breathtaking view. They stood below the plateau, protected by a high overhanging ledge, a nook big enough to sleep in was behind them and off to the right some distance past the bordering rocks, the forest enclosed them in a semi-circle of impenetrable green.

The ground at the edge fell away with a sheer drop into the depths of the valley below and without Axel's supporting hold, she felt as though she would tumble forward into the empty space before her. Stepping back she looked out instead of down, and there displayed in all their splendour, was the range of hills and mountains rolling and melding into one another, over a hundred different shades of green blending into an array of shapes and mounds, with staggered tree tops giving depth and mystery to their canopied web. Sulphur Crested Cockatoos perched on a dead branch jutting out from the green on a smaller adjacent hill, adding a splash of vibrant white and with the endless blue of a cloudless sky the picture was imprinted in her mind forever.

A familiar and much enjoyed fragrance drifted her way and she turned in disbelief to its source. Axel had pulled a metal box from the back of the small cave, extracted a single ring gas burner and was brewing the most delicious smelling coffee.

"I have a fold away chair if you want it, oh and..." He held out a tin. "Or a biscuit to go with your coffee."

Jo shook her head. "Errr... No to both...yes to coffee, thanks." The way her stomach was churning at his friendly attitude she wasn't even sure if she could get the coffee down. Maybe he planned to gain her confidence then throw her over the edge. She shook her head at her own stupidity.

"I guess these were no random coordinates then." Jo crossed her arms over her chest and stared at him, wondering what his game was.

He poured out two mugs. "Didn't know where else to get a coffee round here."

Amusement filled her smile as she accepted the drink and sat with her feet dangling over the edge, breathing in the aromatic scent. A cool fresh breeze fanned her skin and she felt an overwhelming impression of safety and comfort when Axel sat down beside her.

"This is my come-to place in times of trouble or when I feel the need to get away. Sometimes I spend a few nights here. I am pretty well set up. Water's not far away and I have a good supply of what I need." He paused, giving her a significant look. "Even get phone reception up on the plateau."

It was the most relaxed she had ever heard him talk. His come to place in times of trouble, was he trying to tell her something? "Thanks for the coffee and for bringing me here, this place is simply stunning, words can't do it justice."

They sat in companionable silence, lost in tranquil splendour. Shadows danced across the landscape transforming as the sun sank further in the west. All of a sudden, she became aware that he had draped his arm around her shoulder. How long they had been like than she didn't know but he seemed as reluctant as her to break the spell that nature had woven around them. Little by little she became conscious of their closeness and unwillingly she pulled away, accepting the feeling of regret she felt at their parting, knowing it must be so.

"You are so beautiful." She felt his soft warm breath against her ear as she tried to draw away. He removed his arm from her shoulder and stood, helping her to her feet, moving back from the edge and pulling her towards him. "So damned beautiful." The whispered honey coated words sent a shiver racing down her spine. Never had those simple words meant so much. He stood close, his hands resting lightly in hers.

Heat radiated from his body and she knew if she leant forward, ever so slightly, she would come into contact with the rest of his body. There was a hunger in his eyes that devoured her rational thought and when she opened her mouth to say something, he shook his head, silencing her by placing a finger against her lips.

They stood staring into each other eyes, drinking and drawing in as much as the few precious moments would allow, knowing that the fragile peace that had just been acknowledged would not stand the test of time, too many secrets lay between them.

He moved his finger from her lips and caressed her cheek with his open palm. As his head bent towards hers, his other arm slid up her body to frame her face with his hands, Jo closed her eyes and welcomed his kiss with parted lips. Axel paused for a moment almost hesitantly; she could feel his breath light and warm against her skin, then with overwhelming tenderness his lips moved across hers. It was a kiss of infinite delicacy, a warm discovery of love. Her mouth soft and pliant under his, followed every move as his tongue wove a web of silk around hers. It was a kiss from the heart, warm and undemanding, discovering and exploring the hidden depths of each other's gentleness. It felt like it went on forever.

It wasn't enough, the warmth that had been spreading through her body was building in intensity and she took the lead from his exploring tongue, bringing in an edge of demand for him to match her growing desire. Leaning her body into his for closer contact she felt him waver on the edge of compliance, his body shaking with control as he tightened his grip as if to pull her completely flush with him, then slightly he withdrew. She pressed in further increasing her demand.

No! Her body screamed as she felt him pull away.

It was too late. Already he had turned the agreeable kiss of hello into a salute of goodbye, pulling back and pushing her away from him with firm intention.

Jo took a step forward, her body craving for the feel of the possessive security she had never in her life needed or wanted before. Axel's eyes grew hard and glazed and she recognised the shutters as they came down, pushing away his softened features and turning his face back into the granite mask of the Phantom.

"I can't give you what you want Josephine." Axel muttered a curse under his breath as he stacked everything into the metal storage box and shoved it to the back of the alcove.

Confused and disorientated Jo watched him, glad he was putting this space between them, but not understanding why. Her body was still alive with the warmth of their intimate contact and it must have shown on her face, for he came to stand back in front of her, towering with malicious intent.

The kiss had shocked him to the core, changed everything. She was doing things to his insides that he didn't know how to deal with. Didn't want to deal with. He wanted to use Jo to further his plan, now, her taste, the softness of her body and the hunger of her lips against his was imprinted in his mind.

How could he even think to put her in danger when all he wanted to do was hold her, protect her and keep her safe? Love her? He kicked that thought straight out of his mind, needing to distance himself so he could work out what to do.

Cold words hid his lie. There was only a week left and the best thing to do now, was to push her away, he couldn't use her as planned. There had to be another way.

"Keep looking at me like that and I am bound to give you what you are begging for." His statement was as hurtful and cruel as the expression on his face, snapping her back to reality with a sharp jolt. "If you are that desperate, come to my room when we get back, I will give you all the sex you want. As long as you realise that all it will ever be is a one night...f-"

"Oh. No. You. Don't!" Jo cut him off before he could finish the degrading word that was on his lips. Her face seethed with anger. She stood only a few feet from him totally undaunted by the aggressive body language and the malice on his face and let fly with all the pent-up frustration which had surrounded her since they met.

"You just listen to me Axel Stone or Phantom or whatever your bloody name is. I saw the real man behind the mask and that is something you can't make me forget. Inside, you are as warm and as compassionate as the next person. You can't fool me with your cruel exterior. Hide if you like, but I know you are in there and that is something you can't run from forever."

The sharp words pierced his heart and he hid the truth of them behind a look designed to destroy whatever was in his path. And by the shock registering on her face she knew she had pushed him too far, but true to her gutsy form she pulled herself together, stood strong and glared right back at him.

His quiet controlled reply contradicted his inner turmoil. It swam with venom and was as destructive to himself as it was to her. "You're only seeing what you want to see, what you wish was beneath the surface. Well, you are dead wrong. There's nothing more to me than what you see. If you give me the chance, I will take you, fuck you, and then throw you away like an oily rag.

I am not interested in friendship, love, or any other inadequate emotion. I'm in this life for what I can get out of it and if that means taking you on a wild ride for the night, lucky me, but I'm telling you straight, you may be as sexy as hell, but in reality I don't give a fuck about you or anything else happening in this world."

CHAPTER 19

Josephine paled under his prolonged attack. Never in her life had she heard such callous inhuman words. He was so convincing, it made her doubt all she had thought and felt. Speechless, she shook her head, her mouth open in disbelief. Staring into eyes which were dead and expressionless brought home the truth that he was indeed the phantom.

It took long painful moments to snap herself back into reality. She registered his words and temper took hold, causing her to tremble from head to foot with absolute rage. Throwing forward, she launched herself at him, swinging her full weight behind her fist as it shot out in a fast upward stroke towards his chin, twisting it at the last moment for extra power and in the process showing him she was skilled in hand to hand combat.

He only just swerved to the left in time as the deadly missile whizzed past his ear, his reaction lightning fast as he blocked, with a concrete side swipe of his forearm the thrust of her other fist as it followed just seconds behind.

Jo might have been trained to fight with bigger and stronger opponents, but she was also out of practice. Her speed and agility were retained by the constant exercise, but the defensive blow as he blocked her second thrust brought tears to her eyes as forearm cracked against forearm. The hesitation caused by pain was not wasted by Axel as he twisted her around and grabbed the back of her neck in a grip which made her cry out as he applied effective pressure.

The world spun before her eyes and pin pricks of darkness began to grow, engulfing her in overwhelming blackness. Then the dizziness was gone, and she was back taking deep breaths, trying to regain her balance. Soft words drifted to her ears as she tried to claw her hands at the grip which was still like a steel band at her neck.

"Don't move a muscle." He applied a little more pressure and she felt the blackness start to engulf her again.

Instantly Jo complied, she knew the hold he had on her could kill her if he held it tight long enough. The two main arteries at the back of the neck were being very efficiently pinched. The blood loss to her brain was what was giving her the blackout feeling. It was a very dangerous move, if he pinched too long or hard, or the wrong angle he could rupture the arteries.

She breathed a sigh of relief as he loosened the pressure, resting his arm with a casual deceptive ease across her shoulder, his hand lightly massaging the vulnerable area of her neck.

"Where'd you learn to fight like that?"

"That hurt."

"Answer my question?"

"An old lover of mine thought I should know how to defend myself against pricks like you, he just happened to be a black belt in karate." Her improvising was quick off the mark as usual. He already had a pre-conceived idea at how loose her morals were and this was no time to disillusion him. Although she wondered what he would do if she looked him at sweetly and declared she was a virgin. Well he wouldn't believe her that was for sure.

Without changing his expression, he dropped his arm from her shoulder and reached for her wrist un-clipping the device and shoving it in his pocket. Instead of crossing the ledge to leave the way they had come, he disappeared around the side of the rocks to the right.

Unsure of whether to follow she stood indecisive, only to jump into action and follow when she heard his bike rev up.

"You made me climb up all these rocks when we could have used this short path."

Axel purposely looked at his locator, revved his motor, gave her a cold glare, then revved it some more, drowning out her voice before he took off down the hill.

"Shit." Jo scrambled to do up her helmet and fumbled in her pocket for the key, dropping it on the ground once before she was able to fire up her bike. She was going to have to ride like the devil to catch him and she had no idea where the shed was from here, except down.

Jo didn't bother to follow him. If she tried to follow in his tracks, she would never catch him. He had too much of a head start. Instead she trusted her instincts and the fleeting glimpse she saw as he darted between the trees. With no time for second thought she took off at an intercepting angle, refusing to be left behind.

Going down was just as difficult as the journey up. Bursts of extra speed on the clearer stretches was the only way she could forge ahead. It also added an element of danger, not just to her, but to her bike. She flinched as another low branch drew blood along the side of her face, then another as a sharp branch added to the tears in the sleeve of her shirt and the scratches on her arm. This kind of riding needed leathers.

Deep in concentration her focus shifted, and it was as though she was riding in another dimension. Her vision became solid and clear. She hadn't noticed on the way up, but now she could see trails defined ever so slightly, from bikes that had ridden that way before. There was less undergrowth, not as many overhanging branches and a firmer feel under the wheels. Pushing herself hard she took advantage of them, using a dry smooth creek bottom to gain precious seconds.

Another glimpse of him ahead and to the right confirmed her instinct had paid off, she was gaining ground. It spurred her to push herself faster and harder. She slid half sideways down a reasonably clear ridge that must have a torrent of water running over it in the wet season. Almost spinning out of control she came to a halt at the rocky formation at its base. Below, at the bottom of a near vertical hillside, Axel sat astride his bike looking up at her.

She was too far away to see his expression, but by the way he sat so still and intent, she knew he was staring hard. Scanning the terrain to her left and right, she realised by the time she found a track around the steep slope he would be long gone. There was only one thing to do. Picking her route, at least the beginning, she backed up slightly, positioned her front wheel, then eased to the edge and took the plunge. Riding virtually straight down the sheer slope, 'The Man from Snowy River style.' There was no time to do anything but concentrate, picking a course that would see her safely to the bottom.

As she braked, her back wheel constantly wanted to spin out sideways, or lift off the ground completely; she counteracted by standing, throwing her body weight this way and that as she twisted and turned around the boulders and trees, picking the perfect path. Small rocks and pebbles overtook her, tumbling fast as if they were having a race of their own. They played havoc with her traction, so she veered wider as she continued to weave her way to the bottom.

When she was almost down, she let out a breath, and took in a few more, chest heaving, not aware that she had been holding it. She felt ecstatic. A grin burst through her forgotten anger and she wanted to let out a whoop of triumph. Skidding to a halt besides him her elation was short lived as he scowled and took off at neck break speed.

Like a demon she took off after him. As much as he tried, he couldn't shake her, and with a face as black as thunder he skidded sideways into the clearing at the shed, only a fraction before her.

∽

Did that woman have a death wish? Axel did not want to be impressed. She could have killed herself. He had hoped the fast hard ride back to the shed would ease his temper. Not a chance. Refusing to look back at the woman and without slowing his rushed pace, he dismounted, storming into the shed with long angry strides. His bellow of orders had Al staring at him opened mouthed and Jeckle raising his eyebrows with interest.

"Get to the repair shed." The molten steel in Phantoms voice had Al jumping to do his bidding. "Tell Kevin I'm coming down. There's something I want him to do."

Al took off down the hill. Axel's attention turned to Jeckle who, with his leather jacket in hand and dirt weary face had clearly just returned from his own trek onto the range.

Jeckle scratched at his groin and eyed him warily. Phantom walked over and asked in a controlled stilted voice, "Everything go ok today?"

"Yep, it's all set."

Axel gave a tight nod, "Everyone else gone?"

"Yep."

"Take your time finishing up here, then drop this Wildcat back at the house."

Looking over towards Jo, Jeckle questioned, "Wildcat?" His expression turned lecherous and he licked his lips greedily. If Phantom was pissed off, maybe he could have some fun.

Axel cursed. Hadn't meant to call her Wildcat. That was his name for her. She was so deep under his skin he was being irrational and the wicked glint in Jeckle's eyes fired up a surge of alien jealousy that consumed his soul. He leaned towards him until he was barely an inch from the unshaven face and spoke quietly, icy tones dripping from his voice. "Yea, Wildcat. And if you touch one hair on her head you will answer to me. She's mine, so back the fuck off."

The two faced off against each other. Axel half hoped Jeckle would stand his ground. Maybe a good fight was what he needed, get rid of all his frustration. He snarled, tightening his fists into lethal angry balls and glared at his friend.

It was a long tense moment as Phantom watched Jeckle weigh up his options before he backed off just enough to retain his pride.

"Hey man, no bitch is worth being turned black and blue for." He lightened the situation more with a sociable mates' punch on the arm. "Chill bro, she ain't my type anyway."

"Keep remembering that." Axel relaxed enough to put Jeckle at ease, adding a brotherly clap on the back. "Make sure her blindfolds 'on tight, I still don't trust her."

Frustrated anger still chomped and churned in Axel's blood. It didn't matter how stunning she looked standing flushed and indecisive next to her bike. He needed answers, he needed to find out just what it was between Kevin and Jo, why the hell they were here, and he had a good idea how to find out.

He sauntered over, his relaxed body in direct contrast to his inner turmoil.

"Now I know how brave you are, let's see if you are smart as well...smart enough to keep away from me." He watched the colour rise into her cheeks, and he couldn't resist goading her further. "Remember where to come if you get no satisfaction from Kevin."

Her eyes rekindled with anger as she rose to his bait, but he was ready and quicker off the mark. "That's it Wildcat, come out spitting, your anger is definitely more interesting." Before she could reply he was off in a roaring cloud of dust.

Bored waiting for Jeckle, Jo mulled over the day's events. Axel's parting words still burned a path of anger to her heart. What in the heck was he playing at? He started it with his invitation to Ride the Range, moved her with his plateau of peace and beauty, sealed it with his delicate heated kiss, and then finished it with his self-destructing anger. He was a mass of contradiction and confusion.

At first, she appreciated the time to sit and gather her thoughts. Now, with the adrenalin no longer singing in her blood, she couldn't wait to get back to the house and to speak to Kevin. It was time to compare notes and ideas, time to take steps and get this job done.

"How long before we go down?" Jo questioned for the third time in the past hour. Jeckle had taken the wheel off his bike and was replacing it with another one. Like before he didn't bother answering. She sat back down on the upturned box and dissected what she knew about the tracks. The use of the Traversers had shed a whole new light on how they managed to move so easily between the coastal hills and the tablelands. It was a revelation.

There were no tracks, except the ones they practised on and they were interesting enough. Tracks of intricate twisting confusion, definitely the most challenging she had ever been on. But irrelevant, she thought. Mind you they had used parts of different trails on the way to the plateau, often criss-crossing over them or sometimes using them for a short time and out of the blue a narrow bridge would appear over tough or deep creek crossings. The whole set up was elaborate and well established.

It all boiled down to whatever illegal activities they were involved in, being made easy by picking their own coordinates where to come out the other end. So, all she needed now was the link between the house, the elusive upper house and this shed. With what she already knew about the tracks, the locators, and the place they went to today, she was close to calling in the troops. She had the coordinates. The plateau was large enough for a chopper, so they could come in by air as well as road. The links between the houses and shed were all that was left.

At the same time Jo knew she was at the end of her self-imposed servility and, admitting honestly to herself, after today, her nerve. She really felt as if she couldn't cope with Axel for one more day. That was probably the reason she did what she did, although it was unplanned and risky, yet once it was done, she couldn't help feeling proud of herself.

The sun was just beginning to set, throwing the shed into eerie shadows. Jo was sitting trying to be patient, twirling a cheap necklace of beads between her fingers. They had been a present from Patrick when she had been about ten years old and she carried them always, using them since his death as a calming tool, threading the beads backwards and forwards one by one like a set of Greek worry beads. Today the tensions were too great, and the chain weakened by time and use accidentally snapped, spilling the beads onto the ground, their dull red colour contrasting slightly with the brown dirt of the shed floor. Jeckle paid no attention at all as she stooped to pick them up. It was then the plan hit her.

A Hansel and Gretel pebble trail. Looking at the scattered beads, Jo knew it would work. They looked similar to the red berries she had often seen on the forest floor so they wouldn't stand out. As long as she didn't get caught dropping them. Being blindfolded she would have no idea if anyone was watching her, but everyone was gone except her and Jeckle.

Excitement grew, if she could get away with it, they would mark the trail beautifully. She hoped Kevin would be glad also, surely he didn't like hanging around anymore than she did, even if he fitted into in the gang a lot easier than she did.

Chapter 20

"What do you mean he is not coming back tonight?" Axel registered the panic in Jo's voice and savoured the way she stepped back a pace and crossed her arms protectively across her body. She wasn't as unaffected by him as she made out.

"Do I have to repeat myself?" He leaned in closer, taking a small step inside her bedroom.

"Kev's staying in town. The part for your bike won't come in until early tomorrow. He's at a mate's house. Having fun I might add, left him knocking back a few beers."

Bemused, Axel watched anger battle with insecurity. What made him continue to provoke her he couldn't say? She was an irresistible force he was drawn to, like a magnet positive to negative and although he knew he should, he couldn't let it go.

After today he had wanted Kev and Jo apart with no chance to communicate, just for a day to see their reactions. It hadn't been hard to persuade Kev to stay in town and wait for the courier to come through in the morning with the parts they needed for Jo's bike. Telling him it would save another trip in the morning, he had taken him to a friend's house where he could spend the night. When Axel had left Kevin was happily playing cards and drinking beer, with not a thought of his beautiful, sexy, hot tempered girlfriend.

Looking at her vulnerability now, he wanted to wrap his arms around her and protect her, but most of all he wanted to make love to her. It was becoming an obsession he was finding hard to ignore and he wished to hell he could push it aside so he could see the plan through without further complications. He needed her pissed off at him, it was the only way for him to keep his distance.

"What's this, Josephine? Is this where you have a girlie tantrum because your lover has chosen to stay out overnight?" He saw her backbone straighten and her chin jut out and admired the ability she had to fight back even when the odds were stacked against her.

"Thanks for the message, now get out!" She went to slam the door. Axel was quicker, easily holding it open with one hand.

"Are you sure you wouldn't like some company?" Damn it, not only did she look stunning, all freshly scrubbed from the day, but her subtle flowery smell reached out and drew him closer. He gave her a look designed to melt her heart, knowing she would fight back. Lowering his voice a couple of octaves, he leaned forward turning on the charm. "I can think up plenty of things to keep us amused."

Jo felt momentary panic at the thought Kevin wasn't around for backup and there was nothing to stop Axel from shutting the door and...*Stop it.* Getting a grip on her emotions Jo faced him full of all the hostility she could muster. She hated the feeling, she had always hated it, but right now she needed it. Her whole life had revolved around frustration and aggression. They were emotions she knew how to deal with, how to control. She had to keep angry for it held off the tears......and she *never* cried.

"Get the hell out of my room." She met his sexy smoulder with a temper barely under control. Fire flashed from her eyes and her fists clenched into tight white balls at the sides of her hips. That was it, she was going to scream, one minute she felt like she was been thrown to the wolves, the next he was weaving his seductive spell around her.

Hysteria built.

She didn't want any of this and she didn't want to react to his low smoky voice. Oh, god; she just wanted to go home. To be left alone. No, she just wanted to bring down Patrick's killer. God she was confused.

Drawing in a sharp breath and closing her eyes, Jo clenched her teeth in a bid to stop the scream from rising into her throat, it was no good. Flinging her eyes open, the strangled sound changed into a gurgle of frustration. He was gone, the room was empty. Jo flung the door shut with a wild bang.

Not for the first time she cursed that there was no lock. Dragging the chair over and jamming it under the door handle was purely an act of visual protection for if anyone had wanted to push the door open it wouldn't have taken much effort.

There was only one thing left for her to do, she would have to do her plan alone. She couldn't risk leaving the beads until the next day, she would have to do it tonight without Kevin and when he came back, they could get the hell out of here and send in the big guns. She would not stay here any longer, enough was enough!

It was three hours before daybreak when Jo finally dressed ready to leave. She had been sitting against the corner of the wall near the door and had been there since Axel had left. For the long dark hours of the night her mind had tossed over problems and emotions, searching for answers she couldn't find. Her first concession was that she was undeniably and uncontrollably attracted to Axel. It was vital that she kept out of his way and give him no further opportunity to play his deadly game.

She also had to concede that Kevin was not going to be able to provide the protection she needed. Axel was an enigma, he had beaten her at every turn by using his blatant sexual power, opening her doors of awareness and putting a pot of emotions on to boil, only to leave her floundering in his wake as he tossed the seeds of desire back in her face.

Once, during the dark hours of the night, Jo had silently confessed to the fact that the seeds, which had fallen on fertile ground, had grown since the day they had met, and were now ripe and ready for picking.

None of the previous men in her life had prepared her for such a wealth of emotion, nor depth of desire. It wasn't that she expected to be a saint all her life, goodness she was twenty-four years old. It was just that none of her male friends had ever made her even remotely feel like going any further than a light kiss goodnight. As she grew older, she also grew more determined to wait for the man she loved.

Jo smiled to herself as she remembered the sex education talk her father had given Kevin and herself. At first, she had been totally embarrassed at discussing such things in front of the male members of her family. Patrick who had been home on leave had joined in with his usual humorous enthusiasm, interested to find out what their father was going to tell the only female member of the family.

Men were made to conquer and women to submit. As her father had so correctly predicted, the statement had Jo spitting fire in all directions, and an uninhibited, if not at first heated, discussion had been born. Her brothers had laughed as she had left the room vowing never to be conquered by the male of the species. That had been when she was thirteen, just starting the blossom into womanhood. It had also been the first of many open-hearted discussions.

Later as she began to understand the meaning of love, her father had taken her aside and talked about the mother she had never known. It had been the first and only time she had ever seen him melt into a softer soul. He talked of love and laughter and the joy of being together. The unique bonding of a man and a woman in the intimate act of first love, the voyage of discovery and the melding of two lives into one, secure in their love for each other. He opened his heart wide, releasing a flood gate of suppressed emotion for the woman he had lost and Jo had left him hours later knowing she could never settle for anything less. The gift of her body would be her gift of love to the man she wanted to spend the rest of her life with.

Jo never forgot the words of her youth, 'men were made to conquer'. It was this memory that made her strong now, for she had also vowed never to submit. Phantom was a threat to all she held sacred and she knew her body would betray her heart if it was given the chance. He was danger with a bold capital 'D' and she was going to do the only thing possible in the circumstances...Eliminate the danger. She had been at risk ever since her father had talked her into this mission, now it was time to take action.

If a plan was wanted on the tracks and trails of the Range Riders and the access to them, then that's what they would have, along with her additional 'off track' information. Once that was accomplished, she could go and distance herself as much as possible from what had happened.

All thoughts of her home were effectively pushed aside as the excitement she so often denied herself crept into her system, taking over her energy flow. The adrenaline surged as she laid down her final plans.

It was a very simple operation, one she hoped to complete before Kevin was back. The trail bike track which led to the house was through the trees off to the right. She had walked the first part of the steep incline until she had hit the gate, which blatantly declared the no go area. After that the thin trail was hidden from view as it wound precariously around a bend, one side inaccessibly steep, the other dropping sharply away to hide in the depth of the forest below. As far as she knew it was the only access to the tracks and Jo had no doubts of her physical ability to achieve her task.

If anyone was to come down that hill, she would hear them coming a mile away and have plenty of time to hide amongst the multitude of trees, steep as the incline may be, she didn't think it would pose much of a problem. It was a simple task to follow the trail of beads that she had laid from the gate to the small upper shed. Once there she could easily make her way to the two trails she had not been allowed to ride on and check out where they led to. She should be able to make it back down the track before anyone was up, find a way down the steep incline, slip to the creek below and back into the areas she was permitted to be in. Following the creek back to the main river by the bridge she could pretend, if anyone questioned her, that she had been for an early swim or a jog. It shouldn't take more than an hour or so after sunup and with a bit of luck she would be back by seven thirty, eight at the latest, just in time for breakfast.

In fact, she probably wouldn't be missed at all.

The slither of a moon slipped behind a cloud as Jo silently crept out of the back door, clad in dark shorts, khaki shirt and green jungle boots laced almost up to her knees. She shivered in the dark of the pre-dawn. It wasn't cold, quite the contrary, the pre wet season of the tropics was hot and sultry, even at this, the coolest part of the night, the Celsius reading was still up in the mid-twenties.

Using the cover of complete darkness, she sprinted across the open lawn, judging the distance to perfection as she stopped motionless next to the mango tree, ears alert and eyes scanning for any indication she had been heard.

As far as Jo was concerned, getting out of the house was the most dangerous part of the whole scenario and she forced herself to stay stationary for a long time, but all she could hear was the erratic pounding of her own excited heart. Slowly it settled back into a steady rhythm. The reassuring beat rejuvenated her nerves and stimulated her awareness as the minutes ticked by. Satisfied at last that she had not been heard or followed, she turned her back on the security of familiar ground and headed for the track into the unknown, smiling to herself in the darkness as the thrill of adventure roared through her veins.

CHAPTER 21

I t was just past eight o'clock when Axel reached out his hand
to pick up the ringing phone. "Hi Kev... yea...damn!...ok, what
time's the next courier...fine, I'll see you later this arvo then...No,
I don't know, hang on..." Axel put his hand over the phone and
called out to Babs, "See if you can find Jo, Kev the Rev's on the
phone." He laughed as the other man on the other end of the line
said something funny. "It sounds like you had a good night."

Babs came back and stated loudly into the phone Axel held
outstretched towards her. "She ain't around and it don't look like
her beds bin slept in."

There was a long silence on the other end of the phone. Axel gave
a light chuckle, deliberately provoking the other man's discomfort.
Wondering at the same time if Jo wasn't in her room where in the
hell was she? He hadn't seen her since last night.

It was a dangerous game they had been playing and now he had
Kevin at a disadvantage and once again, he used it to the fullest,
needing to see his reaction to the situation. "All's fair in love and
war," he goaded.

"What do you mean by that?"

"Take it whatever way you like, but when I was in her room last
night, she sure was spitting fire. Feisty little thing isn't she?"

The explosion when it came was no disappointment. "If you have laid one finger on her I'll kill you, she has a free choice remember."

"And don't you forget to abide by what she decides," Axel countered cutting off the connection.

Axel sat for quite a while, tapping his fingers monotonously on the wooden arm of the chair. His thoughts were channelled inwards and the silent brooding power which was etched into the contours of his face was enough to deter even the bravest of the people who walked past him every so often.

When Kevin had first contacted the group a few months ago he'd had reservations. People who came into gangs like this usually needed the security of handling life as a group instead of as individuals. Kevin had always seemed a bit too sure of himself. It was one of the reasons Axel had been so hesitant about his acceptance into the Riders. Something about the man was a little too powerful, a little too clean. He was more leadership material and hiding it, and that was a threat. He knew by past experience you kept threats where you could see them.

Then of course there was Josephine. The temptingly elusive Jo, blowing hot and cold all in one breath. He rubbed his hand frustratingly along his upper thigh trying to ease some of the tension he felt when his thoughts drifted her way.

From the moment he had first seen the defiant tilt of her chin and wild flash in her eyes he had trouble concentrating on little else. After racing against her, seeing her exhilaration, defying danger and battling alongside him, flying free and wild with the wind, he had wanted her in the group for more than the obvious reason.

When he had purposely thrown the race and witnessed her outrage at the unfairness of it all he knew she could be the link he needed to make his plan work. The fact that he wanted to throw her on the floor and make love to her every time she came within ten metres of him was not helping him to think clearly. He didn't even want to analyse how he had felt when she had ridden kamikaze style straight down the hillside. He shoved that thought straight back out of his head and concentrated on what he did know.

It was plain to see Jo and Kevin cared a great deal for each other, but somehow the relationship didn't seem quite right. Jo was clearly a woman who could look well and truly after herself and Kevin, well, Kevin was playing some game and Jo was his bait.

Still, regardless of how he felt it would soon be all over, one way or another. His plan came first and foremost. The wheels were in motion, over the last twenty-four hours enough fuel had been added to Kevin and Jo's fires, now he would stand back and see which way they burned. With a bit of luck it would be in his favour. What he needed was for them both to not react to this situation, if they just carried in a normal manner all the better. But that led to the question, where was Josephine?

He was so lost in thought, the sound of the phone made him jump. On the third ring he answered it with his usual grunt.

"That you, Phantom?" came the sleazy voice of Viper, the leader of the Range Riders.

Axel grunted his affirmative.

"We have someone up here that might interest you."

CHAPTER 22

From the time she left the haven of her room under the cover of darkness, Jo found little chance to give her actions a second thought. Swept along on a roller coaster of events she had no control over, it took all of her courage to fight back simply to stay alive.

Her plan fell apart from the very beginning. After navigating the road up from the gate, she found herself confronted by a mass of overlapping tracks, at least ten of them leading off in different directions. It took her way too long in the dim light to find the first of her discarded beads. In hindsight, she should have been content to find the right track and finish the rest tomorrow with Kevin, but with stubborn determination to achieve the goal she set out to do, she didn't give a thought to the foolhardiness of trying to do the job on her own.

Waiting until the first threads of dawn begun to show, Jo systematically ruled out at least half of the tracks as they wound back on each other. Another half an hour ruled out two more as they finished in dead ends. Choosing one of the remaining three, finally met with success and with the dull red bead in her hand, she had set off at a light stepped jog, senses alert and alive to all that was around. The track lead up hill, not steep but constant, one side like the road, dropped off at a sharp angle. She came to another junction, three tracks leading off to the left of the steep drop off to the right. No beads, she would have to eliminate them one by one again.

The centre track looked the most worn, so she walked slowly eyes down searching.

Silent as a ghost the trail bike glided around the corner taking her completely by surprise as it almost ran her over. Jumping sideways, she missed her footing and tumbled head over heels down the plant encrusted embankment, lodging painfully in the tangled thorns of the wait-a-while vine.

Stunned, she lay still. Cruel hands grabbed her and pulled her painfully and callously free, dragging her backwards up the slope by the scruff of her neck and a hand full of hair, depositing her unceremoniously onto the dusty track. A leather boot jammed into her back pinning her to the ground.

"Well, well, well. I caught me a wildcat." Jo recognised the gruff voice of Jeckle.

All-consuming was the thought of getting free, and for the first time in her life panic almost took over. She was in deep trouble and she knew it, and she had to fight not to let it smother her ability to think quickly on her feet. Letting her body go limp and exaggerating her cough as dust swirled around her mouth, she tried to talk.

He released the pressure from her back with a warning to get up slowly and carefully. She did just that, until she was halfway up. Then with a speed which left him unable to react, she used the momentum of her upward rise to punch him full in the solar plexus. As he doubled over, Jo lifted her knee to connect with his nose, before she turned tail and ran back the way she had come, with only one goal in mind, to warn Kevin and get the hell out of there.

Her troubles had only just begun. From behind, the tinny whine of a trail bike caught up with her at an alarming rate and she only just flattened herself against the trunk of a tree as it skimmed passed. Jeckle had recovered fast, not stopping to stem the flow of blood that ran from his nose and she cursed herself for not thinking of using the bike.

He turned the machine in an aggressively tight circle and glared at her, murder in his eyes. Giving her no time to think, he slowly and purposefully rode back towards her. She turned and ran back in the opposite direction, searching franticly sideways for an opening in the thick forest. The bank was too steep, and she had no choice but to keep on running.

Staying directly behind her, he let her run and too late she realised he was herding her back to the destination he had come from. Breaking into the clearing she stopped dead in her tracks as he turned off the motor and waited, successfully blocking any escape from the path.

Jo was stunned, the area was quite large and circled by a brown brick wall which blended in perfectly with the forest that grew right up to its edge from the other side. In the middle of the compound stood a single roomed hut with no visible windows and a door which was slightly ajar. A thick wooden beam used to lock the door lay discarded on the ground. There was a gap which ran around the connection between the roof and the sturdy looking walls which must let the air circulate, but there was no doubt in her mind that it must be like a sweat box inside.

From above, only dull dappled light shone through and Jo realised the whole area was covered by a camouflage net, protecting it from airborne observations.

Her attention snapped to a flash of bright colours as Spike dropped the bucket of water she was carrying, spilling the contents onto the dusty ground. With an angry cry of protest, she was roughly pushed aside by the man who had followed her from around the corner of the hut.

Jo felt well and truly trapped as the most formidable form of a man she had never seen before came towards her. He was bulky, not with fat, but with hard full muscles compacted by his short height. Dirty and unkempt, his long matted hair clung to his scarred, unshaven face. It had to be Feral. There was no doubting the wild, animalistic aura that surrounded him.

Sickened and frightened Jo backed away without taking her eyes off him, manoeuvring herself around in a circle in a desperate attempt to keep some distance between them.

He hissed a profanity through a twisted sneering mouth as he circled closer. "Heard all about me huh...an' couldn't keep away?" He made a swift lunge in her general direction, his laugh of torment grating in her ears as he anticipated which way she moved.

Not wasting any energy on answering his taunts, but concentrating on his every move, the stalking continued. This time she realised she was being herded in a certain direction but was powerless to prevent it. Every time she tried to move where he didn't want her to go, he lunged at her again forcing her to step back to fall in with his wishes. Each time he came a few steps closer, shortening the distance between them.

She had no idea what his plans were. A swift glance had shown that Jeckle had stayed at his post by the track. Spike was nowhere in sight. Jo hadn't even seen her move, but the bucket still lay upturned where it had been dropped. It was close. Maybe she could use it as a weapon. Inching her way towards it, she realised Feral wanted her to go that way otherwise he would have leapt towards her again. Stopping to gauge his next move, she saw his body tense ready to strike. He would expect her to jump to the left as the wall of the hut was close to her right and as he moved, she jumped backwards in a bid to out-manoeuvre him.

Too late she felt her feet slipping from under her as they struck the mud caused by the spilt contents of the bucket. Feral's blood-curdling cry of victory crashed inside her head as he grabbed her legs, and as she clawed at his hands, he twisted them viciously so she had no choice but to flip onto her stomach.

After trying to avoid close contact fighting with him it now seemed a relief to be able to strike out. As he wrenched her legs, she rolled with it, grabbing his in the process and bringing him down into the mud with a thud.

He was short, compact and heavy, and with his surprising speed he was a horrific opponent. Laughing with hysterical glee, not at all put out by her resistance, they rolled around moving from the mud to drier dust, covering themselves thoroughly from head to foot in a fine brown coat.

It would be only a matter of time before her strength ran out against him. They both knew it, and he took every blow she managed to land like it didn't matter. As her fingernails racked down the side of his face it was only a small victory to hear his howl of pain as he retaliated by wrenching her arm so high behind her back, she thought it would break.

"Stop it, Feral." The strong voice bounced around the compound.

"No." Although his voice betrayed a strong denial, his grip on her arm loosened, allowing her to turn to the sound of the voice.

Spike was standing feet apart some distance from them as if aware how dangerous Feral was. A Winchester 303 was aimed in their direction, the butt of the gun firm against her shoulder, her stance strong with shrewd eyes fastened on them both.

"I said it's enough. Let her go, we are gonna take her to Viper."

She knew the words to control him. At the mention of the leaders name he released her arm completely, letting fly with a string of cursing words at them both. With a sly look he went to move away.

"Don't move, Feral, I'll fuckin shoot if I have to." Spike apparently knew his character well as she continued, "Do as I say, or I swear I'll shoot you as well as her. This is important. We gotta take it to Viper."

Feral apparently knew her too well. Not doubting her word he shrugged his shoulders in compliance.

Jo stared at Spike but didn't see a shred of compassion as she waved her rifle to emphasise her next words.

"Now take off her boots, use the laces to tie her hands behind her back." It was done painfully rough with as much touching as Spike allowed, which fortunately wasn't much.

"Jeckle find a blindfold, rip off ya shirt if you have to, we don't want to show her any more than she's already seen."

Feral dragged her to her feet. The intense reek from his unwashed body made her gag and try to pull away from him. He wrenched her back hard and she stumbled, turning from the rancid smell. A figure stood in the doorway to the hut, but Jo's attention was snapped back to Jeckle as she heard him swear at the woman to get back inside.

He walked straight up to Jo dabbing at his nose with the bottom of his shirt. "What the hell do we need a blindfold for?" And before anyone could stop him, he punched her full on the jaw. As his fist collided with the contour of her cheek all she saw was a flash of pink as the woman in the doorway disappeared before instant blackness took hold.

A low moan escaped Jo's lips as she felt her body being unceremoniously dumped onto a hard unyielding surface. A small flood of light surfaced in the blackness which enveloped all conscious thought.

It hurt.

She pushed it away, unwilling to let it invade the dark peaceful void of nothingness. This time noise interrupted the quiet haven, echoing down a tunnel so it rang around her head in an incoherent mumble. Slowly jumbled sounds formed legible words and with the recognition came the realisation of the trouble she was in. Full consciousness came in a blazing shock, yet she was still reluctant to open her eyes to the reality that would unfold.

"I think we should keep her for a while."

A sliver of fear shot through her and she resisted the temptation to move her body into a more defensive position. There was a sharp pain in her hip and shoulder as she lay at a strangely uncomfortable angle. The following words pushed all other thought out of her mind and cold fingers of fear crept into every crevice of her body.

"I say we kill her. These roads are dangerous, accidents happen."

She recognised Jeckle's hard angry voice.

"I want her as my pet, someone I can play with in the long lonely hours of the night."

Jo was almost physically sick at the slavering animalistic sounds that came from Feral. She almost panicked, turning her sudden gasp into another moan as she fought to gain control.

Someone came over and poked her none too gently in the ribs with a boot clad foot. The tension inside her was too great. With a scream of fear, she flipped over onto her side and tried to scramble clear, realising too late in her confusion that the reason for her discomfort was that her wrists were bound tight behind her back. With difficulty she stood.

The light blinded her eyes, and she was momentarily stunned as they swam in and out of focus. A hairy tattooed hand clawed at her arm as she tried to shrink away, and she could smell rotting flesh as he breathed close to her face. This was it; she was going to die. He was going to rape her and then they would kill her.

Unexpectedly once she had admitted this to her sub-conscious, she felt surprisingly numb. Everything seemed to be happening in slow motion as if she had all the time in the world to react. Viper was sitting relaxed in an armchair, about ten feet away from her, slightly to the left, hands clasped and leaning on his chin as if amused by the whole affair. Spike was standing expressionless beside him, her hand possessively on his shoulder.

Jeckle was dabbing at his nose which evidently had refused to stop bleeding. The woman from the hut came in with a cold compress and even in her vulnerable state, Jo felt a touch of pity as he roughly shrugged off her help. What reignited her terror, was Beth, as she encouraged the woman sitting next to her to call out profanities, goading Feral to do some very nasty things.

Jo forced down rising panic. Feral, lapping up the attention was the immediate threat. I am going to die and the last thing I will remember is this... this gross excuse for a human being. Out of the corner of her eye she saw Viper lean over and pick up the phone. Her attention snapped back in a flash as a loathsome hairy arm grabbed at her shirt, ripping off the buttons and tearing the sleeve leaving her shoulder exposed.

Slowly she backed away as Feral stalked closer. The look of animal lust in his pale beady eyes sickened her soul. He was filthy, unshaven, long haired and badly tattooed, with black crooked teeth and he smelt as if he hadn't showered for a least a month. Jo shuddered in revulsion at the thought of him touching any part of her body.

'Oh, God I need help,' she acknowledged silently, 'I can't get out of this on my own. Axel, I need you.

Not questioning her line of thought, she just accepted that it gave her a new surge of courage. Jo remembered every feature of his face; the strong hard masculine curves of his body, the heat of his passion and the steely strength of his arms as they wrapped around her. Revitalising her thoughts, it gave her the strength and courage to fight for her life.

With a slow smirk of a smile Jo stopped her retreat. Cocking his head, Feral stopped his advance. He had been edging forward every time she moved back, playing with her like a cat with a mouse as she moved around the room.

Her half exposed breasts, made more prominent by her arms tied securely behind her, rose and fell with her erratic breathing and his eyes were glued to them. Licking his lips in anticipation, he made his final lunge. Jo, using his momentum, stepped forward into his move, lifting her knee and ramming it into his groin with as much force as she could muster.

As he fell frontward clutching between his legs with both hands, his groan of agony was drowned as Jo let out a yell of her own. Expelling all her breath as a driving force for her foot as it connected with his down turned face, he was flung upwards before he fell in a painful crumpled heap at her feet. Feeling sickened, she quickly backed away. The kick hadn't been anywhere near powerful enough to render him helpless for long. It had been hard to balance with her hands tied.

Viper still hadn't moved from his chair, he just watched her through slitted beady eyes, as he motioned for Jeckle to block the door, her only means of escape. Except for her heavy breathing and the painful gasps of Feral as he tried to get to his feet there was silence in the room. Everyone was watching her as she backed into the wall trying to put as much distance between herself and her attacker as possible. In the background she heard the high pitched whine of a motor bike roaring full throttle and her eyes darted apprehensively to the door.

CHAPTER 23

She wasn't disappointed, Axel filled the door frame and her eyes drank in the sight of him. Beginning to step forward she stopped, uncertain halfway through the motion, as her eyes caught the cold uncaring brief flicker of his before they scanned the room taking in every detail.

Feral, now almost on his feet, was off to the left, half hidden by the long three seater couch which he was using for support. Viper was sitting relaxed and watchful in his chair, Spike was standing possessively behind him, rubbing her fingers through his hair in small excited circles. Beth and the other woman remained on the couch. Jeckle having moved off to his right as Axel had taken up position by the door, finally accepted a drink from the nervous, twitching woman who hung at his side. She had to be Mouse.

Axel rested his eyes back on Jo, unrelenting in his cold stare as he leaned back, casually resting his shoulder against the door jamb. Reaching into his boot he pulled out a short sturdy knife and proceeded to clean his fingernails with an air of disinterest.

Jo concentrated her entire attention on him, willing him to do something to help her. She couldn't believe he would just stand by and do nothing. Even now, as disgusted as she was by her reactions, she could feel her body calling out to him. His icy gaze dropped briefly to her heaving half exposed breasts and her nipples tingled, pushing against the silky lace of her bra. For a moment she saw a slight thawing in his body language and her heart leapt into her mouth. It didn't last more than a couple of seconds. His eyes clouded over, his expression blank and cold.

Her heart sank into the depths of despair as the silence stretched out to an unbearable pitch and the urge to scream as Feral finally made his stumbling way back towards her was overpowering. Gasping at the air she desperately tried to draw in enough to breathe.

It was no use moving away any further, there was nowhere else to go. So she stood her ground willing her legs to hold steady and not show any of the terror she felt inside. With jumping eyes, she flashed from Axel to Feral and back to Axel again and she noticed a change in his stance as he held his knife balanced loosely in his right hand.

Phantom now had her full attention. The constrained power that radiated from him took a hold over the whole room.

Viper lifted his weedy eyebrows in interest.

Even Feral paused as he drew close to his quarry. "Don't interfere, Phantom." His wounded pride blazed across the room. "Me and this wild bitch have a score to settle."

Phantom moved further into the room with the grace of a sleek Black Panther ready to spring, flipping his knife casually in the air and catching it blade first in the palm of his hand. "You got it wrong, Feral. A bitch is a dog. She is a wildcat and all you have done is rubbed her fur the wrong way."

There was only about eight feet separating them now, Axel at the furthermost point of the triangle. With a movement that was as swift and controlled as the throw, the knife flew out of his hands and lodged in the wall just a whisker's width from Jo's ear.

"Rub her the right way and she will purr like a kitten," he continued, reaching into his other boot and pulling out a second knife, tossing it just as casually in the air. "Either way, Feral, untie her first, at least make it a fair match."

Not knowing what game Axel was playing, Jo started to edge herself away from the protruding knife. It was as though he was trying to goad Feral into continuing his attack. Even if it meant her arms being free, she didn't want that animal to come any closer.

"Freeze!"

The other knife whizzed past the opposite ear and lodged itself into the wall with a positive thud and all bravery was lost as she was paralysed with fear. He hadn't even been looking at her when he had thrown that second knife; his attention had been fixed onto Feral in a duel of clashing eyes. Jo didn't know whether he was trying to help her or kill her. Either way she knew she was still in danger.

Feral started to wilt under the dominance of the taller more athletic man. Shifting his glance sideways to address Viper in a protest that spelt defeat, "Come on Viper... she stinks of trouble, we found her on the track heading towards where we are keep..."

"Enough!" barked Viper from deep within the folds of the chair. "We are yet undecided on what we are going to do." Next he addressed himself to Jo. "Well, Wildcat...what are you doing up our neck of the woods?"

Momentarily stunned, Jo struggled to find her voice. Viper was the last person she had expected to get a reprieve from. Sensing it was her only chance, Jo looked from Axel to Feral. The decision wasn't hard, but it was frightening none the less and she was relieved to hear her voice sound steady and surprisingly strong.

"I came to find Phantom."

"Why?"

The question threw her into turmoil, how did she answer that without getting herself any further committed to a single course of action. Not knowing where to look, she dropped her gaze to her feet only to feel the beginning of a flush as her attention was brought to the devilish state of her clothes.

"Why?" Viper snapped impatiently.

"I... um..." She looked at Axel in desperation, unable to say the words which would deliver her into his arms.

He acknowledged her defeat with a smile like she had never seen one like it before. It was a smile of sadistic victory and it made her powerless to move as he came purposely towards her.

"Despite their spitting images, wildcats are really rather shy creatures!" Axel's tone was deep and seductive. "Let me show you what she was after."

Holding her eyes, he reached for the knife stuck in the wall to her right. "Turn around Josephine."

Like a mesmerised rabbit she looked up into the unyielding lines of his face, not knowing what to do or think. Her senses were completely overridden by his closeness, by the towering presence he commanded, making her small and vulnerable before him. She wanted to melt into his chest, to feel the strength of his arms as they enveloped her and protected her from all this hurt and pain, to hear his heart pound a steady beat beneath his chest as she rested her head. But most of all she craved for him to hold her steady against his solid frame, letting the rise and fall of his rhythmic breathing bring stability back into the world and she would be safe.

"Now." The words cut through the fantasy as she swayed unknowingly towards him, eyes beginning to flutter closed. He gripped her shoulder and spun her around to face away from him, his hand splayed deep and firm between her shoulder blades pressing her into the cold surface of the wall.

Jo thought he was going to cut the ropes and she could feel the first stirring of anger flow back her veins when she realised he was going to do no such thing. He moved in close, his warm breath whispering a light breeze across her half naked shoulder and his body surrounded her like a sheath. His teeth nipped in a pleasurable pain at the exposed line of her neck and anger surged through her body in self-protection against the sensations he was able to provoke so easily.

Ignoring the tense rigidity of her body, he worked his hand deep into her hair at the crown of her head. The pressure changed and it was now her head held imprisoned with deceptive softness against the wall. His free hand reached out to pull the other knife from the wall and with a quick flick of his wrist he cut the bands that held her hair in place and it tumbled in a knotty cascade of mud and dust down her back, hiding his hand from sight.

This time he did cut the bonds to her wrists and they fell lifelessly to her sides as the rope dropped to the floor at her feet. He slid his hand slowly down the back of her head until it rested at the base of her neck. Applying a steady pressure, he turned her back towards him, watching the anger rise on her flushed face as she recognised the hold.

"We have been here before. Now you must take your chances on me, there will be no smart tricks...or you are on your own."

Anger, it was the only thing which kept her from melting into his body. As long as she had her anger, he could never possess her mind. She, who had abhorred the aggression that had been so prominent through her life, was now clutching to it, making it the very essence of her survival and she hated herself for it as much as she hated the sensations that racked through her body at his touch. Gritting her teeth, she stared defiantly at him with eyes flashing fire as his head descended towards hers.

Before she knew what was happening, he crushed his lips against hers and she was unable to deny him access as he clenched a fist full of her hair and wrenched her head backwards.

A triumphant growl rumbled deep in his chest as his tongue re-introduced itself to her mouth, exploring every moist avenue with its deep thrusting impatience, devouring her anger with a greedy violence of its own.

Jo was powerless to do anything but surrender. So total was his possession. Trying to raise her arms to push him away, she let out a cry of refusal as he changed his attack. He tightened his grip and pulled her head further backwards to expose the long lines of her neck. And before she could protest any further, he renewed his sensual attack, following the deep blue veins, biting, licking and sucking at the soft succulent skin until he reached a fading bruise at the sensitive dip of her shoulder.

His hand slid from around her waist, down over the curve of her hips before travelling up again to enclose over the swelling mound of her breast. Jo was almost sobbing with controlled effort not to join him in his aggressive assault. There was no denying what he could do to her body, but she was still fighting it every step of the way. Raising her numb, rope chaffed hands in an attempt to ward off the moulding, squeezing fingers, she cried out in pain as she tried to use them. The blood which had rushed back into the veins was now causing them to tingle and sting as they came back to life.

Her cry of pain made Axel catch his breath and he released the pressure from her breast and hair, stepping slightly back so there was only the slightest hint of body contact. Looking down with a soft expression, he brought his hands gently up behind her ears, his finger massaging into her scalp. Then ever so tenderly he lowered his head, bringing his lips to hers in the sweetest, most delicate kiss that literally took her breath away. The contrast was so shocking it dispelled all other emotions as she yielded to his empathetic sensual demand.

Turning her, as he had done once before so that he was pressed up against the wall, he teased her with the tempting rotation of his pelvis, letting her come forward to press her desire into his. She followed him willingly, raising her painful hands high to clasp round the back of his neck in a bid to bring the tantalising pleasure of his lips into a more fruitful contact. Complementing her move by lowering his hand to her buttocks, he tucked her tight into the heated shaft of his erection.

A low moan of willing compliance escaped her lips, causing a hoot of approval from Spike as she called out crude encouragement to the passion inflamed couple. For Jo it acted like a douse of cold water, for Axel seemed to ease his tension. He gave a warm-hearted chuckle and as she struggled in his arms, he enveloped her in his protective embrace until she stilled against his beating heart.

Its racing tempo matched the flood of despair which whelmed up inside her and she felt physically sick as well as disgusted by the way she had acted. Every time he had beaten her in their unwanted game of desire and each time she found it harder to resist his demands, always turning her anger back on itself, feeding her until he called a halt. How far would it have gone just now if they had been alone? A shudder of unknown origin and feeling shimmied down her spine and Axel clutched her tighter to his chest. Slowly his heart returned to a normal steady rhythm and for the briefest of moments she felt the safety she had sought before.

As her body relaxed, moulding itself to his form, Axel moved his hand under her hair to clasp the back of her neck again. She stiffened in apprehension. This time the pressure was light, but the threat was there even though he still held her close to the solid stance of his body.

Jo felt like she had been from Hell to Heaven and back to Hell again. Everything and everybody were still in the same positions as before. What had felt like a lifetime to her had in fact been a few fleeting moments, only the expressions on their faces were different. They were all looking at Axel as if they had never seen him before, except for Feral who was scowling in angry protest.

"Well, I'll be," said Viper with amusement. "Phantom has a human element after all."

Jo flinched as Axel's grip tightened on her neck. He moved with her to stand in front of the leader. Risking a glance up at her captor she expected to see the same expressionless face as usual, to her horror he looked smug and conceited, a slight smile twitched at the corner of his mouth.

"Viper, I don't believe you have met one of the newest recruits to our group, Josephine. It had been my intention to wait until after next week before I brought her up here, but she is an impetuous little thing." There was a slight trace of sarcastic humour which no-one seemed to notice or care about.

Giving Jo a nudge as if he expected her to exchange polite greetings with them, she just stood there barely able to comprehend what was going on.

"Sorry, she is not talking much today, I think a cat has got her tongue," Axel continued smugly, as if he didn't have a care in the world.

Viper unfolded himself from the comfort of the chair, rising before them with a fluent grace and ease which showed off his muscular physique to its best advantage. It was impossible to take a single step away from him as Axel made her stand firm, but inwardly she cringed at the hidden power he emitted. His whole body was poised as if ready to strike.

"I think the Phantom has taken all the fight out of our little Wildcat, well not all, I can see it smouldering in those green cat eyes." Reaching out he ran a hand, which was rather small for such a huge body, down the side of her face, under her jaw and across the exposed line of her breast.

She tried to jerk backwards but Phantom held her tight, pushing her slightly forward away from his chest, placing his other hand in a rock like grip on her shoulder. It was almost like he was offering her to his leader.

Her mind screamed out in protest as Viper's caress lingered on the rapid rise and fall of her chest. She was at an emotional end, any moment now she was going to collapse in a crumpled totally defeated heap at their feet. Then the touch was gone, his attention left her as he concentrated his hooded eyes on Axel.

"In all the time you have been with us, I have never yet seen you take a woman from our group. You've always gone to the outside. It looks like with this one you didn't have much choice."

Axel dropped his hands and walked away from her and over to the bar to pour a drink without a backward glance at Jo, who now stood unprotected in the middle of the room. Feral automatically circled closer, but Jo didn't take her eyes off Axel's towering figure, not knowing quite what to think or feel.

Protected, yes that was it, she still felt protected. A knight in shining armour had rescued her from the brink of a revolting death, huh, a knight indeed, more like a mysterious phantom from the dark depths of the forest. Stop it! She admonished as she felt her emotions tremble on the brink of hysteria, think of something rational. But no thoughts would drown out the sense of apprehension as Axel walked back towards her, his eyes ablaze with an inner depth she couldn't quite fathom.

Looking up at him with wide questioning eyes she wondered who was going to rescue her from him.

"There's no escape" he whispered close to her ear, reading her expression correctly. "You are as far into my territory as you can possibly go." A hot flush of unwanted excitement flooded her body as he possessively grabbed her hand and held it tight. She stood rigid, refusing to look at him as he chuckled softly to himself.

"I want her with me, Viper, I would have waited..." the sentence was left hanging, but the leader apparently knew what Axel meant.

Silence stretched out long and tense, all eyes on Viper waiting for him to speak.

"We all know the timing is lousy, but by the looks of things it was taken well and truly out of Phantom's hands, and if it had been left up to him, well, we all know he would have done things in the right way. I say we except Wildcat into the Upper circle..."

He didn't get the chance to finish as Feral exploded into a fit of frustrated rage. Protesting with crude violence, he took his temper out on the nearest piece of furniture, smashing it into a display of angry fragmented pieces.

"How do we know she didn't see the child?" The malicious question was out before anyone could stop it and a deadly silence fell over the entire room. "She," he stabbed a pointed finger at Jo, "was on the track which leads... "

"Feral!" Viper intervened cutting him off with a sharp command similar to how you would call a rampant dog to heel. He obeyed instantly but didn't back down. Instead he came forward to stand closer to his quarry. Viper turned back to Axel, "She's your responsibility. Make sure she doesn't leave the upper circle until this is finished."

Jo began to shake as Axel placed a protective arm around her shoulders, pulling her in close to his side. She couldn't believe what she had heard. She wasn't going to be raped and killed, emotionally she let go, and barely registered what was happening around her.

Her knees began to shake, and her body went cold as if there was no blood pumping to keep her warm. Swaying slightly, she relied heavily on Axel's support to keep her upright. He turned her slightly and looked into her face. Her eyes unable to focus properly thought they saw a fleeting expression of compassion and understanding in them.

Protest died on lips too tired to move, as Axel hoisted her effortlessly onto his broad shoulders in a fireman carry. The last thing she registered as he strode out the door was his large hand grabbing a bottle from the table as he passed.

Draped unceremoniously over his shoulder Jo began to stir in protest, the blood rushing to her head as it sloped down towards his backside. There was nothing she could do, the hold was designed to be effective and it was.

If she had bothered to tilt her head sideways to look down past his swinging buttocks, she would have seen the way they had come, which even from an upside down prospective would have looked original and characteristically unique. They had left the central core of the main building and were now walking down a large veranda. The rainforest grew right up to the edge and visually overflowed into the hanging baskets and potted palms which were placed with abundance in every nook and cranny.

She didn't have the energy. Her eyes barely registered the floor as it changed from the wooden planks of the veranda to the cork wood tiles of his room. It was the loud click of the lock turning in the hardwood door that snapped her back into reality.

In the middle of the room he waited until she was fully aware of where they were before he released her arm and pulled her other leg close to its partner so she could easily slide down over his chest.

It was a slow tantalising descent, prolonged and provocative as his left hand nestling firmly on her waist stayed stationary. Her shirt bunched and rippled beneath his palm as her body glided over his pounding chest, leaving her back bared to the whisper of a breeze that fell from the slowly turning overhead fan. His right arm which still held the bottle of liquor pressed her hips and buttocks in close to his.

Jo's hands slid over the top of his shoulders, resting lightly on his chest, as her feet touched solid ground. Automatically looking up into his down turned face, she read the hungry desire etched into every feature. Panic surged and she pushed her hands against the unyielding wall of muscle, arching away in a desperate effort to place some distance between them.

His warm chuckle of genuine pleasure invaded her senses, sending waves of rolling delight rippling down her spine. She was rocketed back into his arms and lost in a sea of sensation as four things happened in such rapid succession, they all merged into one mind shattering erotic invasion.

The shock of the liquor bottle as it touched her bare flesh made her arch her chest away from the cold glass and deeper into his embrace. The concave curve of her back allowed him to slip his hand under her bra strap and release the clasp. Simultaneously his large hand moved around to close over the soft flesh of her breast as his mouth came crashing down on hers.

The effect was instant, and she was powerless to do anything other than respond with an open hearted passion of her own, meeting his urgent demands with a tender willingness designed to leave him breathless in return. Her lips moved in gentle rotation against his, her tongue lightly dancing around his hungry thrusts. Tracing her slender fingers in soft sensual circles over the back of the hand that was greedily moulding at her breast, Jo showed him the way into her heart.

She'd had enough of violence and demands she couldn't meet, and she found peace and harmony in the gentling of his caress as he answered her unspoken need. This was what she wanted, what she had sensed in him from the very beginning, a soft loving tenderness hidden beneath a toughened exterior. This was what he was hiding every time he drew down the shutters over his eyes.

CHAPTER 24

Slowly Axel moved forward, taking Jo with him until the back of her knees met with the soft resistance of his bed. Releasing her mouth, he looked down at her closed eyes, placing kisses on each one in turn, watching her lips quiver with sensation as she turned her head to guide his mouth across her cheeks and down the side of her neck. He skirted around the sensitive dip of her shoulder, teasing her again and again before he suckled long and deep into the graceful curve. Her moan of delight almost sent him wild and he fought for control to keep his passion reined wanting to give her every ounce of pleasure possible.

This was the side of Josephine he found impossible to resist. She was pure woman.

Pulling away to trace a line down the bruising on the side of her face sent a flare of sympathy surging through his soul. He searched her face, her eyes, and found them alive with emotion and desire, wanting everything he was capable of giving.

Slowly he undid the remaining buttons to her shirt, tantalising the silky skin beneath as he pulled it from her shoulders. Discarding her bra in the same erotic fashion it dropped to join her shirt in a crumpled heap on the floor at their feet and with both hands he reached out to trace circular patterns around the outside edge of her sensitised nipples not watching them spring into renewed life, but instead fascinated by the display of rampant emotion flashing across her features.

She confused him. His wildcat, with the fiery temper and lightning fist, was now a bundle of quivering sensations in his arms. He had expected their love making to be as explosive as their relationship. This was as far removed as possible. She was a mystery that fascinated and frustrated him. Revelling in her sweetness and light was driving him to the peak of his control, all he wanted to do was throw her down on the bed and make wild passionate love, driving her to a point of abandonment before he gave her release.

He wanted to get the sexual tension out of the way before he questioned her. It had been building between them for too long and he thought their release would be quick and aggressive.

Now he knew he had to wait, she was a contradiction of personalities, a paradoxical creature and he had to find out what she was up to. She had been controlling his actions ever since her feet first touched the floor and he had almost fallen for it, not anymore. His heart had almost been taken with her soft tender approach, and it unnerved him. It encouraged the feelings he didn't want to acknowledge, and he finally admitted it to himself. It scared the hell out of him.

Releasing the sensitive tips of her rosy nipples from between his thumbs and forefingers, Axel sighed a deep regret letting his hands fall to his sides. Scrutinising her flushed face, he frowned slightly as a look of confused bewilderment puckered at her forehead. Gathering his own emotions and shoving them back into the deepest recess of his mind, he brought back Phantom.

"We both know you didn't come looking for me, so now it's question and answer time." He made his voice cold and hard to match the expression on his face. "Tell me, what you're up to?"

Axel was prepared for anything and he fully expected a swing back to his aggressive Wildcat. As it was, his mask almost slipped when her eyes flew open, hurt, vulnerable and full of unreleased passion. The rosy flush of her cheeks vanished, leaving behind a bloodless white sheet and she swayed uncertainly as if she was going to faint.

$$\infty$$

It was just how she did feel. Though never having fainted in her life before Jo didn't quite know what was happening to her. Small pinpricks of black rushed towards her face growing in size until they almost filled her vision, then they vanished as if they had passed through her head and out the other side, only to be replaced by new ones in an ever continuing spiral of giddiness. The buzzing in her ears distorted his voice as she tried to decipher his face between the black balls of nothingness and a trembling started in her knees, systematically working up her body until she was shaking all over.

His arms came towards her and she tried to fend them off with hands which wouldn't do as they were told. Strong fingers dug into her shoulders forcing her to sit on the edge of the bed and a hand came down with equal strength, pushing her head between her knees.

Normality crept back into her consciousness. The world stopped spinning and her breathing became less erratic. She struggled against the pressure of the hand at the back of her neck then gave up, as it was unrelenting, and she felt too weak to protest any further.

Unwilling to accept the fact that her shirt and bra were in a heap at his feet, she concentrated on his boots. From the corner of her eye she could see her naked breasts, but she refused to acknowledge them as they moved freely with each calming breath she took.

The top edge of the knife handle was just visible where the black leather of his boot met his jean clad calf. If she reached out, she would be able to grasp it in her hand, but what then? She had no more fight left, she just felt like curling up in a ball and letting the world pass her by. The boots shifted and the pressure on her neck was released. Before she could reach out for her clothes he had bent down, picked up her shirt and draped it over her shoulders. Even in her wounded vulnerable state, her pride wouldn't allow her to show how utterly defeated she felt. Sitting up, she squared her shoulders, staring straight ahead unable to meet what she might find in his eyes.

Muttering under his breath he stomped away. For a moment she thought he was going to leave but then the clink of glass on glass jarred the silence and sharp tang of cheap scotch fill the air. Inwardly she cringed with renewed anxieties, she felt as though she was on the very edge of screaming hysteria. Her limbs were heavy, and her head pounded with the tension of the last twenty-four hours. With no food or sleep the night before, her reserves were at their lowest ebb.

For all her forward planning she certainly had acted like the unprofessional she was. What on earth had made her think she could pull off a stunt like this on her own? Sinking her head into her hands she silently panicked as she realised she had now put both herself and Kevin in a very dangerous position indeed.

"Drink this."

Jo licked her dry lips and looked at him with eyes that would barely stay open. Taking a deep shuddering breath, she tested out her voice in a cough and a deep swallow before she felt able to use it for words. Thankfully they came out clear although rather husky. "I would rather have a drink of water."

"Drink it," he commanded in a voice which allowed no argument. His temper was at a terrible pitch, the veins in the side of his neck were protruding and Jo swore she could see the blood rushing through them at a thunderous speed. He thrust the glass into her hands.

As she thought, it was whisky, and she silently thanked her father for insisting she drink the fiery liquid along with the rest of the family. With a slight shrug as if to indicate the unimportance of his request, she downed the lot in three quick swallows without flinching or changing her expression. If he thought anything of it, it certainly didn't show. He just continued to stare at her with his blank mask.

The fiery ball hit her empty stomach leaving behind a warming, revitalising trail as it fled to every part of her body. Her face buzzed with warmth, but the alcohol didn't help to clear the fuzziness inside her brain.

Axel grabbed her by the shoulders and made her stand before him, his grip biting into her flesh as he held her an arm's length from his body. "I want answers and I want them now. And just so there is no confusion, I will remind you just how dangerous a position you are in. All I achieved this morning was to stop you from being raped and killed on the spot. Now we are here and alone, just you and me, so you can tell me why and what you were doing. And don't give me any crap about trying to find me. We both know that's a blatant lie."

He shook her shoulders hard as she just stared blankly up into his face. He looked tired she thought and very stressed. The gap between his eyes at the bridge of his nose supported two parallel furrows which ran deep causing his eyebrows to hood over. It emphasised the deep intensity of his brooding eyes as he glared down at her. And she remembered how it looked when he laughed in genuine pleasure on the day they first met. She smiled at the memory, a slight sweet smile which turned up one corner of her mouth. It seemed so long ago, and she tried to remember how many days it had been, wishing he would smile like that again.

Jo knew her thoughts were rambling, and she tried hard to concentrate on what Axel was saying. The whisky invaded her weakened state. No food, little sleep, the shock and aggression she had endured, all compacted into a tight, rickety unstable ball in the pit of her stomach.

In fact, she felt absolutely awful. The man in front of her was barely containing his fury as she tried desperately to remember the question he had asked. She didn't want his anger. All she really wanted was to melt into his arms, snuggle up to his chest and fall asleep, safe and secure. He didn't scare her at all, that feeling was beyond her. Not even now as he was shaking her harder, spitting out something about whether she was with the police or a member of another bikie gang. His voice receded to a distant echo and the ball in the pit of her stomach lurched in such a way that he froze at her expression.

"Going to be sick," she managed to stammer between the tightly clasped fingers at her mouth and she turned wildly looking for somewhere to relieve the contents of her heaving stomach.

"Bathroom." He unceremoniously pushed her towards the door to the left of the bed.

She heaved into the bowl.

"Here, rinse your mouth with this." After passing her the glass of water, Axel leaned against the cabinet watching with confusion as the woman on her knees before him rinsed her mouth and spat out the contents into the toilet. He had held back her hair as she had retched violently into the bowl. That she hadn't eaten for a while was obvious. Now she rested against the cool wall as if the very thought of getting to her feet was beyond her comprehension.

Unmistakably she was running on her last reserves. What he should do now is ruthlessly bombard her with questions until she gave him the answers he required. Yet a strange compassion took hold of a heart he thought had hardened to anything life could offer him. Over the years he had been able to detach himself from situations of a sympathetic nature with an ease that bordered on the side of callousness but looking at this defeated woman before him blew all the unemotional cold-heartedness of the past years away. She was a danger to the stability of his entire existence. He recognised it since the day they met and had tried to distance himself against it.

There was no way he could get the answers he required while she was like this. He needed to let her fighting spirit rejuvenate itself.

Then he could justify to his suppressed morality, the necessity to match his aggression against hers.

It was a strange scene. If anyone could have observed them at this moment, they would have found two motionless people staring sightlessly, both lost within their own thoughts. Surprisingly it was Jo who moved first, rising with a quiet dignity to her feet. In a dreamlike state she walked into his arms and rested her head against his chest, wrapping her arms around his waist with a sigh of long sought contentment.

Axel reacted as if he had been prodded with a red-hot poker, wrenching his body away with a sharp sound of regret. Grabbing her arm, he powered into action, dragging her the short distance to the shower. He reached across to turn on the taps, then quickly and efficiently he stripped off her dirt encrusted shirt and shorts, refusing to look at the cuts and abrasions on her long shapely legs. Hooking his thumbs in the top of her brief lacy knickers he hesitated, watching her expression as a slight flare of awareness surfaced. With an inward groan of self-control, he released the flimsy lace and shoved her unceremoniously under the shower, knickers and all.

She gave her absolute compliance and it almost drove him wild. Stripping off his own shirt, he soaped her body as best he could without climbing under the shower with her. Although he tried his best to detach himself from the task, his soap lathered hands slid over her skin with a satiny sensuality they both found hard to ignore. Seeing her wince slightly as his thorough cleaning brushed over a growing bruise on her hip, brought him out of the infatuation of his task. Wrapping her up in one of his over large towels, Axel sat her on the edge of the bed, bending her head forward so he could vigorously dry her long thick hair. In the end he had to leave it damp and unbrushed as he didn't have the necessary equipment to finish the job.

Leaving her sitting, dwarfed within beige folds, he went over to the wardrobe, pulling out a bunch of keys, selecting the appropriate one and unlocked the door. Looking back over his shoulder he could see her watching his every move with those slightly out of focus eyes. Positioning himself so it was hard for her to see past his body he reached for the small but comprehensive first aid kit.

Locking the door and returning to the bed, he found Jo had laid back and was almost asleep, knees still hanging over the edge, arms curled protectively over the towel at her chest. "Oh no, not yet my ferocious Wildcat. First we have to see to all those cuts and abrasions on your legs and arms."

"No," she murmured, attempting to pull her leg away from his grasp. "It hurts."

His thumb rested on another deep purple bruise spreading on her leg, wondering, not for the first time, how she had arrived in such a battered state. Before her shower she had been literally covered from head to foot in dirt and dried mud. The water had washed it away, leaving all the bruises and scratches exposed for him to see. It was evident that some of her injuries had been inflicted by Feral and possibly Jeckle going by his bloody nose, but the scratched and bruised appearance of her skin suggested she had also had a battle with the forest itself.

Well, he would clean her up, smother her in antiseptic to stop the infection that was bound to set in if left unattended. The tropics was notorious for infections and fevers and the last thing he wanted was a sick woman on his hands.

Standing up he stared down at the now sleeping woman. Attending to her wounds had been another internal battle. He had pulled her up on to the pillow so she was lying flat and comfortable on the bed. It probably would have been better if she had fallen asleep before he had started. After removing the towel, she had lain there excepting his administration with the minimum of complaint, gritting her teeth as he pulled out some broken thorns of the Wait-A -While Palm. Apparently, she had not waited a while to get free but had ripped at the spikes as their curved angles hooked into her skin. Once the painful part was done, she relaxed under the gentle application of the healing cream and it turned again into a sensual exercise of self-control.

Task completed he sat snugly against the curve of her hip, leaning over to lift the bulk of damp hair from under her shoulders to spread it out so it could dry easily in a fan over the pillow. As his face came close to hers, she reached up with shaky arms to his shoulders, invitation obvious on her soft, pale features. He shook his head in negative reply and as she opened her mouth to protest, he placed the lightest of kisses on her parted lips.

Drawing back to watch her dreamy expression, he took her hands off his shoulders and placed them down by her side. "Time to sleep, Josephine. But first there are two things you must realise." Axel spoke clearly, emphasising each word with slow precision. "Number one. You will answer any question I ask... I will not leave you alone until you have answered to my satisfaction. Is that clear?"

Green lifeless eyes looked at him. "Yes."

"And number two. I want you fully awake and aware of what you are doing when we finally scratch this itch that has been bugging us both." He didn't need a confirmation. It was written in the bright flush that crept into her cheeks. Even though the heat of the day had already warmed up the room, he covered her with the lightweight sheet, then turned and left, locking the door carefully behind him.

CHAPTER 25

I t was nine am and the day felt oppressively hot. Small grey-white clouds reflected off the still waters of the South Johnstone River, while deep underneath the surface the lazy current drifted towards the river mouth a few kilometres away. Earlier this morning the esplanade had been alive with joggers and dog walkers, now there were only the odd die hard fanatics prepared to battle the growing heat of the tropical sun, sweat drenching their shirts as they pounded the concrete pathway.

Kevin took a mouthful of his coffee and grimaced, cold coffee tasted disgusting. He put it down on the grass next to where he sat waiting impatiently for his phone to ring. Worry about Jo was eating him up inside and he had spent the last half an hour on his mobile discussing options with their father. The unease that had settled on him early this morning was now on full blown red alert.

Last night he had sent a text message to Jo, knowing she checked her phone and reported in on her morning run. He hated the fact there was no service at the house and that Jo had not contacted him could only mean two things. Axel and some of the gang had run with her as they sometimes did and she had been unable to get away to use the phone, or she was in trouble. When he hadn't heard back from her, he had rung the Range Riders house, just to settle the niggle of unease he felt. It was probably nothing, no doubt Jo was fine, and Axel had just been stirring him up when he said Jo could not be found and her bed hadn't been slept in.

He couldn't afford to act rashly, but not too complacent either. Which was why he had rung his father and requested to set in motion a plan they had devised. Sir Robert should now be in discussions with the appropriate authorities, once they agreed on a course of action the elite squad of MICO would be on red alert and in position for a storm and rescue operation somewhere between forty and forty-eight hours from now, probably spear headed by his oldest brother Robert Junior.

A sparrow hopped on the grass by his feet searching for any leftover food. It was soon joined by another. Kevin barely noticed them, they would be out of luck anyway, coffee was his usual breakfast, it wasn't often he could eat first thing in the morning and today was no exception.

Standing he finished the last of the bitter brew, made his way to the waterfront balancing the empty container on the top of the overflowing bin. Phone in hand he followed the footpath. A few trawlers were tied at the docks, but most berths were empty as the vessels were not yet back from their hard work out at sea. When they came in, they would be laden with their catch and Kevin had to admit the seafood in this town was the best he had ever tasted.

As he walked, he looked at the colourful mosaic plaques tastefully placed along the low wall that separated the path from the river. He didn't bother to stop this time, on his first pace along the river's edge he had investigated and read each one, as well as stopping at the statues of the early cane settlers and paying his respects at the war memorial that stood as remembrance for those who fought and died for their country.

The paved river front walk was only short. He turned and headed back the way he had come, away from the noisy playground where parents watched as their young children raced energetically about beneath the protective sunshade. The sounds coming from the park were loud and happy, but he didn't need that right now, he needed to listen to what was in his head and to his gut so he could follow through with the best possible course of action to make sure his sister was safe.

Sitting back down under the dappled shade of the tree, he looked at his phone willing it to ring and nearly jumped out of his skin when it did. He let it go to message bank, listening to the message as it did.

'Sorry wrong number,' was what he was waiting for. He smiled when he heard the message then deleted it, fondly remembering his brother Patrick as he took the back off his phone, removed the battery and inserted a new sim card. This kind of anti-tracking had been Patrick's idea. He had been the real undercover expert along with Matthew and this was a method they all used in certain situations so calls could not be traced or link back to a particular person.

His two oldest brothers, Robert Jnr. and Stephen were more into the training and operations command control, Patrick and Matthew excelled in deep undercover work and as for him and Jo, he didn't really know where they fitted in. This was his first mission, the recon had sounded easy and fun, but now the reality of the situation had taken hold and turned it into a deadly game with an unpredictable outcome and he wasn't sure he liked the feeling. Losing one brother had been enough, he didn't even want to consider what life would be like if he lost Jo as well.

Snapping the case back on the phone he waited for the sim to activate, then dialled his father again. It answered almost immediately. They spoke quietly for a few minutes before Kevin hung up, letting out a sigh of relief. Plan C was in place for 0400hrs. Forty-three hours from now. It was a good safety backup plan, giving him time to suss out the situation before deciding whether to send in the troops.

After reinserting his original sim, he dug a tiny hole in the grass with his pocketknife, wiped his finger prints off the card, snapped it and buried it, not that he really needed to go to those lengths. The sim was unregistered and therefore untraceable.

All he had to do now was hang around town until the afternoon courier came. He already acquired the part, but Axel didn't know that. It was all he could think of as a ruse to call. Now he wished he had been smarter; said he was ringing to see if Jo wanted anything from town. It reinforced his annoyance at his inability to think fast.

He decided to send her a text message, designed, that if everything was ok and she eventually did get it, she would just be a bit confused and respond, at least then he would know she was fine. If she was in trouble and someone had her phone, he had to phrase it so they would just disregard the message as unimportant. Message sent he lay back on the grass. Waiting around all day was going to be hell, a real exercise in patience. About an hour later his phone buzzed a message alert, he read it smiled and relaxed, it seemed Jo was fine.

CHAPTER 26

For once the upper circle house was quiet. Feral had been sent to take care of the lower house. Two of the others were at the hut looking after the brat. Phantom and his pussy wouldn't surface anytime soon. She felt a twinge of jealousy, she had been told to make a play for him once, way back when she had been instructed to join the gang. Rejection didn't sit well, and she never forgot. That just left Viper and his drug induced orgy, he would be strung out for a few hours so he wouldn't even know if the house fell down around him. It had been easy to extract herself from the tangle of torsos and limbs.

She took Jo's phone out of her pocket and decided to walk up the hill a bit so she could pick up reception. If you got up high enough and in line with the gap in the adjacent hills, reception could be quite good.

Not caring about the breathtaking view of the rich green valley below that was dotted with farms and a meandering creek snaking around the base of long line of hills. She waited for the signal to catch. The phone buzzed a message alert. She looked at the time it was sent, an hour ago.

'Hey babe, ur sista rang last nite bin trying 2 contact u, asked if I wd pass on a message. She plan c u soon, pls contact her.'

Interesting she thought, Jo didn't have a sister. With information from her contact, she made it a priority to find out as much as she could about the family once they showed an interest in the group. And they had been interested for a while. Dear dead Patrick was Jo's brother, Paddy. Pity he had to die, she'd had the hots for him and that didn't happen very often, she basically despised men, scum, the root of all evil.

Something about Paddy had piped her sexual interest and he had been pretty free complying with her demands. She had been fuming when she had found out he was an undercover operative, all that did was enhance her hatred of men. Liars all of them. But that was in the past, she shrugged it off, the dead don't tell tales.

Thinking about whether to send a reply or not, she climbed and sat on a large boulder trying to catch some sort of breeze. Damn it was hot, and it wasn't even summer yet. Her own phone buzzed. It could only be one person and the reason she needed to come up here in stinking heat of the day of the first place.

She typed back. *'Ring now.'*

"What?" she said sharply into the phone.

Listening for a moment, she answered, "Yep, she was nosy and got caught. Phantom has her nice and secure." Thinking, *holy shit, if he knows this quick, he certainly does have friends in high places.*

At least she knew he didn't have another person other than her in the gang, otherwise he would have known Jo was in trouble not just asked if she knew where she was...unless he was just making her feel secure, or fishing for information. Damn this was getting messy.

She said yep a few times before questioning, "What plan?...oh their plan. Not a problem, what time is it set for?"

The raspy voice answered, "0400 hours Sunday."

She decided quickly, even though last minute glitches were annoying, they were not impossible to work with. The key to success was flexibility. "Ok. I will make sure her brother has no chance to call it off. That way we will know what we are up against.

Just make sure my whole payment is in my account before then, or it's a no go."

As usual she held the phone away from her ear as the rasping voice broke out into a violent wheezy cough, she held her breath hoping he would comply with her demand. The usual was half before, the rest after the job was done.

Her smile turned cynical as she stood firm. "Full payment, I've been on this job a long time and it holds a lot of danger. They will be snapping at my heels as it is with these plans running so tight together, just this once I want my payment secure, I may need it to disappear fast."

The pause drew out and she was determined not to be the first to talk, she had him over a barrel and they both knew it.

"Fine," he finally wheezed, coughing once again.

"Good, I'll let you know when it's done." She hid the surprise in her voice, she hadn't expected him to agree. It also made her suspicious. Cutting the connection, before he could say anything else, she sat for a while mulling over her own plans.

She had her own agenda. By the time it was finished she would be long gone. Once the money was secure in the account he had help set up, she intended to transfer it to a second offshore account, the one he didn't know about. She had learnt a lot in the years she had been working for him and didn't trust him at all. When the funds were in and just before the mission she would transfer the lot and over the last fifteen years and with investment it was a nice fat nest egg.

A new identity and a new life, Erika Solberg, a filthy rich Scandinavian heiress.

Typing quickly, she sent a brief reply to Kevin. *'Thanks, busy right now. Plan C her l8r.'* That should keep him calm for a while, until she worked out how to get rid of him.

CHAPTER 27

The transition from the deep sleep of exhaustion to full awareness took its ime. Jo stretched and yawned, the scrub fowls' loud and noisy notes came from somewhere within the dense jungle outside, and the song of the cicadas filled her ears with an insistent high pitched monotone buzz. Feeling cool and comfortable, she snuggled deeper into the wonderfully soft pillow, not wanting yet to rouse for the day.

Errant thoughts flashed through her brain, slowly bringing it to life. She could hear Kevin moving around the room. It made her wonder what he was doing up so early, for the last few days she had always been up before him. Still reluctant to relinquish her mind to full consciousness, she listened as he turned on the shower, whistling a soft tuneful melody.

She frowned. The noises from the forest were all wrong. A Red Necked Crake let fly with the short sharp repetitive note of its melodious coot-coot-coot, shooting an icy shaft of remembrance through her body, bringing it to full awareness. It was the dusk chorus. She could hear the sounds of the day birds settling down for the long night ahead.

Disorientation was only momentary as the full flood of realisation hit; it was evening. That wasn't Kevin she could hear in the bathroom, his whistle had no melody, in fact it had grated on her nerves while they were growing up and intensified since they had been thrown together on this mission. The whistle she could hear was warm and tuneful.

Her eyes flew open as she sat up. Axel. A flush darkened her cheeks as the sheet fell away to reveal her near naked state and a tingle of excitement rolled in a slow wave down the entire length of her body. Despair followed close behind as she recalled how pliant she had been in his arms. How gentle he had been and how she had desperately wanted him to make love to her.

It scared her. Not the thought of making love, but the soft tender feelings he was able to provoke. They spelt disaster. She must never allow him to let her feel like that again. If he did, she knew her heart would be lost forever.

Her sharp mind jumped into high gear. There was only one solution. She had to get out of here. Get back to Kevin.

Shit...Kevin.

She hadn't even given him a second thought. He would be worried sick, and he would be furious. Wouldn't even know where she was. Was he ok, had they hurt him? She must to get back to the lower house, find out what had happened, and then they needed to get the hell out of here.

Feeling a little lightheaded, she slipped silently off the bed. She quickly scanned the room looking for anything that might help her out of this dilemma. The huge bed sheet was too big and restrictive to offer the right kind of protection. She needed to be able to move. Her clothes were no-where in sight. At least she still had her knickers on. Never before had she realised how protective a small flimsy piece of lace could feel.

And never had she seen such a plain sterile room. It was devoid of any personality. With a sinking feeling Jo realised her escape from her square prison was not going to be easy. The huge bed overpowered the wall opposite the door and the wardrobe. Both of course were locked. There were two windows with plain dark brown curtains. One was on the wall which ran at right angles to the wardrobe and the other filled the space in-between the bed and the adjacent bathroom. Both were meshed with a tough, high quality security screen which covered the whole frame, not just the glass section which slid open. The walls, although painted a nice shade of light green, were absolutely bare of any adornment and the only other furniture was a table and a chair which sat uninviting against the wall that held the bathroom and a bed side lamp clipped to the wooden rail of the bed head.

Her assessment was lightening quick and decisive. If she was going to escape, there were three things she needed to accomplish. Some clothing and the keys to unlock the door, and to get both she must put the mighty Phantom out of action.

Any minute now he would be finished his shower and her advantage would be lost. With her plan of escape formulated, she moved the chair next to the half-closed bathroom door, near the door handle so that when he emerged his eyes would be slightly angled away from her position. Climbing over the bed and unclipping the lamp, pulling it from the socket and placing the unscrewed bulb noiselessly onto the floor, Jo moved swift and sure, pausing only for the slightest of moments as the shower was switched off.

Silence.

Controlling her breathing into deep slow steady breaths, she felt the familiar rush of adrenaline accelerate her already pounding heart. The whistling stopped. A glance at the door showed he couldn't possibly see her from this angle as she moved silently across the floor to take up her position on the chair. Wrapping the thin electrical cord of the lamp around her left hand and securing the base in a balanced two-handed grip high above her head she waited.

Uncertainty crept in as her ears tuned for the small noises from within the bathroom. A flare of doubt erupted as she realised she didn't want to hurt Axel, she didn't want to hurt anyone, she just wanted to find out if Kevin was ok, go home and put this all behind her.

Almost abandoning her plan of attack, Jo gritted her teeth and mentally prepared herself for what she must do. Encouraging anger and frustration to take over her emotions as she silently cursed her father for getting her into this mess, she cursed Axel for all the feelings he provoked. But most of all she cursed herself for allowing these feelings to flourish in her body until she wanted nothing more than to be in his arms. Then he was coming through the door and she had no further time for thought as she flung herself into action.

Propelled by a desperate need to escape, Jo slammed the lamp with precision down on the vulnerable side of Axel's head, just above the temple. He fell like a ton of bricks, sinking to his knees with a groan of pain, before slumping to the floor semi-conscious.

Cat like she leapt from the chair, hesitating for a split second as a flash of regret fled across her mind. He looked so vulnerable lying there with only a towel wrapped around his waist, the broad muscles of his back waiting to have her hands running over their tanned bulk, trace the lines of his tattoos. Jo chased the thoughts away by another memory of last night. No way could she stand up to his questions about why she was here and once that was done, he would find out how much she wanted him.

Time was of the essence. Nimbly she leapt across his inert form and wrenched his unresisting arms behind his back. Dropping the lamp and grabbing his wrists in her right hand, she straddled his back locking her knees together to hold his arms firmly in place, wrapping the cord from her left hand around his wrist in a fluid circular motion.

Phase one complete.

Elated and running on overdrive, she looked down at the powerful man on the floor at her feet, effectively bound and unable to stop her from escaping. All's fair in love and war and it was not as if she loved him or anything. He was not the sort of man she wanted to love. *Keep your mind on the war,* she admonished, *it's not won yet, you still have to get out of here in one piece.*

Axel started to growl as he lifted his head with difficulty, shaking it from side to side, blinking his eyes as they started to clear. At least, after she had gone, all that would be hurt was his pride, of that she was relieved. For a moment she had been worried that she had hit him too hard. Now that he was coming round, she spurred herself back into action.

Dashing into the bathroom and grabbing his discarded cotton shirt, throwing it over her head and shoving her arms into the sleeves, she was grateful for the bulk of the man to whom it belonged. It hung halfway to her knees, offering the much needed protection to her body. It felt safe to be covered again even if the musky masculine smell of his shirt tantalised her senses. His jeans were far too big to wear as she knew they would be, but she rummaged through the pockets looking for the key to the door. Groaning to herself, she realised he had put the single key onto the jangling mess she held in her hand. There must be at least a dozen to choose from. Picking out the most likely one and holding it firmly in her fist, she squeezed her hand tight.

Phase two complete, now to get away.

As she moved swiftly back into the other room, Axel was half up on his knees struggling with the wires that constricted his wrists. Half turning, he paused in his efforts, the black thunder in his eyes and an angry set to his jaw would have stopped a runaway locomotive at full throttle.

Not Jo. Committed to her plan, she pushed her foot against his backside in a bid to knock him off balance again, shocked to find her own legs being kicked out from under her as he lurched out sideways. Jo made a desperate bid at the chair with failing arms, only to miss it completely as she hit the floor with a heavy bump. The keys flew from her grasp and slid across the room well out of her reach.

It was a slow-motion pantomime to see who could recover first, and as her head cleared she could see him rise to his feet, hands still trapped behind his back.

Roaring like an angry bull he charged.

Having no time to analyse what she was going to do next, Jo acted on pure instinct. She dropped to the floor and rolled deftly out of the line of fire, grabbing the keys as she came back up in a fluent motion onto her feet.

Axel's reaction was as fast as hers and he changed direction a split second after she rolled and before she was halfway to the door he charged again. This time using the force of her momentum against her, he lowered his head as she ran full speed into his solid body.

In winded agony Jo collapsed in a crumpled heap onto the floor, clutching her stomach unable to draw a breath and she drew her legs up to her chest in an effort to relieve the pain. Through tear streamed eyes and gasping breaths, she watched in horror as Axel shook the last of the wire from his wrists. He threw the lamp across the room with a violent motion that portrayed the intense danger of his temperament before he leaned back against the door gathering breath of his own, his eyes deathly cold as he watched her acknowledge defeat.

Jo, her breath finally coming easier, rose proudly to her feet. She was angry, more so than she had ever been in her life. Fury seethed and raged inside her looking for an outlet it could not find. Watching him close the short distance between them with formidable determination, she knew she was going to lose her virginity in a way she had never dreamed. Everything else seemed irrelevant.

The towel dropped from his waist to reveal the potent evidence of his arousal. His penis proud and erect mirrored the powerful solid frame of his body.

Wide eyed she stared. She had seen her brothers naked many times. Shyness had not been encouraged in her family, she had shared a room with Kevin for goodness sake, but never in her dreams had she prepared herself for such a magnificent sight. Sensations exploded into a million fragments of individual desire as Axel brought his mouth crashing down on hers.

Time ceased to exist as her anger found its release in the form of undeniable passion. She answered the primitive thrusts of his tongue with an equal fever of her own. This was what she was wanting, what she had been yearning for.

Keys dropped forgotten to the floor, their vibrant jangle lost in his groans of pleasure as she reached trembling hands behind his neck, fingers digging deep into his black unruly hair, still damp from his shower. Wrapping some strands around her fingers, she tried to pull him away from the stormy kiss. He responded by delving deeper into the crevices of her mouth demanding all she had to give. Strong hands clasped her buttocks, bringing her sharp and firm against his lower torso, as he devoured her moan of agreement with simultaneous thrusts of his probing tongue.

Melting into his body, Jo rubbed her sensitised breasts against the solid wall of his chest and his first words of desire cascaded down her spine.

"Take off your shirt," he demanded in sexy whisper against her ear. "I want to feel you naked in my arms, feel your breasts caress my chest, show me how much you want me."

Jo fought against the desire to do his every bidding. She wanted to detach herself from the feelings that he was drawing out from her. There was no way she could stop their love making, in truth, she didn't want to. There was nothing she wanted more. He had started a smouldering fire in her the day they had met. It was now a raging inferno that devoured all forms of resistance.

Except one.

Her heart was protected by an impenetrable wall of anger and defiance. As long as they both stayed hostile towards each other she was safe. It didn't matter that he was going to take from her what no man had ever dared, she wanted him as much as he wanted her, but he wouldn't get near her heart, she was saving that for love.

"It's not my shirt," she challenged, pulling slightly away, deliberately fuelling the fire at her refusal. "And I'll not be the one to give, you will have to take what you want."

Nostrils flared and dark eyes flashed pure heat as he accepted the gauntlet she threw down. With slow sensuality he reached for the shirt and without hesitation pulled it up and over her head in a lingering caress across her body.

"I don't have to take anything from you, my little Wildcat."

Her body now naked except for the tiny lace knickers, stood strong and proud almost trembling with impatience as he took his time devouring her with his eyes.

"One look at your body tells me you are more than willing to give me anything I ask."

It was true. Jo squared her shoulders, raising her chin to read the naked desire etched into every feature of his face. His words excited her beyond belief and for a fleeting second she wanted things to be different. She wanted to be in another time and place, where life and love were simple and easy. For a moment she thought she saw an echo in his eyes. Then it was gone, and they were cold and hungry as he slid a firm hand down the front of the fragile lace panties, deft fingers working their way between the moist warmth of her thighs and she was lost again in the glorious world of sensations.

Pulling her closer into his body with a firm arm across the length of her back, he leaned over her whispering the words onto her lips. "I made you a promise when you first arrived. Be prepared to retract your words Josephine. By the end of this night you will belong to me...body and soul." With a confident downward wrench of his hand the fragile lace broke, falling to the floor in a soft forgotten flutter.

There was nothing soft about the two bodies now locked in a passionate duel, a duel of demand, of give and take. Him trying to dominate and her refusing to let him by giving him all he demanded and then demanding more from him in return. Teasing and provoking, Jo pulled away from him, denying him the contact and access he was wild for, only to have him retaliate as he caught her, she arched against him, only to be denied with what he refused to give.

The soft mattress hit the back of her knees and she let herself fall, still clinging onto Axel as he fell with her. He took the weight of his body onto his hands giving her the freedom to move. Jo bent her legs, placing her feet on the soft mattress and curved her body away from his in an attempt to put distance between them, laughing with him as the move placed them perfectly on the bed. With a growl of triumph he towered over her, slid his hips between her legs and pinned her arms to either side of her head.

All movement ceased as the mingled current of aggression and desire danced between them. Axel was shaking with restraint as he towered over her. Pulsating and poised at the entrance to her womanhood, he hesitated as she let him see all that was her. Fear, apprehension, anger, uncertainty, denial, all overridden with a pure naked provocative yearning that sent a fierce flood of boiling blood rushing through her entire body. She showed through her eyes how much she wanted him.

"I agree, the time for fighting is over." His words whispered down to mingle with her plea for release as the sexual tension built to an unbearable pitch. "I want more than you have given any other lover." And as she felt his body tense for the first powerful thrust, she rose to meet him. Her cry was of both pain and ecstasy as he broke the barrier of her virginity.

Gaining a moment of sadistic satisfaction at the shock and disbelief that flashed into his eyes, she moved against him in a motion that was hard to resist. Her legs enclosed his hips in a vice like grip as her feet pushed down on his buttocks demanding in no uncertain terms that he continue.

With a growl of pleasurable anguish, he moved against her and into her again and again as he fought for control over his actions. He tried to kiss her, to gentle her motion, but she refused him that as well, turning her head away and biting hard into his shoulder in protest.

Ignoring the pain, his mouth came down on the sensitive side of her neck and she moaned long and deep in unashamed pleasure as he moved to her ear, whispering soft words of encouragement into her soul. Jo soared to new heights as he gave up the struggle by taking charge of the tempo with firm controlled thrusts as he hugged her body close to his, enfolding her within his strength.

Sensation upon sensation exploded around her like a kaleidoscope of vibrant colours and she gave him back as much as she received, sending them both into a heaven of rapture, until the kaleidoscope burst in a blaze of fragmented glory around them. The pieces slowly falling back down to earth scattered, never to be assembled again in the same aggressive pattern.

Chapter 28

The room was silent except for the light, relaxed snoring of the man lying next to her. Soon the first rays of the sun would appear to chase away the stillness of the night. Faint moonlight lifted the edge off the darkness as Jo extracted herself from with-in the loose circle of his arms. This time there was no murmur of protest, no automatic tightening of protective muscles encouraging her to stay safe and warm in his embrace.

Moving the wooden chair over to the window, she returned to pick up the sheet that lay unused at the foot of the bed and wrapped it around her shivering shoulders. She wasn't cold, but her body shook with the emotional impact of what had transpired. Tears fell in silent streams as she let them flow unchecked over her cheeks, hoping they would bring some sort of stability back to her thoughts.

Going over their aggressive, but highly passionate lovemaking in her mind, Jo tried to refuel her anger, but she found she couldn't. There was only an empty space where it had been. Other emotions tried to fill it only to have her push them away recognised, but unwanted. The emotions didn't go far, she could feel them hovering in the background waiting until she relented and acknowledged their existence.

The tears abated as she remembered his compassion as they both fell back to earth. She had tried to pull away, but he had wrapped his arms around her and drawn her gently back to him, lifting and carrying her to the shower, letting the soothing waters wash away the last of the tension. After tenderly drying her and laying her back on the bed, it had been evident he wanted her again. When she had reached out to him, he had smiled, shook his head and drawn her softly to him, moulding her back and buttocks deep into his chest and groin bringing up his knees behind hers so they were locked in the foetal position together. Soothing her with whispered words as he wove his protective shell around her, she had fallen asleep to the peaceful rhythm of his hand stroking her hair.

Sinking down into the chair, resting her chin on her drawn up knees, Jo wrapped the sheet around her like a shroud. Positioned so she could watch both the waking dawn and the man on the bed with a flick of her eyes she finally relaxed, realising that this was the first time in the last twenty four hours that she had had a moment to gather and nurture her bruised emotions.

The man on the bed turned over in his sleep so that his face was towards her. His peaceful features were dappled by the fading moonlight. He was strong and powerful and so damn sexy she almost felt in awe of him.

Last night their lovemaking had been full of anger and frustration, although she had hurt him, scratched him, bit him, he had responded with a sensual passion guiding them to a fulfilling release. Not once, even in the blackest depths of their tempers had he overstepped that boundary and abused his power. Ironically, it had been her unwanted feelings for him which had made her behave so rashly in the first place. Her need to escape the situation between them had only thrown her deeper into his territory.

It didn't matter that she could see the keys on the floor by the end of the bed, dimly outlined in the growing dawn light. That she could just pick them up and walk out while he slept. There was no more escaping what could happen between them and that was what she had been trying to run away from. He had said she would be his body and soul and he wasn't wrong. She ached for him now, for the soft tender contact she knew he was capable of.

A slight smile crossed her face as she finally acknowledged he had also broken down the barriers to her heart and the emotions she had pushed aside came flooding in, demanding she look at them too. She loved him. The feeling was clear and defined. It didn't surprise her. She had known it for a long time. Since the day they had met and raced side by side, united, yet wild and free, joined by a frozen moment in time as their hearts had beat as one. It was only ten days ago. It felt like a lifetime.

"I don't want to love you." The words were just a tiny whisper in the soft light, and she knew it was true. Just as she knew that while he was involved however deeply in activities outside the law, he was as kind and compassionate as a person could be. He had known she hadn't come to see him, yet he had saved her. There *was* good inside him. She could feel it and recognised she would have to confront him about it. The same as he would confront her about herself, about Kevin. Maybe now they could finally talk without anger and aggression getting in their way. Dare she tell him she was with the law? Could she use it as a tool to convince him to help her and in return, she would give it her all to help him get off as lightly as possible.

The thought of him going to prison sent a shard of despair to her heart. One step at a time she steadied her resolve. First, they needed to talk. For the moment all she could do was protect herself as much as she could, keep her feelings hidden and work towards getting them out of this in one piece.

Her natural assertiveness rose to the occasion, be damned if she was going to just sit here and watch him sleep the day away. She hadn't eaten since yesterday...no, it was longer...and that was the priority she would deal with now.

"I'm hungry," she stated, watching with concealed amusement as he jumped awake at the sound of her voice. It wasn't until after she had said the words that she realised they were both naked. Well, she had realised, but hadn't given a thought to what would happen when he woke. Once again she had put her foot in it, and she vowed it would be the last as she saw the answering gleam in his eyes. She flushed, tucking the sheet closer under her chin.

Axel laughed deep and genuine as he swung his legs over the side showing not a shred of embarrassment. Instead of getting up he sat where he was, hands braced on his thighs, watching her with amused eyes, saying dead pan. "So am I."

Jo jumped to her feet, clutching the sheet tighter to her chest, the smouldering look on his face had her spluttering. "Food. I was talking about food."

He roared with fresh laughter. "Oh, the joy of finding such pure innocence in the most unlikely place on earth."

"I...I..." she faltered, frowning, not knowing what to make of the way he was joking around. This was not what she expected and a side of him she had only glimpsed the day they met at the racetrack. She shook her head and stared at him.

"You really are a rare gem amongst the coals and whether you liked it or not, you're stuck with me."

Refusing to acknowledge the statement, she stood tall and strong. "Well, do I get anything to eat, or are you planning on starving me to death?"

All that achieved was to send him into renewed fits of mirth, as he imitated her regal stance by pulling the sheet from under him and wrapping it around his shoulders, throwing his head in the air.

"Is madam requesting sustenance from her humble servant?" he asked in an over the top British aristocratic voice.

She opened her mouth as if to say something before snapping it shut again, shaking her head and squashing her lips together to stop herself from laughing. She almost cracked, her laughter hiding just beneath the surface. Squashing the feeling she let wariness creep back into her face. She didn't know how to take him and was out of her depth and unsure of how to act, but try as she might, she couldn't conceal the glint of amusement in her eyes.

"There are a few things I'm going to have to teach you." His eyes shone in return. "Like, on how to say good morning before demanding food."

Trying hard to regain at least some of the anger from last night and failing, Jo finally laughed. Looking at the man standing wrapped in an extremely over-large sheet did have its funny side. Especially when in her smallness, she must look even funnier. For a brief moment her eyes shone back at him. Then the reality of the situation took charge and a deep furrow dented her brow.

This was for keeps, there was no getting up and walking out of the door, her life depended on this man. She was confused, wanted to find her anger, to scream defiance in his face and wanting at the same time to wrap herself secure and snug in his arms. He was being nice enough now, but what happens when he wants to make love again...Oh god, not now...

Flashing her eyes up to his she knew instantly she had left her emotions wide open and he had recognised her line of thought and she shook her head in denial. Stepping away, turning her back on him to look out of the window wasn't the right thing to do either. Even before he touched her, she felt the warmth of his body close to hers. She tensed as he moved her hair to one side, then shuddered in delight as he placed a delicate kiss on the side of her neck, softening beneath his touch.

Rotating her slowly in his arms and cupping her cheeks in both hands, he gently lifted her face, searching the green depths in an investigation so intense she almost melted into the folds of his body.

He overpowered her senses and he overpowered her. He filled her vision as brilliant blue eyes devoured a way into her heart.

Well aware his sheet lay crumpled at his feet, Jo fought the urge to drop her own and run her hands along the golden swell of his shoulders wanting to feel them ripple beneath her touch, wanting to trace the outline of the tattoos that fascinated her so much. She swallowed and licked her lips, blinking as she tried to lower her eyes from his.

She was caught, mesmerised by their hypnotic strength and as his mouth came down on hers there was nothing she could do. Nothing she wanted to do other than kiss him back.

Undemanding, yet sensually erotic, he moved his mouth over hers with such silky finesse it was like kissing the morning sunshine. His friendly tongue flicked a hello along the line of her lips before parting them to enter the silky depths.

She met him and frolicked lightly, enticing him deeper into her warmth.

He complied, exploring every hidden crevice she led him to, before inviting her back into his own mouth. She went tentatively at first, nervous and shy. Teasing her, gently coaxing, he drew her into the warm seductive cavern, encouraging her to explore.

Jo embraced her sensitive side responding on pure instinct. Feeling the passion rise she poured it into her kiss, deepening it with such a fever, she was totally surprised, then utterly disappointed as he broke away to hold her by the shoulders at arm's length.

Before she could utter a word of protest, he shook his head, and his words closed her mouth up tight.

"Tisk tisk, Josephine." He cocked his head to one side. "You are greedy, but it's one step at a time. There are many types of kisses. This morning was an introduction on how to give a good-morning kiss. Later..." With a quick waggle of his eyebrows, he left the sentence wide open as to what other kisses she might like to try.

She had never played sexual games before and was highly aware she would probably mess it up somehow, so she stuck with what she knew, trying but not quite succeeding for an annoyed tone. "I don't like being called Josephine."

His expression made her toes curl "Well, you are way too sexy to be a Jo. Hell, you are all woman." He deepened the smile, her name rolling off his tongue like silken honey. "Josephine."

They were words of magic giving her a warm glow deep inside. No-one had spoken to her like that before or said her name in such a way that it made her feel so feminine and sensual. Others had tried to call her Josephine and she had slammed the door in their faces but coming from his sexy lips it sounded just perfect. "Say it again," she said.

"Josephine."

Hell yea, she could compromise if he kept saying it like that, for the first time in her life she felt like a woman.

Axel leant in and gave her smiling lips a soft fleeting kiss sealing the deal and before she could react in any way, he silenced her with a finger to her mouth, spoiling the moment with his next words.

"Don't forget Josephine, we still have our question and answer time to come, and after last night I have a few more to add to the list." A slight steely tone had crept back into his voice and his expression took on a slant which brooked no defiance.

Jo squared her shoulders, lifted her chin and stared right back into those sensual blue eyes. Trying as hard as she could to project some form of anger into her voice. It didn't quite work, although she did manage to put a touch of strength into the words. "And I have a few questions for you also, so you had better get your answers ready." She went to put her hands on her hip in a gesture of defiance. The action brought a smile of amusement to his face as she made a desperate grab for the sheet as it started to slip off her shoulders.

"Having trouble admitting defeat, well I don't mind operating on two levels. Looks as though we are in for some interesting discussions, power and passion. If I can't get answers out of you one way, maybe I'll try the other." With that Axel leaned over and placed a delicate kiss on the tip of her nose before turning to walk to the wardrobe, picking up the keys on the way.

Hell, he confused her with his hot and cold tactics, but there was no doubt about it, this man was body beautiful. That he must spend a fair amount of time outside with his shirt off was obvious by the dark tanned span of hard muscle which rippled as he unlocked the wardrobe door. Tapering down to a nice slim waist, the stark whiteness of his bottom was an alluring contrast that was very pleasing to the eye.

There was no way she would give him the upper edge. If he could read her thoughts, he would realise she had turned to putty deep inside. She was hard pressed not to just melt back into his arms and try as she might the anger she'd felt towards him had vanished, disappeared with the aggression that had been a part of her life for so long.

Shutting and locking the door, Axel must have felt her scrutiny. He turned slowly, the clothes in his hands fell across his stomach and hung down his legs, covering the most interesting parts of his body. Sauntering back to the bed, in what Jo could only describe as a highly seductive swagger, he dropped the clothes onto the bed. "If you keep looking at me like that, we might skip lesson two and jump right into lesson three."

Fire rose in Jo's cheeks as she turned away, she wasn't embarrassed by it, but Axel and nudity together, was entirely something else.

"You can turn around now, it's quite safe," Axel mocked softly. "I have left some things of mine on the bed that will have to do until I get your clothes from the lower circle."

"Kevin." The word was whispered, but her heart carried a thousand cares and worries as she belatedly remembered how worried her brother would be, and concern about him flooded her thoughts. What he would do when he found out where she was?

"Ah, yes, Kevin." Axel stared at her intently but spoke softly. "I have no idea what he is to you, but one thing is certain, he's not your lover."

Jo retreated a few steps, her outstretched hand finding the bed. Suddenly, weak in the knees, she sat. She hadn't thought about the implications of explaining Kevin to him.

By the determined look on his face, question time had come. Too soon for her liking.

"I doubt you have been sent from a rival gang...being a virgin and all."

Jo felt sick to the stomach. It was out in the open. What should she say? She opened her mouth and shut it again trying to formulate a solid sentence.

A puzzled expression caused his eyes to draw closer together as he studied her. "That leaves the cops, but would they have sent someone so green and..."

A loud knocking made them both jump.

Jo didn't catch his mutterings as he strode to the door and wrenched it open but it sounded angry. It was Beth.

"Viper wants to see you. Kevin is kicking up a stink wanting to know where his lady love is."

Axel stepped through and shut the door behind him before Jo had time to register the words. She sat in shock. Seconds later the door thrust open again.

"It's ok, Feral. Don't look like much fight left in her after a night with Phantom." The look Spike gave her was crudely assessing and much to her distress Jo felt her face flushing.

Feral came from his hiding place around the corner and leaned against the open door, a rifle slung loose in his hands. "Pity," he snarled, "I wanted her to make a run for it."

Refusing to look at him Jo was glad she hadn't even thought of trying to overpower Spike. Her mind was still reeling over what was going to happen to Kevin. Instead she addressed the woman, using her voice to project strength and command. "What do you want?"

Spike was not intimidated "You don't have much time, if ya not ready, Feral can give ya a hand." With a sideways smile she threw a plastic bag towards the bed, the contents spilled out onto the floor as the half-hearted aim fell well short of the mark.

"Thanks for your kind thoughts." Sarcasm dripped as she held the other woman's eyes, making no move to pick up the contents of the bag.

"It weren't me sweetie, I had to. Phantom wants you 'lookin' pretty. Some of the stuff is new, and there's no way I want it back, so you'd better get me some more."

The door banged shut and the lock clicked into place. Jo sank onto the bed and looked at the assortment of scattered underclothing and toiletries on the floor, then decisively flung into action. She didn't know what Axel had in mind but what-ever it was she intended to be dressed for it.

CHAPTER 29

Jo was still trying to brush the knots out of her tangled hair when the door opened again. She was sitting on the chair with her head bent over towards her knees, her hair falling in a fiery curtain hiding her face from view. The awareness that tingled through her skin told her it was Axel who had arrived.

After showering with lightning speed, she dressed in the clothes provided, trying hard to ignore the tension which was building up inside her. The undergarments she had on were far removed from anything she would ever wear. She liked lacy knickers, but these could hardly be called pants, they were just a small triangle almost covering the fine downy hair at the front, narrowing to a thin strip at the back, so her buttocks were just as good as bare.

The garment which Spike had provided instead of a bra was made from the same material as the pants. A fine silky threaded fish net weave that fitted rather like a thin strapped vest, except it finished just above her navel. It was also a lot tighter on her more muscular frame and moulded to her like a second skin. At least they offered some form of protective barrier for her modesty and they wouldn't be seen as the dark grey t-shirt Axel had left her hung almost down to her knees.

It was obvious to whom the shirt belonged, with its large imprint of the comic book Phantom's head on the front, the outlines of his mask face almost lost in a swirl of pale grey giving it a mystic appearance. Also obvious was the fact that by wearing it, it made a statement of possession and in truth she didn't mind, it made her feel safe.

Determined to seem strong Jo stood, flicking her hair back over her head. "I suppose it will do until you bring me my own clothes."

"I don't know," he used a deep charming drawl, slowly moving towards her as he pulled a scarf of brilliant green out of his back pocket. "I think it states the fact in a sexy kind of way." Reaching out he moved her closer towards him as he tied the scarf deftly around her waist, tight enough to hint at the slim line of her figure.

"That was handy. Do you always keep spare strips of cloth in your pocket, just in case you need it?" Her scornful tone didn't quite come off as her voice rose a couple of octaves on the last few words as Axel seductively slid his hand down over her hip to the bare skin at the back of her knee. Trying to take a step back was countered by the strong hand still at her waist as he gripped the belt holding her firm.

"Don't you recognise your own scarf, Josephine?" He raised his eyebrows in question as she stared down at him not answering. "You never did ask for it back." A calculating smile crossed his face, as if daring her to react as he traced intricate circles up and down the back of her legs.

Aware of the skimpiness of her underwear but unable to stop him, she watched his eyes darken and flood with primitive desire as he touched the under swell of her near naked bottom with a feathered caress.

"What in the heck did Spike give you to wear?" Growling with delight he slid his hands around the firm swell of her buttocks before tracing the thin strip up to her hip.

"Stop it." came her whispered plea.

"Say please." he teased softly as she melted against him.

She turned her head to one side, clenching her teeth against the exquisite pleasure as his fingers snaked around towards her inner thigh. She had to stop this, she couldn't fight him anymore, she didn't want to, she couldn't even feel angry at him, she just wanted him with a desperation that overrode all else.

"Obviously Kevin wasn't your lover, so what's your relationship to him?"

The words acted like a dose of cold water and Jo shuddered in his arms. Oh god, again she hadn't given Kevin a second thought, she was so busy fighting her own feelings she had completely forgotten why Axel had been called out in the first place.

"Won't answer that?" Axel cut through her transparent concern. "Well, try this for size, he's here and we are going to see him."

Jo visibly paled as if all the blood drained from her face. She looked up at Axel as she pulled away from him. "Please don't let them hurt him. I give you my promise I will obey your every word. I won't fight you any more...I'll give you whatever you want, tell you whatever you want, just don't let them hurt him."

It had cost her a lot to say those words, but she was beyond caring about her pride. Kevin was her lifeline. If anything happened to him another piece of her would die. Losing one brother was enough. She couldn't bear the thought of Kevin being hurt, or worse. It wasn't the first time she doubted her father's wisdom in insisting she accompany her brother. Just look at the trouble she had landed him in now. She owed him everything, and she had to clear him of her latest stupidity.

Dark thunder flashed in Axel's eyes as he stared back at her, then as suddenly as his anger appeared, it disappeared, and the inevitable mask of self-concealment was back in place. His voice was deceptively calm as he ran a light finger over the bruise on her cheek.

"Your loyalties are about to be put to a test, Josephine. Somehow I think the decision on what happens is on your head not mine."

A terrible tension was rapidly building as she walked or was rather led with the familiar hand resting on the back of her neck, into the same room they had been in yesterday.

Just before they went through the door, Phantom stood still, eclipsing and commanding all her personal space as he pulled her closer to his body. For an elated moment she thought he was going to envelope her in his protective arms offering her the support of his strength and love. Her hopes died as quickly as they rose as she realised she was fooling herself, she did not want love from this man. Protection maybe...but not love.

His expressionless face finally cracked but not the way she had once hoped or desired. It was just a small chip in his impenetrable armour. A flair of his nostrils, a tightening of the jaw and the deepening of the furrows on his brow, was all he allowed before he tightened the firm hand of control on her neck.

Jo kept her head bowed as she was guided into the room. Not knowing what she was going to find, she took the few seconds it gave her to control the fear and tension which strung out through her body like an over wound elastic band.

When she lifted her head she was prepared to face the worst. As expected, all eyes were turned on her and Axel. On their right, Viper sat as before in his comfortable chair, a glint in his eye as if he drew a vast enjoyment from other people's discomfort. Spike in her pre-ordained position behind him, a possessive hand playing patterns on his shoulder. She was also amused by the situation, giving Jo's attire the once over with raised eyebrows of speculation. Mouse and Beth sat on the couch to the left.

Jeckle was perched on the arm rest, his murderous anger of yesterday had vanished, although he touched his nose as if reminding her he had not forgotten. Beth looked on with sour interest. Mouse lived up to her name, head bowed, hands twisting nervous circles in her lap. In between and more towards the back of the room stood Kevin and behind him lounging against the far wall was Feral.

It was a perfectly arranged arena, with her and Axel on centre stage with the others spread out in a semi-circle around them. Positioned as such, no-one could hide an expression from anyone else, apart from Feral, but Jo wouldn't even look in his direction, the evil intent emanating from him could be felt and she had no desire to acknowledge it at all.

Finally, her eyes rested on Kevin, the thrill of seeing him unharmed, standing free without restraint, released a lot of tension and she almost took an involuntarily step towards him, her eyes shining with relief and affection. Jo winced, raising her shoulders slightly in defence as Axel's iron grip of control tightened on her already tender neck.

CHAPTER 30

"Let her go man." Kevin spoke with steel-like authority. He was a powerfully built man, taking after their father in more than just looks. Moving with a menacing step towards them, it was Jo's sudden secret sign for stop that made him check the move rather than the omnipotent stance of the self-assured giant at her side.

Kevin looked at his sister deeper this time. When she had first walked into the room, head bowed in total submission he had felt the anger build. Then when she raised her face to stand tall and look at her captors with defiance, he felt proud. But when her eyes rested on him, he had seen her open need for his love and protection. Nothing would stand in his way to give it to her.

It had never been planned for her to be so deeply involved, not like this. Her bruised and scratched appearance and the paleness of her skin emphasising the dark circles around her eyes had sent an arrow straight to his heart. What had his father done? What had they done? His reaction had been rash and looking closer now he could see the strength and courage in her eyes and his pride was renewed at her ability to think quickly in a very explosive situation.

He always wondered how she would handle the pressures of undercover work. Now he knew. And he knew why his Father had insisted she join him on this venture despite his first initial objection. Her clever decisive mind was not inhibited by pressure, it was enhanced by it. As they were growing up, it had always been her quick thinking that catapulted them out of trouble. How she had got herself in this position he had no idea but now in the middle of the toughest and most dangerous ordeal of her life she was coming out with flying colours. With the simple flick of her wrist she had stopped him dead causing him to re-assess his actions.

'You OK?' He signed, abbreviating and using as little movement as possible, his concerned brown eyes connecting deeply with hers.

'Yes, good see friend face.' For Jo it was easier to 'talk', as she portrayed nervous symptoms that were pretty appropriate to how she felt.

Kevin shuffled his feet, aware the time they had stood staring at each other had drawn on a little too long. He turned to Viper, acting out his part of jealous lover to perfection. "We had an agreement, that the choice between us would be hers." Disguised by the movement towards the leader as he signed, 'You with me, Jo?'

Viper's mouth lifted at the corners in some semblance of a thin lipped grin as he looked at Axel. "Not my fight." Kevin could see by his expression he was enjoying the clash between the titans immensely.

Turning back to Axel, Kevin dropped his eyes for a quick look at Jo's fingers before confronting the inevitable antagonism from the man at her side.

She was smiling and ready with her reply. He had asked, in their old school day terms if she wanted to continue with the original plan. She signed 'Yes,' and quickly followed with a statement of her own. 'Trust me.' He acknowledged with a flick of his eye, unwittingly falling back into the pattern of letting her lead the way out of trouble.

"The choice was hers." Axel challenged. "She came to me by her own free will."

His flashed his eyes to hers with surprise, reading the confirmation in her face. He signed an angry 'why' checking his expression of annoyance as she replied with a question rather than an answer. *'How you get here?'*

What answer was she looking for? Was she hoping he had some form of escape?

'Back bike.' He disguised his delay in answering both Axel and her, by rubbing his hand across his eyes, shaking his head slightly as if he couldn't believe what he had heard. As he knew she would be, Jo was ready, as sharp as ever, and impatient. She always had been when he couldn't match her train of thought quickly enough.

'Blindfold?' Although they had their own secret signs, they were also reasonably proficient at Australian sign language, Auslan, often using the two combined. For 'blindfold' she had to revert to Auslan by opening one hand and putting it palm side to the hair line of her forehead and bringing it down so it briefly covered her eyes, that signified blind. To add fold, she lowered her hand turning it palm outwards to about waist height, then turning it over so the palm was down and placing her other hand on top. It looked as though she was loosely clasping her hands in front of her.

***

The movements Jo made were bold and dangerous, she covered it with a confidence she didn't know she had. Reaching over her shoulder to the hand which was still uncomfortably tight on her neck she turned so she could see Axel's face.

He was staring at her with such a strange expression that she almost faltered. My god, he is clever, everyone else thought this was a duel between two jealous men. Axel, she realised didn't know quite what to believe. He knows we are up to something. Sharply she turned back to Kevin, picked up his quick *'yes,'* and scanned the other faces in the room.

A thrill ran through her body, no-one had guessed, all the time she and Kevin had used the secret signs, no-one had ever had even an inkling of an idea what they were up to. Axel still didn't know what was transpiring between them, but he knew something was happening and it gave her an exciting rush of adrenaline to try and accomplish all she had to before he realised what was going on.

Feeling totally in control of herself and her actions it spurred her to take the biggest risk of her life. She no longer felt the need to flee. It was obvious that they didn't intend Kevin much harm, they had left their options open by blindfolding him. It showed they had every intention of letting him return to the lower circle. If she could convince them that her loyalty was with Phantom, Kevin would be free. And she would be installed deeper into the group that they had ever planned. Realisation dawned on her that Axel's train of thought might be on a different track, but he was one step ahead of her.

Before this meeting he had said to her. "Your loyalties are about to be put to a test and I think it will be you who decides."
How had he known? She looked at him with new eyes which he acknowledged with a devastating smile that sent her hormones into back flips.

"What else did you two decide when I wasn't around?"
she questioned huskily, hoping she was giving the opening he required. Letting out a breath of relief as he loosened the hold, she knew she had followed the right track.

It was to Kevin he directed his reply. "The other must accept your decision." With that said, he released her neck and took a step away from her, his eyes not leaving Kevin's.

A subtle change came over the room as Axel moved past Kevin over to where Feral was still sulking against the wall. He took a friendly swipe at his fellow companion before moving to the table which held the remnants of breakfast. Picking up an apple he threw it at Jo, calling, "catch" as he had done once before.

It was like a symbol for people to start moving.

Viper unfolded himself from his chair. For one scary moment Jo thought he was going to come to where she stood. Instead, he went over to talk to Axel, their voices low and soft, Jeckle joining them and although he flicked his head to Feral, the latter refused, preferring to continue throwing evil looks in her direction.

With an air of indifference Spike moved to sit at the far end of the couch, tucking her legs up under her, disdainfully picking at her bright red nails. Still twisting her hands in her lap, Mouse sat head bowed, Beth continued to watch with interest.

Something flashed into Jo's mind. A flicker of bright pink clutched tight by a small child who was nestled in the arms of Mouse just before Jeckle had blacked her out with his punch. Feral's words flashed back. *How do we know she didn't see the child?-* Who was the child? Surely it wasn't being kept in that hut. Pink? Axel? Fluffy bunny? Child? She felt compelled to find out more.

Jo took a huge bite from the most delicious, crunchy red apple she had ever tasted, it tantalised her taste buds, stimulating the growl of hunger in her stomach.

It was obvious what they were doing. They were leaving the choice up to her. When really from her view there wasn't any. Under no illusions, she knew what would happen if she decided to side with Kevin. He would be stuck here as well, there was no way they would let her go after what she had seen. Possibly they would even kill them. Axel could not help her if she rejected him now. He had given her the means to protect Kevin and by the gods she would use it.

With slow deliberation Jo moved to the couch, sitting next to Mouse, never once taking her eyes off Phantom. All the time she was talking to Kevin, her hands tapping as much information *as* she could about the hut and the confusing trails which led to it. Turning the apple nervously was a perfect camouflage as her fingers relayed messages while she ate.

CHAPTER 31

Kevin grappled with the concept he was going to have to leave his sister. It manifested into one of the hardest things he would ever have to do. He was under no illusion; both their lives depended on his next move.

One look at his sister and you could see what kind of violent man Phantom was. Yet she could evidently cope with what had happened. He did not want to not leave her here to fend for herself, he always looked after her in the past, and that wasn't going to change now. He took strength in knowing the backup plan was in place.

Watching her sit there casually in control, munching on her apple as if she didn't have a care in the world, Kevin realised his sister was right, the course of action she suggested ensured he would be free to arrange help and blow this group right apart.

"Jo...?" Kevin's voice was deep with emotion and he knew they had run out of time as out of his peripheral vision Phantom start to move. He held out his hand towards her. Fortunately to the others it sounded like a plea for her to choose him. Quickly he signed with his other hand close to his body using his outstretched hand as a decoy. A straightening of his hand, thumb briefly to the third finger...Plan C, he gave her a very brief thumbs up to indicate it was in place.

"Her name is Wildcat, and by her choice she's with me." Axel strode towards them glaring at Kevin as he pulled Jo ungraciously to her feet, spinning her around, and almost shoving her into his arms. "Make your choice Josephine and you had better be quick." With that he turned, nodded to Viper and strode out of the room.

Feral showed interest for the first time, thrusting his compact body off the wall, his eyes positively gleaming. Jo's inward cry almost broke his heart as he accepted, he must leave his sister, there was no time to think, he saw her slight nod to say she understood his last message. He managed to give her an encouraging smile as she mumbled, "I'm sorry Kevin," and fled the room after Axel.

Kevin walked a few steps towards the door watching it close behind her, trying to stay calm and relaxed hoping they accomplished enough to survive. Plan C was in place, and there it would stay, glad, not for the first time that he had set it up before he returned to the house. Forty-four hours, well, twenty-four of those had already gone. As much as he had kicked up a stink when he got back last night, Feral had assured him they would take him to Jo in the morning.

He would use the rest of his hours wisely, following through with the information Jo signed. Could he and Jo still pull this off? He wouldn't stop worrying about her until this mission was done.

The blood chilling double click as the cocking of a lever action slipped a bullet into the chamber shattered the silence of the room. Kevin's hairs stood on end and his heart picked up pace as adrenalin shot to every fibre in his nerves.

With dread he turned to face his foes.

The Winchester 303 nestled confidently in Spike's shoulder aimed steadily at his chest. Viper and Beth were at her side and Jeckle moved to stand in front of the door effectively blocking his exit. Not that he was going anywhere whilst he was staring down the barrel of a gun. Feral grinned wildly, twisting his hands together in glee.

Chapter 32

Axel didn't wait or slow his pace as he strode across the veranda. Jo trotted at a fast pace to keep up with his determined gait. At the door she hesitated but with his patience at an end he shoved her unceremoniously into his room.

Once inside he didn't stop, he stomped towards her, eyes flashing with anger. She tried to stand her ground but was no match for his bulldozer attitude as he ploughed into her, forcing her to walk backwards until she came up against the table. He stopped their bodies just a hair's breadth apart, his voice low and threatening.

"What in the hell are you two playing at? Who in the fuck is Kevin? How could he just leave without a fight, doesn't he care about you at all? What would have happened if one of them had realised you are not lovers? What do you think would happen to you?" Bracing his hands on either side of her he breathed in deeply a bid to gain control.

Stunned, she looked straight through his anger and saw genuine concern battling to surface and knew in that instant her love of him was right and that she could trust him with her life. He just helped her save Kevin, without knowing the answers to any of those questions, and she recognised in him a raw aching need to be able to trust in return. Finally, the Phantom's mask had been removed.

Reaching out with one hand she smoothed her fingers on his face, a soft gentle caress that sent a shudder through his body. He closed his eyes and rested his forehead on hers.

"Who are you Josephine? What are you doing to me?" His words scented with sweet apple whispered freshness over her soul as he held his face just a fraction above hers.

She tilted her head wanting to talk, to tell him she loved him and knew he was a good man, that they could get through this together, but she craved his touch even more, wanting to show him through actions rather than words.

Her lips brushed lightly over his offering him all that she was. Unable to refuse he lowered his head fitting his mouth with perfect unison over hers, the taste of her chasing away his anger and concern.

Lifting her so she could sit on the table and tuck in close, he savoured the softness and the honesty she offered with her kiss, only breaking away as he lifted his arms to help her drag off his shirt. His breathing deepened as tender hands traced his snake tattoo up his arm and over his shoulder and around to the head which rested just above his nipple. A ripple arrow-headed straight to his groin as his nipple sprang to life reaching for her touch.

Mesmerised he watched her fingers slowly creep inch by inch across the smoothness of his chest to repeat the same tantalising motion around a smaller more personal tattoo. She leant forward and placed a delicate kiss on the little heart as if knowing the tattoo held a piece of his own heart from his troubled childhood.

Overcome with emotion he placed his hands on her shoulder as if to push her away and she lifted her face to look searchingly into his.

For an instant he saw vulnerability, not just in her eyes but in her whole body. She painted a picture of pure innocence wrapped in a layer of sexy mystery.

Axel's heart went out to her. Undeniable compassion took hold and with that came the full realisation of what he felt for his Wildcat. Love. His heart was full of warm, unfamiliar emotions, all for his Josephine.

He had known from the first time they met that they would end up on the same side. He had seen it in those beautiful eyes, the out of kilter body language and deep down he had realised that she was cut from a different mould than the others.

Uncertainty surfaced. What did she see in him, how could she love a man who had done the things he had done? Obviously, they were attracted to each other, but he wasn't dumb, she was not who she seemed and not here with him on her own accord. Just where did she stand and what was she after?

And then there was Kevin.

Seconds ticked silently by. Tension started to build. He drew in a breath wanting to talk but not knowing where to begin, seeing the same indecision mirrored in her. A loud and prolonged rumble broke the intensity as her stomach protested its need for more than just a few bites of an apple. It was a well-timed intervention, just what they needed to relax the moment between them.

Axel smiled deep and genuine. Lifting her off the table and putting some distance between them he stepped back. The rumble grumble came again and this time they both laughed as she clutched at her stomach.

"Sounds like the perfect cue to go and get us something to eat." He paused giving her a thoughtful look before walking out.

Temptation in the form of the open door stared her in the face. She ignored it and sat down on the rough wooden chair, committed now to seeing this through to the end. Information was what she needed, especially about the child and talking to Axel was the only way. And then there was the unfinished business between them on a personal level, she craved the soft tenderness only he could give.

It was necessary to talk first. She must set aside her feelings so she could evaluate information on its merit. Plus, she really needed to find out where Axel stood in all this. She could help him, but she needed to show him he could trust her and that she would do anything to help him when all this was over.

A small scream escaped her throat as a duffel bag slid violently across the floor making her jump. Beth stood in the door frame, wiping her hands together a few times before taking a hands on hips stance. Spike stood just behind her gun in hand.

Beth spoke. "That's your shit from the lower house." She pulled a typical mean girl snigger. "You won't be going back there again."

Jo did her one eyebrow raise combined with a condescending 'as if I really care' head tilt, taking pleasure from Beth's deepening scowl as she turned and walked away.

Axel nudged past Spike, gave her a glare and kicked the door shut with his foot. "Making friends with the locals?" He held a tray laden with colour and wafting with mouth-watering aromas.

Not bothering to answer she glanced at her suitcase and at the food, saliva pooled on her tongue. "That smells so good."

He rested the tray on the bed, ignoring her apprehensive look. "Give me a hand." He lifted one end of the table and waited for her to grab the other. Once the table was in position he went and brought over the only chair, offering it for her to sit on. He walked back to the door. He locked it with a loud click, came back and sat on the bed, tucking his legs under the table.

"Wow, did you cook all this?"

He smiled as he passed her a plate. "Been on my own since I was fourteen, learning to cook was part of survival, wait till you can see what I can do with seafood. Five years on a trawler teaches you things about the sea's supermarket."

Such a long personal sentence had Jo savouring every word, letting it set the tone for the meal ahead.

"Fourteen's pretty young to be out on your own?" Jo tried not to probe too deep as she loaded her plate with bacon, scrambled eggs and mushrooms and tucked in with gusto.

"Coffee."

It wasn't a question as he passed her a perfectly poured cup and she found it just a little disconcerting that he knew how she liked it. He popped a piece of bacon in his mouth chomping on it as he answered. "Better than where I came from, and before you ask, no parents, was abandoned at birth in a railway station toilet right in the heart in Melbourne, pretty dramatic hey."

Realising he did not want to go down the sympathetic path, Jo kept her tone light, "Rough foster care?"

"Mostly." He automatically touched his shirt where his heart tattoo was, and she didn't think he realised he had done it.

They were silent for a while as they demolished the hot food and started on the fresh fruit. Jo had the impression he didn't want to say anything else about his past. She felt grateful he had told her that much. It gave her a small insight to the life that shaped the man.

The table between them acted like a buffer zone and before she could plan where she was going with it, but knowing she had to start somewhere, she said softly, "Kevin is my brother."

Shock registered on his face, then disappeared just a quickly as he leaned forward to rest a loose fist on his chin in a listening position, placing his other arm on the table in front of his chest and raising his eyebrows slightly.

Jo relaxed and let out a breath feeling more comfortable; she may as well go the whole hog. She felt she only had something to gain and she had promised if he helped keep Kevin safe, and he had.

"Kevin works for a covert intelligence organisation; I was asked to help." Not knowing how he was going to react, she dropped her eyes, barely breathing and toying with the uneaten crust of her toast. "Kevin didn't have access to the smuggling trails so they bought me in as his racing mad girlfriend, hoping I could map them..." She swallowed deeply and took in a breath. This was it, make or break, before she lost her nerve she continued, "And...and to bring you down for murdering my brother Patrick a year ago."

Jo didn't know what to expect as she raised her eyes, but she didn't except to see him with a Cheshire cat grin and a sparkle in his eyes, holding back a laugh. Not knowing how to react or what to say, she stood, pushing back from the table. She turned away, only to find he moved with lightning speed, pulling her in close to him. Tight fisted she lashed out to no avail as he picked her up and rolled them both onto the bed, pulling her in even tighter against his chest and throwing a leg over hers to stop her from struggling.

Shhhh, shhhhhh, he hushed, kissing her gently on the forehead. "I didn't kill your brother." As she stilled against him, he kissed her again. "If we are talking about the same person, he's my friend. I can't promise he is alive, but I can tell you he didn't die in the boat accident."

Releasing her he rolled onto his back, giving her space and time to take it in. After a while he continued "Ok, I am presuming Paddy and Patrick are one and the same. I knew he worked undercover, but I didn't know..." His words were cut off as she rolled on top of him and planted a tear moistened grin of a kiss on his lips and then a more serious controlled passionate one that that told him in no uncertain terms she believed him.

She leaned back and looked down at him. "I knew you weren't a killer." He expected her to bombard him with questions about Paddy, but he didn't anticipate the verbal confirmation she showed him. He seemed to be the focus of her emotion and the honesty of it went straight to his heart enveloping him in her happiness. He sat and drew her into his lap wrapping his arms around her and returning her kiss with a fervour that left them smiling and breathless.

They pulled apart at the same time, totally in sync with what was the next step. Words weren't necessary as they stood. Axel packed the breakfast dishes back onto the tray, flicking at a few little sugar ants that had already started a feast of their own, and placed the tray by the door.

Jo picked up her case, rummaged around inside and headed for the bathroom, her mind a buzz with the news of her brother. By the time she came out Axel was sitting with his legs outstretched and his body resting against the head of the bed. Happy to be back in her own clothes, Jo resisted the urge to sit next to him as she made herself comfortable sitting cross legged by his feet so she could look at him. She didn't waste any time. "You have to tell me everything you know about Patrick. He *has* to be alive."

CHAPTER 33

K evin groaned long and deep, almost choking on the putrid gag stuffed in his mouth. Rough hands grabbed his feet, causing him to fall sideways, cracking his head on the floorboards adding an extra spin to his semi-conscious state. His arms had been bound tight against his body and his split lip dripped a red pattern down his shirt and onto the floor.

Out of half-closed eyes he watched Jeckle's boots stomp purposely towards him. His bonds were tight and there was nothing he could do to avoid the vicious kick to his gut, except try and ride the pain by tightening his stomach muscles and curling into a semi ball. He fought the urge to vomit, coughing and spluttering into the gag.

"Enough!" hissed Viper's voice of authority. "We don't want him dead. Not yet anyway."

The accompanied laugh sent a new wave of despair rushing through Kevin's body. He had heard enough in the last few minutes to know that the mission had been compromised, and that could only mean one thing, there was a traitor in MICO.

Working on blocking the pain, he let cold anger keep him rational. Refusing to think about Jo and the extraction team who would walk into an ambush, he concentrated on himself, his surroundings, and any information that might help him escape.

Voices swam in and out of his consciousness, then became clearer as the pain faded and he grasped onto every word he could catch.

"Feral, go stand on the veranda, watch Phantom's door, he has already been out once to the kitchen, can't risk him coming in here. If he wants to leave his room, delay him, till we get this rat out of here."

"How in the fuck do I do that"

"Who gives a shit, tell him you wanna fuck his wildcat." Spike sounded annoyed. "Just don't let him come down here till we've got rid of the agent man."

Viper pulled rank, "Feral. Veranda. Spike keep an eye on Feral. Jeckle tell Mouse to get the kid's things ready, she's to stay at the hut till we move out, and if anyone sees Beth, tell her to get her ass back here."

Kevin's heart started to pound, sweat dripped in his eyes blurring his vision as Viper walked towards him. He tightened his muscles and gritted his teeth as boots stopped close to his stomach, flinching as they only nudged him.

"Hey Jeckle, help me get him outside. You can bag and drag him to the compound, but remember, I don't want him dead. Not yet. The plan is to kill him and his sister together."

Jeckle's laugh sounded manic. "Her first. Let him watch while I get even with the bitch."

Even though it was futile Kevin couldn't help but struggle as they hoisted him to his feet. It was short lived as Jeckle's elbow connected to his cheek bone with a jarring crack. As he slumped forward, the two men started to drag him. A clod of congealed blood dripped from his lip to the ground and earned him a kick in the shins as it almost landed on Vipers boot as they juggled him through the door.

Jeckle spoke. "What about Phantom?"

Viper brushed the question off. "Leave him to me. He'll be fine once he gets his Wildcat out of his system. More important, you still ok about them taking Mouse with the brat? She's been with you forever man."

"It's all about the money. She's young, pretty, about twenty I reckon. Damaged goods, but she'll fetch a good price on the market. A good fuck, just bored with her now."

Kevin's yell of anger at their words mixed with his cry of pain as they dragged him down the steps and dropped him on the dirt behind Jeckle's bike. They tied a rope around his waist, and looped it through the bindings at his feet, leaving two long ends to tie around each side of the handlebars.

Mouse appeared, shoulders slumped and clutching a backpack. He tried to get her attention, hadn't she heard them? but she refused to look at him stretched out behind the bike. She climbed on behind Jeckle. Viper tied off the second end of the rope to the other handlebar, giving each side a tug, as if to show him what was going to happen.

Kevin felt helpless. He tried not to let despair take hold as a hessian bag was dragged over his head and shoulders, plunging him into darkness. Air became almost non-existent. His muffled yell sounded dull even to his own ears. Someone smacked at the bag with a violent swipe catching him on the side of the head, and the muffled words, "Let's give this bastard a ride he won't forget," exploded his fear.

Noiselessly the bike free wheeled down the track, dragging him painfully behind. He knew what was happening, every time Jeckle turned the handlebars, it loosened one side causing him to almost flip before bouncing back again. There was nothing he could do but endure the horrifying ride, holding himself in a stomach crunch for at least some of the time in a bid to protect his head. Even with the freewheeling keeping the speed down, he felt every bump and turn the rough track had to offer and by the time they pulled to a stop he was delirious with pain.

CHAPTER 34

"You look a bit like him you know." Axel folded his arms in a bid not to reach out and pull her to him. She seemed relaxed and comfortable, sitting cross legged on the end of his bed. He liked the fact she had chosen to sit opposite him, as much as he wanted to pull her into his arms, they needed some distance.

"Not so much look, but you have some of the same mannerisms. That's why I laughed before. It's been bugging me since we met. You and Paddy tilt your head the same way when you are questioning something, have a similar expression as well." His lips curled in a half smile. "I should have picked it earlier."

Silence stretched for a while as they looked at each other.

"Tell me about Patrick. What did you mean you don't know if he is alive?"

He took a while to answer, appreciating the way she waited until he was ready.

"It's a long story. It starts way before Paddy came into the gang."

Axel rubbed his chin thinking about a place to begin. Took deep breath and jumped off the deep end.

"Welfare wasn't working out, so I jumped a goods train and ended up in Innisfail. Broke and hungry, I enquired round town looking for work. Viper's father Snake took me in."

"How old were you?" Her soft voice was full of concern.

He lightened his tone, not realising how sad he must have sounded. His life dramatically changed with the kind generosity of Snake. It hadn't been easy, the work had been long and hard, but it was the beginning of a new life.

"Fifteen. Snake took care of me, helped get a fake ID, and changed my name to Axel Stone." Axel laughed. "He let me pick the name, I got it from a video game I used to play in one of my foster homes. Axel Stone was a tough street fighter and I wanted to be like him." He shook his head at the memory, it seemed a lifetime ago.

"So, did he teach you to ride?"

"Not straight away. He had a motto, stay out of trouble and trouble won't find you. Threatened to kick me out if I didn't work hard and stay clean. He secured me a cash job on a fishing trawler. I was away for weeks at sea, then back with Snake and his bike shop during my times off. I learn to ride then."

"Tough but fair, hey."

"Yep. Taught me not to squander my money and to stay clear of drugs and booze. Wasn't hard. I'd lived with a drunken abusive foster family; I wasn't interested, and I never liked the clouded mind of drugs. After eight years I stashed enough money away to be independent. I bought a boat to do my own fishing and stayed with Snake. I liked what he was doing. Always bringing stray kids under his roof and setting them straight."

Axel admired the way Jo let him tell the story at his own pace. She smiled at him and everything in the world seemed ok. He cleared his throat.

"Viper and Snake never got along, always fighting when they got together. Then out of the blue Snake died. With him gone Viper turned hard and mean, formed an alliance with the Hell Raisers and expanded the tracks and trails between the groups and the criminal activities that went with it. Created the upper circle. I didn't like the change and toyed with the idea of hitting the road, but didn't want to leave the kids behind, Freckles was barely sixteen then. I couldn't desert them, so I took charge of the lower house.

That's when I met Paddy. We hit it off instantly, I never told anyone about my past before, but with Paddy it felt right.

The Hell Raisers liked the idea of us Range Riders being 'clean,' it gave them a good front for their activities. They brought crime and distrust, where Snake was running a clean, almost refuge type thing, for troubled teenagers. Paddy helped me see the big picture, he confided in me he was undercover, but after the big guns. He was fanatical about it. The Hell Raisers were into drugs, smuggling, but when they turned to kidnapping the child of a customs officer so they could get goods smuggled into the country, Paddy knew we would have to intervene and save the child."

Jo sat still, barely breathing, not wanting to disturb this free flow of words that so obviously came straight from his heart.

"We set up a plan for his organisation to raid the place, but something went wrong, the gang knew about the plan, but not that it was Paddy who put it in place. We worked out who was the mole from our side and using my boat set up an accident to make it look like Paddy was dead, killing the traitor at the same time. I took the child back to safety and Paddy went deeper undercover, moving from the Hell Raisers up to the next level."

He looked across at her as she interrupted.

"Wouldn't they have known him...Patrick I mean?"

"All contacts are by phone. Security, with codes. They'd never seen the traitor or Paddy, so he simply switched identities."

Maxed out from sitting still, Jo jumped up off the bed and started pacing the room, processing the information. She came back to stand in front of him. "So, you saw him after the boat blew up, you know for sure he is alive?"

Axel swung his legs off the side of the bed and sat looking up at her. God she was beautiful. He could see Paddy all through her now, the sparkling intelligence in her eyes, the quirk in her smile, her self-assured character. But where Paddy was patient and controlled, she was impulsive and restless.

He watched her almost unable to stand still, wanting to know everything so she could act upon it. Carefully he stood, taking her by the shoulders and swinging her around and pushed her to sit on the bed, barely hiding his smile as she jumped straight back up again, determined to have her answer.

He took the keys from his bedside table. "No, I didn't see him." Her face visibly dropped as he hurriedly continued, "But, he has contacted me through a person named Willow." Turning away he didn't see her surprised look at the mention of the name. He went to the cupboard, unlocked it and took out a small box and brought it back over tipping the contents on the bed.

Patting the place next to the paraphernalia, he let her investigate it while he stood on the bed and reached for a phone that was high on the window's sill. He smiled as he sat down on the other side of the contents. "Lousy phone coverage, up there on the window is the only place I can get reception inside. I was sent this package after everything with Paddy settled down. I didn't know until then if he had pulled off the infiltration or not."

Jo looked at the phone, the charger and four small envelopes each bearing a numbered one to four. And at a tiny thin disc like object that looked like a bug of some kind. "So how do you know Patrick sent it?"

"It wasn't really sent, it just appeared in my backpack one day, when we were out riding. I got back and it was in there. I can't remember leaving my pack unattended, not for long any way."

Axel picked up the phone, shook his head as he checked it for messages and placed it back up on the window. "I also received a note which I was told to destroy once I read it. I'm meant to wait for a message saying, 'call me,' then change the sim using the one in the first envelope, destroying the old sim and ring a number I had to memorise. Once I have spoken to a person named Willow, I am meant to change the sim with the one in the second envelope and wait for her to contact me back."

Jo tilted her head smiling softly. "It's all very intricate and has a typical complex Patrick ring to it. My brothers used to tell him he was always a step above MICO, he set up most of their systems.

Always loving subterfuge the most out of our family, and excelled at it. The best in his field."

Axel nodded, reaching out and tucking a strand of wayward hair behind her ear before he continued. "The last thing he said to me was, I could trust Willow and I would hear from her. He said, time means nothing, but to wait and if I didn't hear, I would know when it was right to act on my own and..." He hesitated, only two people had known his actual name and Snake was dead, so that left only Paddy. "Willow called me by my birth name, only Paddy would know that. That's how I knew he was still alive."

He picked up the stuff on the bed, putting it all carefully back in the box. Now someone else knew. He looked at her and it felt alright, felt good to share this burden with her, to trust her. It had been over a year and the phone had stayed silent, now it would be good to have help to do what he planned.

She reached out and took his hand in hers adding her warmth and strength to him. "And now you know," he added softly, looking directly at her. "My real name is Brodie Mathews, given to me by the state of Victoria."

Axel was astounded, when without warning Jo reached across and kissed him gently on the lips. Mouthing quietly who each of the three sweet kisses were for. One for Phantom, one for Axel and the last and most lingering, she stated, was for Brodie.

They sat in thoughtful silence for a short time, before Jo questioned.

"So you haven't heard anything since receiving the phone and instructions?"

He shook his head. "Time's running out, I can't wait any longer, it's all going down with-in the next two days." He pulled Jo into his arms and looked down at her. "We have to save the child."

"A priority," Jo stated. "You will have to tell me more, but first it's time I tell you my side and what I know and then we need to formulate a plan. I think Patrick is indeed still very much alive," her face radiated happiness, "or at least Willow knows his whereabouts."

She pulled away and started to pace again. "Just after I accepted the assignment, my father gave Kevin and me some information for our ears only. He was quite mysterious. I just filed it away at the time. He said *'If you hear the names Brodie or Willow, I want you contact me asap. Not through the regular channels, but on my private number.'* He obviously knows something and typically he is keeping it to himself until he thinks we need know." She stopped in front of Axel again and said in earnest, "I have to get a call to him."

Nervous energy radiated from her as he watched her resume her pacing. It was setting him on edge as she walked back and forth. He sat on the end of the bed and waiting until she walked past again, reaching out to grab her hand. Indicating with a tilt of his head that she should sit, to his surprise she did, but two seconds later she was up again and after a full circuit of the room she was back in front of him.

"You know why Kevin and I were sent in, but what you don't know is when I didn't turn back up at the house Kevin put in place a backup plan with MICO. I am not sure of the timing, but we can make an educated guess." This time she sat down next to him on her own accord, angling herself so she could look at him. "He put in place Plan C, which is a 44-hour window for a storm and rescue. We can presume he put it place once he got back..."

"Maybe not," Axel interrupted. "He called me about eight am and didn't arrive back at the house till late afternoon. If it had been me, I would have put it in place straight away. That would leave plenty of time to find out what was going on with you and time to stop it if everything was ok."

Jo jumped up and the pacing resumed. "Right, let's say 0800 hours on..." She stopped dead in her tracks, putting her hand to her head. "holy shivers, what day is it today?"

Axel had to think for a moment himself first. "Saturday afternoon, which means Plan C was put in place Friday morning. Sunday morning will be show time." He stood up and questioned, "Unless Kevin has cancelled it already?"

"I don't think so, otherwise he wouldn't have told me." A visible shiver of dread flooded her system. "Kevin will be ok now won't he? I mean, they will just take him back to the lower house?"

He walked over to where she stood and pulled her into his arms. She felt so good, small and compact fitting perfectly into his embrace and a fierce protectiveness overcame him. He would let nothing hurt her. Running his fingers over her cheeks, he lifted her head so he could fall into the beauty of her eyes. "We need to do three things." He placed a soft kiss on her lips. "Call your father, find out what he knows about Willow." He gave her a second kiss. "Find out if Kevin is ok so we can set a plan in motion." He stood mesmerised in the depths of emerald green.

"That's only two." Her voice was low, husky and inviting. She stood on tip toes stretching up so he could reach her lips easily.

A soft moan of delight met his kiss as his lips slid over hers with sensual assurance. He gently pulled her body closer angling his head to make the most of the moment, kissing, releasing and kissing deeper again in a tempo that was a prelude to what he wanted to follow.

Her parted lips were a welcome invitation for his tongue, and he revelled in the sensation as she allowed him to lead, lips meeting lips, tongue tasting tongue as he devoured her softness.

He pulled back almost as breathless as she and smiled. "Now that was a kiss of promise, a taste of what's to come." He lent back and gave her a mini version, lingering just a little in his reluctance to stop.

"We have to make plans." He put his hands on her shoulders. "You realise you are going to have to stay here, Viper won't let you leave." He could see she didn't like it, but she gave a sharp nod. "I'll call your father and see what I can find out about Kevin."

Jo gave Axel her father's private number, reminding him to say his name was Brodie and watched him walk out the door before she shut and locked it quietly behind him. She didn't want anyone coming in. Restlessly she began to pace.

CHAPTER 35

A stale humid smell blanketed the air. In the dim light Kevin could make out a windowless square space, the muted sunlight filtering through a small gap running around the ceiling. Tight bonds bit into the skin on his wrists and dug into his back where he leaned against the wall. Methodically he moved every limb in turn, assessing the damage and to his relief nothing felt broken.

His head hammered as if a hundred bikes were revving it up and his body hurt as though they had run over him again and again. Despite the pain he felt reasonably clear headed, but it was barely enough to fight down his rising panic. He had to get away.

His eyes followed the woman as she walked to the far side of the room, dust flurries dancing around her feet. She was making crooning sounds as she rocked her arms. The small child was quiet now. When they had arrived, it let out a howl that was only drowned out by Jeckle yelling at her to shut the thing up. Jeckle also took his temper out on him and a few well aimed kicks saw the relief of darkness take hold.

He had been awake for a while leaning uncomfortably against the wall. The bag had been taken off his head and Jeckle was no-where in sight. Hopefully gone; he didn't think his body could take much more abuse. Thirst took hold and he licked at the dried blood on his lips watching as the woman put the sleeping child to bed.

After swallowing several times to coat his parched throat he croaked, "Water." The woman ignored him, so he tried louder. "Water...can I have some water...please?" She still went around her business of tidying up, head bowed, putting all the child's belongings in a bag. The quick sly glances she stole in his direction were not long enough to get her attention. Too tired to resist his eyes desire to close, he relaxed, sinking deeper into the pain releasing darkness.

Consciousness came in a swift motion. One minute he felt and thought nothing the next he was instantly awake. He had the most bizarre feeling. His eyes were still closed but he felt a presence close by, so close he could feel breath on his cheek. Tentatively he opened a swollen eye.

It was as though he looked into the eyes of an angel. Pale dove grey with tiny shimmering highlights of soft blue, they belonged to a sweet compassionate face that offered him a tentative smile. The woman gently wiped the dirt and dried blood from his skin with a cooling damp cloth before she held a cup to his mouth. He drank greedily, not caring that his lips didn't seem to work properly, causing him to dribble over his chin and onto his shirt. The water tasted like nectar, rejuvenating his bruised body and helping to clear his throbbing head.

"Can you untie me?"

She watched his face as he spoke, then shook her head, darting a purposeful look towards the door. Her next move astounded him, she held her left hand palm up out in front of her, palm facing inwards, clenched the fist of her right hand leaving the index finger pointing out straight and moved her fist over her upturned palm from wrist to fingertips. Using Auslan, she had signed 'later.'

There wasn't much time to register she must be deaf as she jumped and put her hands on the ground, her face clouding over with trepidation. She put her finger to his lips and pulled the hessian sack back over his head plunging him back into a world of rank darkness.

What came next he wished he could block from his mind. Jeckle had been in a foul mood, totally ignoring him, as he gave Mouse all his attention. The way Jeckle spoke to her, made it clear she was used to his aggressive sexual attentions and fortunately for her they were over in record time. The guttural sounds she had been demanded to make would be imprinted on him forever and anger seethed deep inside at being unable to stop it from happening.

The bag stayed over his head. Jeckle had long gone and the room was relatively quiet. He knew she was not badly hurt, as she had attended to the child again when it had started to cry. The baby had been awake for a while, making soft gurgling noises and playing happily with some kind of jangly toy.

Cocking his head, he listened as the sound of a bike in the distance grew louder and louder, coming up a hill. Where he was? He had no idea except that the journey had been down, across, then up from the upper house. It was as much as he could remember. He had tried to memorise the route, but it had been too hard, and he barely remembered the end.

He listened again. It wasn't Jeckle's, unless he had changed bikes. The tone was different, but familiar. One thing Kevin knew and that was bikes. This one was Phantom's and a spike of dread fled to every bump and bruise he had, as thoughts of his sister flooded each crevice of his mind. Mouse's soft touch to his shoulder almost made him jump, and he sighed with relief as she lifted the bag from his head.

Kevin blinked as his eyes adjusted to the brightness of the late afternoon sun as it shone through the open door. Fresh air played with his nose and he breathed deeply.

Mouse went and stood next to the door as Phantom skidded to a halt in front of the hut.

Ducking as he came inside, he gave Kevin a surprised glance and then looked at the woman, placing one hand on her shoulder, the other he touched lightly to her cheek. "You ok?" Kevin heard the words and saw her nod. "Sorry," he said, and Kevin saw the woman straighten a bit and take a deep breath as she nodded again.

Axel turned his attention to Kevin, shaking his head and muttering. Taking the knife out of his boots, he manoeuvred Kevin away from the wall and cut away the bonds from his hands and feet, signalling for Mouse to come closer and help lift him to his feet.

When he had seen the knife, Kevin had thought he was a dead man. When he felt the bond release his limbs, he had an overpowering urge to fight back and find Jo. Surprising Phantom by lunging to his feet, he took a swing and totally missed as both his legs and arms refused to cooperate with his thoughts. The action sent him sprawling to the floor.

Strong arms lifted and half dragged him to the bed, sitting him on the soft mattress. When it looked as though he would try again, the woman stepped in-between and signed 'friend.' Kevin watched again as her two hands came together, palms inwards, clasped one on top of the other front of her stomach, she moved them sightly twice in quick succession, mouthing at the same time, 'friend.' It sank in.

"Josephine's fine." Axel stated bluntly, understanding it would be the first question Kevin would want to know the answer to. "She is confined to my room, but she is safe."

Kevin stared, Josephine? A million questions rolled around his head, but he just sat and stared. Life was coming back into his blood deprived limbs and it wasn't a pleasant feeling at all. He moved them about trying to hurry the blood along. Tentatively he stood wobbling a bit, then biting back the pain limped around the room. His right knee was up like a balloon, he could feel it stretching and pressing against his torn and tattered jeans. Every muscle ached and he felt like his body was on fire. He came back to stand in front of Phantom and the woman. Noticing a large bruise deepening on her swollen cheek he clenched his fists vowing to pay back Jeckle tenfold. "Jo's safe?"

"She was safe when I left her, I need to get back."

Axel looked directly at Mouse and said clearly, "Drink." Made the motion with his right hand of having a drink and pointed to a bottle on the cupboard shelf.

Mouse returned quickly, holding an empty glass and the bottle out towards Phantom, she asked the question with her eyes. He shook his head and motioned towards Kevin. He needed one to boost his reserves; it looked as though he had been to hell and back. Axel didn't want to cloud his own mind with alcohol, he had everything he needed in Josephine and he was impatient to get back and make sure she was still ok. Something strange was going on between Feral and Jeckle.

After leaving Jo he had headed to the lower house hoping to find Kevin, planning to ride out into the valley together to make the call to their father. Once at the lower house Feral informed him no one was to leave the property until Viper gave the order and that he didn't know where Kevin was, gone for a swim with the others maybe. Axel had checked out the swimming hole, but no one had seen him, Babs said she hadn't see him since Jeckle had taken him somewhere, they hadn't seen Jo either.

He could tell they were a little uneasy and Axel encouraged them to stay at the house until things settled down. He would have liked to have told them more but too much was at stake. They would be safe enough at the lower house. It was well away from the compound and from what was going to go down.

Not being able to ride out into the valley put a damper on his plans to ring Jo's father. Being second in charge he could have overridden orders from Feral, but he didn't want to raise their suspicions. Things were strange enough. He had an alternative spot, but he needed to go back to the upper house and climb the hill

First, he called back into the lower house. There was still no sign of Kevin, Axel pretended to be light-hearted about it saying he just wanted to clear the air, it was no big deal. Jeckle had turned up in one of his darker crueller moods, laughing as he scratched his groin, imitating Mouse's noises.

Although he wanted to get going, Axel forced himself to act natural by hanging around for a while before telling the boys he would see them at the compound at six the next morning. He hoped it would be well and truly over by then. He wasn't sure yet what he was going to do. His original plan was to take Mouse and the child to the plateau cave, lay low for a few days before getting them as far away as possible, then leaving them with the authorities somewhere.

Mouse would be fine; she couldn't be held accountable for anything. Maybe they could find her true family. He on the other hand had a lot to answer for and didn't want to spend the next twenty years in prison.

The upper circle were all from the Hell Raisers, except him, Axel didn't know all of Mouse's history, but it had taken him quite a while to convince her to trust him and take the plunge to help him. Being friends with Paddy had warmed her to him. Apparently, he had done a lot of work with her communication skills. She would be very happy to find out he was still alive.

He had no choice but to call into the compound on the way back. He had left Jeckle and Feral, feeling a little uneasy at their smug behaviour. After Jeckle's disgusting display he needed to make sure Mouse was ok. There was no telling the amount of relief he felt at seeing Kevin, he may be in a bad way, but he was alive.

Kevin looked a bit steadier on his feet now. Obviously, he had backbone. A lot of men wouldn't be standing after the beating he must have taken. By the torn and tattered state of his clothes Axel knew they must have dragged him here. Puffy slits of blood shocked eyes looked back, assessing him.

"Josephine... Jo, really is ok. We are working together; my birth name is Brodie and I was a friend of Paddy...Patricks." He didn't want to go into details that Paddy might be alive, what if he wasn't, they hadn't heard from Willow yet. Besides that information was up to Jo to deliver.

Kevin took his time taking it all in and with a voice laced with pain he finally said. "What's the plan?"

"Priority one. Get, Jo, Mouse, the baby and you to the plateau. It's safe there and even if your father's organisation can't make a rescue in time, it's a good place to lay low. After I leave here, I need to get to a spot with mobile reception to contact your father. The gang's plans are set for six am, we are hoping MICO can come earlier." He hesitated, not proud to be associated with the next bit, but pleased within himself that he had helped stop the previous one and would not let this one go ahead either. "That's when they come for Ruby." He indicated towards the child with a nod of his head. "She is meant to be released as her father followed instructions, but the Hell Raisers have other ideas. She gets taken from here and 'shipped' to her new owner."

Kevin struggled to open wide his swollen eyes as he half jumped towards Axel. "Shit. What in the fuck are you involved with?"

Axel placed a reassuring hand on his shoulder. "I don't have time to explain. You will just have to trust that Mouse and I were never going to let it happen. It's complicated, but I must get back to Jo. I don't trust the others and although she is safe in my room, I want to be sure."

They stared at each other for a few long seconds before Kevin gave him his trust by nodding. "What do you need me to do?"

"Stay with Mouse just in case anyone comes back, I don't think they will, Jeckle's done his damage for the day."

Mouse must have been following the conversation by lip reading and she dropped her head to her chest. Axel gently lifted her chin so she looked him in the face. "If anyone else comes tonight, Kevin will take care of them. Ok? It's nearly over Mouse." He looked over at Kevin and directed the next words to him. "If Jeckle comes near her again, you can kill him. It won't matter any longer."

Kevin nodded. He wouldn't kill him, but he would make sure he was never able to use his dick again.

"Be ready, we will come back and get you as soon as we can. Don't worry." He saw more questions ready on Kevin's lips. "I have this covered." With that he was gone.

CHAPTER 36

J o paced trying to work off her restless energy. Axel had been gone for hours and the room, although a good size, was constrictive. She wanted to know what was going on and didn't like being out of the action. It was exasperating and pushing her patience to the limit. Was Kevin ok and had Axel spoken to her father?

After he left she indulged in a long soothing shower. Happy to have her own belongings and be able to wash and condition her hair, she spent a frustrating time working the knots loose. She shook her head letting the fresh soft waves catch the breeze of the overhead fan. It felt good to be clean and tidy, and nothing felt better than wearing her own clothes.

Never having been one to deliberate over what to wear, she found herself in new territory and for the first time felt self-conscious and indecisive, finally settling on the light green loose flowing skirt and pale green embroidered short sleeved shirt; remembering the appreciation in Axel's eyes when she wore this before. Besides cool and comfortable justified her choice. This room was hot and stuffy now the afternoon sun hit the walls in full fury.

On top of her case she placed clothes she would need for later. Dark jeans and the long-sleeved shirt she had worn on the tracks.

They would give her plenty of camouflage and protection for the task ahead. Socks, boots and gloves she rested next to the case, along with the bands for tying back her hair. That done, there was nothing left, but to start pacing.

It was almost dark by the time he came back. One minute she paced restless and bored and then he walked through the door. Desire, adrenaline and anxiety danced in her blood. Anxiety won and she couldn't help but impatiently blurt out, "Kevin, father? Did all go ok?"

His eyes never left hers as he sat on the bed taking off his jacket and boots, telling her the day's events, not holding back about Kevin and the condition he was in. Reassuring her all was going to be fine and he had left Kevin armed and looking after Mouse and that they would be ready.

She looked steadily back at him, at first shocked about Kevin, then trusting Axel completely when he said he would be ok. He finished talking and his expression changed as she watched him stand and devour her with his eyes. His voice, husky and soft drifted to her ears.

"How about a kiss of hello?"

It felt like a dream as he walked towards her. Reality took over as he clasped his arms around her in a powerful possessive embrace. Automatically she lifted her arms around his neck, running her fingers through his hair, pulling him towards her to draw their bodies closer together. Holding her back teasingly, he smiled his desire at her, his hands ever so slowly following the line of her spine to the firm round contours of her bottom.

Instead of bringing her close into contact with his body, he surprised her by running a tantalising trail up over the slender curves of her waist, dipping his hands under the hem of her blouse to trace a delicate path to the silky skin beneath her breasts. He coaxed them into life by running soft teasing lines below and to the sides of them, lifting his thumb in a fleeting contact as the peaks became ridged, throbbing for the sensation only his hands could give.

Lowering his head, he finally kissed her hello. It was a kiss full of passion and promise as he enfolded her deep into his embrace. Tantalising, he offered her a tiny taste of what she knew he could give.

He pulled back, eyes sparkling with delight, "Hello."

Jo was breathless. This man sure knew how to kiss. Each one proved to be special, how he applied different emotions and passion to each type was a skill within itself and she couldn't help but to encourage more, "What kind of kiss comes next?"

He laughed. "You'll have to be patient. First, we must make that call to your father." Grabbing his boots and jacket and hastily pulling them on, he looked back at her. "Do you want to come? You'll just need boots. I'm going to walk up the hill so I can get enough reception to make the call."

Jo didn't need to be asked twice, by the time Axel had the other things he needed out of the cupboard and his phone off the window sill, she was ready. She tied her hair into a simple pony tail, eager to be doing something, her smile matching his. Patrick, maybe now she would find out about Patrick.

Opening the door Axel looked down the veranda, music could be heard from the other end of the house. Taking Jo's hand, he pulled her into him, throwing his arm around her shoulder and casually sauntering towards the kitchen. He opened the fridge and pulled out a beer, passing one to her as well.

No-one was around, the music changed to the next song covering the sounds of their footsteps on the leaf strewn path. Once around the back, they followed a small trail up the steep hill behind the house. Later tonight, the moon would be almost full, but now there was enough of the dying daylight for them to avoid tripping over loose stones and branches. They left the music of the house behind as they climbed, winding around the side of the hill. A large boulder blocked their path. Axel took off his jacket and put down the beer. "They won't hear us from up from up here." He leapt up onto a deep flat ledge at the side of the boulder. "Do you want a hand?"

Without even bothering to try and be ladylike, she tucked her skirt hem into her knickers and climbed, sure footed up and past him, onto the next ledge then grinned from the top as she smoothed down the folds. "No thanks."

In no time at all he was besides her giving her a quick sexy kiss. He passed the phone across. "You may as well call now."

Before she had the chance to dial, the phone buzzed, not loud but sharp and vibrant.

She showed him the message. 'Call me.'

Elation illuminated his face, the stress lines disappeared, and he was like a small boy in a candy store, so long he had waited for this message and now it was here. He beamed at Jo. "This is it, it's Willow."

He grew serious, then it was all business as he sat down, changed the sim and made the call. "Willow," was all he said when it answered. He hung up. Steady fingers changed the sim again, and it rang almost instantly. "Brodie," his voice was charged with suppressed excitement. He listened for a while, grunted a few affirmatives, spoke quietly into the receiver, listened again and hung up.

Jo sat down a little distance from him, giving him privacy. She was silhouetted by the rays of the setting sun as it added an ambient glow over the houses in the valley below. A few yellow lights blinked on as the families prepared for the night to come. She looked up at him as he came to stand in front of her. He reached out, pulling her to her feet when she placed her hand in his.

"Willow already knew your cover had been blown. She's been trying to contact me for hours. I must have lost service on the ledge. Sometimes it just not reliable. But we were right, I don't know how she knows, but there is a traitor high up in MICO."

"And Patrick?" Jo was literally holding her breath.

"Willow wouldn't mention any names for covers sake but did say she was permitted to tell us her contacts code name is Thor."

Jo's eyes shone bright, and she put her hand over her mouth to stop from shouting out. "That's too much of a co-incidence. We used to play superheros when we were younger, he was always Thor." She threw her arms around him. "He's alive. I just know it."

Axel had to agree. It certainly looked that way. "So what superhero were you?"

Jo ignored the question and stated. "We'd better ring dad."

"We can't. Willow says all contact has been suspended, the traitor is in deep and no phone can be trusted not to be tapped or traced."

He watched as Jo processed the information.

"I know," she said. "I'll try Robert Jnr's private number. It's worth a shot."

Axel raised his eyes in question.

"My oldest brother. He's stationed up the tip of Cape York."

"Three brothers?"

"Five, including Patrick," she grinned. "All older, no sisters. Stop getting distracted." She pushed his hands away from where they had crept up under her shirt.

"Distraction therapy will help the time go quicker, now we have to wait for Willow to call back. She is going to try and get in contact with Sir Robert and tell him about the plateau." His fingers began their explorative journey back under her shirt.

"Axel," she gasped as his hands changed direction and clasped seductively around her butt. "I have to at least give it a try."

He looked down at her and placed a delicate kiss on the tip of her nose, hell she was beautiful. "Of course," he said passing her the phone.

Service disconnected. She passed the phone back, screwed up her nose and shook her head.

"There's no doubt that your father won't send help. You, Mouse and the baby, whose name is Ruby by the way, must go to the Plateau. Willow said it is possible they may come in by chopper.

If that's the case, they can take you all to safety." He drew her close silencing her protest with a smooth kiss.

He pulled back slightly and continued, "If not you will be secure there until it's all over..."

"Oh no..."

His kiss, deep and long, smothered her objection, finally lifting his head, both a little breathless he continued. "I gave the GPS coordinates to Willow, so they know where to find you.

"I'm coming with..."

A third prolonged, highly seductive kiss was necessary.

"I reckon once help arrives it'll be over pretty darn quick. Kevin should be fine at the hut, we'll leave him armed, unfortunately his knee won't take much walking."

Jo gave him Buckley's chance for a fourth kiss. Pulling away and holding her arms loosely by her side, she studied him in the growing moonlight. A slight smile graced her face. "Anything else?" she asked a little too sweetly, cocking her head to one side.

Suspicions aroused, he said cautiously, "We can't let Kevin and Mouse know, it's too risky to take the bikes out now. It will be different in the middle of the night; everyone will be asleep. We will just turn up earlier, they'll be ready." His eyes widened as she popped the lowest button to her shirt.

"So now we wait for Willows call?" Another button opened.

"Yes." His voice turned a little husky. God she was a she devil, turning the distraction game back on him.

She undid the third button. "I wonder how long..." And the fourth. "She will be?"

He devoured her with his eyes, picking up a nervous edge to her voice as she undid the last button and let the shirt hang open and said, "I guess we have time for that beer then."

"Forget the beer." Axel took a step towards her.

Jo retreated, adding distance between them. "I don't think so. Don't want to be wasteful."

This woman was driving him to the point of no return. He tried his best to keep his expression encouraging, wanting to show her he liked what she was doing. The bulge in his jeans drew her attention and for a moment he thought she was going to call out to stop him as he turned away to do her bidding.

A croaky, "Sure," was all he managed as he jumped onto the lower ledge and then the next one to where they had placed the beer. On his way back up, she stopped him by calling.

"Stay where you are, I'll come to you."

The lower ledge put him at waist height and when he looked up, she had moved her skimpy shirt aside so it hung open bathing her breasts in moonlight. Her discarded skirt lay near her ankles leaving her dressed only in tiny lace panties and calf high riding boots

"Leave the boots." His voice thick and heavy with desire.

With sexy provocation she stepped over her skirt, reached up and released her hair from its restraints so it tumbled around her shoulders.

Walking with a sensual roll to her hips across the top of the rock to where he stood on the ledge below, she could see only from his chest upward and gave him a greedy once over when he lifted his arms and took off his shirt revealing his chest in all its magnificent glory.

Stopping close to the edge she looked down into his face. "I'm coming to get the beer." She placed her hands on her hips. "But first I need to clarify a point."

Axel grinned. His love of her sass radiated through his eyes. Reaching up with both hands he hooked his thumbs through the lacy sides of her knickers, pulling her so close to his mouth she could feel his breath caress her through the thin material.

"Clarify away."

A small moan of pleasure flirted with his ears as he peeled down her underwear, leaving his mouth just millimetres from where he knew she craved it to be. Her, "I am not staying on the plateau," wasn't said with any conviction as his hand pulled at a boot clad ankle while he breathed the word into her pubic hair. "Lift."

She complied, watching as he slid the one side of her panties over her boot. Her quiver when he put her foot back down wider than before teased his control.

"Sorry, what did you say?" He breathed long and hard as he tapped at her other ankle. "Lift."

"I'm not staying..." She gasped as his tongue investigated the widened gap between her legs. "...on the plateau." She resisted the temptation to hold onto his head for support. He took it a step further running his hands up her legs to join his mouth, pulling her thighs apart so his tongue had better access to the delicate pink skin inside. She let out a deep moan pushing her pelvis towards him.

Taking advantage of the angle, he suckled hard on her nub of pleasure, then left it exposed to throb in the cool air and he gave her no time to mourn the loss of his mouth as his fingers created sensations of their own.

"Oh. Yes. You. Are." He punctuated each word with a kiss as he made his way to her belly button. As he moved his hands, intending to place them on her hips to lift her down to him, she stepped nimbly back out of his reach. Her backside swayed as she turned and walked away. He let out a growl of pleasure as she brazenly bent over flashing her white cheeks at him as she picked up her discarded skirt.

"Sorry, what did you say?" She turned, sauntering back towards him, a small cheeky grin gracing her lips and speaking again before he could open his mouth. "Doesn't matter." She jumped down next to him. "Subject's closed."

"The hell it is." He muttered under his breath, delivering a kiss that was both possessive and demanding. He wanted her safe, hell he just wanted her. He didn't deserve her, but he wanted her all the same and would do anything to protect what was his.

Stepping away, he turned and jumped to the next level. It wasn't a big distance. He looked back, placing both his hands on the ledge saying, "Maybe a bit of trust is in order."

The ledge was quite deep and not as high. She walked over and put her hands on his shoulder. His head came just above her breasts and he kept eye contact reinforcing how important this was to him.

"I do trust you," she said, honest and straight forward. "But trust is not the issue here. It's about letting a person make their own choices, life or death. It is their life. A person must follow their own code of ethics and morals, without that we are not the people we proclaim to be." She leaned down, kissing him gently on the mouth. "For the record, I trust you with my life."

Axel's return kiss stifled her yelp as he swept her of the ledge and into his arms, she instinctively wrapped her legs around his waist for stability as he swung in a circle.

Not breaking eye contact, he hoisted her a bit higher, so the support was just on one arm. He reached for his leather jacket and smoothed it out on the ledge, lowering his arm until she was sitting on his jacket, legs dangling over the side. "You started this," he said, stepping in between her legs.

"No, it was you with your distraction therapy," she countered, feeling sexy and sassy.

"Did it work?"

"I don't know, I'm still waiting to find out."

"It worked for me." He drew attention to the bulge in his jeans, at how perfectly he was positioned. "In fact, I think this ledge will work fine for both of us."

The emotions that crossed her face fascinated him. She was so expressive, holding nothing back. The flare of apprehension, then excitement flash to the surface made him remember how inexperienced she was, and he realised she probably hadn't thought this far ahead. Hell, he had. Seeing her standing before, almost naked, glistening in the moon light with the light breeze teasing her hair, he had almost come on the spot.

The moon slipped behind a cloud. He stepped back, letting her watch him in the half-light strip off his clothes, letting her see the evidence of how much she aroused him.

"Oh yea," she whispered huskily as he stood tall, proud and naked. "It sure is working for me now."

CHAPTER 37

Axel took off her shirt and laid all their clothes on the rocks behind, providing a thin buffer against the stone before pulling his jacket and Jo close to the edge so she had to cling onto him for support. Then, secure in his arms, he kissed her long and deep. It went way past the kiss of promise and accelerated into full blown hot lust.

"Lie back." As if the moon agreed with his whispered words, it broke away from the cloud and into the star-studded sky, bathing them in glistening light. Axel watched in admiration as tight stomach muscles controlled her descent, not needing his steadying hands, but taking them anyway.

Mesmerised he ran lingering fingers over her soft skin. Beginning at the dip in the neck, all the way to where calves meet boots, savouring the hungry arch of her back that followed his journey.

Lifting smooth legs one by one and bending them at the knees, he placed her boot clad feet on the ledge either side of his hips, totally turned on by the feel of the cool leather in contrast to the heated skin of the beautiful woman that lay before him.

Bucking and surging, his penis close to the prize, nestled against her folds. Tantalising, he rubbed it up and down her length a few times, holding in restraint as he let it sit on top of the junction to her thighs, a solid reminder of things to come.

He reached out and picked up his phone. Choosing a song he thought she would like. This was her night, she had given him so much, and he wanted to make this night perfect. He wanted to show her how soft and sensual making love could be. His gift to her in case things went bad.

Watching her relax as the seductive sounds of the soft music filled the air, he listened to the ebb and flow of the notes as his gaze took in every detail as she lay open waiting for his touch. He memorised the fine lines of her body, the smooth contours from hip to waist, and the firm graceful rise of her chest as she breathed, delighted in the way her nipples tightened and puckered as his hands hovered close.

She raised her head and held out her hand encouraging him to come to her. Gently he placed it back above her head, weaving the magic of the music into his voice, blending with the gentle rhythmic flow, he whispered how beautiful, strong and sexy he found her.

He danced light fingers over her body, down to the downy hair where his penis lay, twitching, almost beating a rhythm of its own on the soft curls. Lifting his hands, he studied her again, watching the cooling breeze, the magical light and the music drift over her heated skin.

She squirmed under his scrutiny. "Axel..."

"Shhhhhhh, relax, enjoy the ride."

He saw her quiver of anticipation, watching as his hands floated, then spanned her waist leaving a warm tantalising trail as they moved upward. His teasing fingers danced an erotic path as they skimmed the outside of heated breasts.

She moaned deep and long as he deliberately ignored the twists and turns of her body's requests. Avoiding the straining nipples, he paid homage to the firm ripe flesh around them. His fingers fluttered in time to the music, leaving in their wake a path of pleasurable torment as they set forth on a venture of discovery. He used his experience and played her body like an instrument, knowing exactly where to linger and tease without touching any of the places she offered up to him.

It was wonderfully erotic watching her discover how many sensitive places she had. Mesmerised by the music, he felt her let herself be absorbed by his touch and sound as they blended into a perfect sea of sensation.

His mouth laid claim to skin, glorifying in the taste of supple salty flesh and when she cried out her need for him, he surrendered, moulding sucking and feasting on pliable mounds, pulling nipples one at a time into his mouth, suckling strong, then releasing, watching them bounce back to glisten in the moonlight.

Leaving a silvery wet trail, he took his time, savouring the taste of her skin, working his way to the junction between her legs. Groaning in delight as she raised her hips to meet his marauding mouth, letting him feast on what she offered, opening knees wide to give him better access, moaning anew when playful fingers joined, plucking at the soft folds and dipping into the place she wanted them to be.

Tucking his hips in close to hers, he admired the woman laid out before him, his woman, eyes closed, mouth open, arms thrown wide, rapture evident in every move she made as he held himself in check, probing gently at her entrance. It was almost killing him, holding back, but he had been her first and it was something to be treasured. Last night had been aggressive and demanding on both sides, now this woman offered him her trust, bared her body and soul to him and had let him take control. She was rare and special, and an overprotective urge to never let her go gripped his heart.

Placing steadying hands on her hips, he slowly entered, letting her adjust, before pushing in to the fullest. Strong muscles contracted around him, squeezing, pulsating, pulling him deeper. Leaning forward, he rocked his hips at the same time, up and down. Her moan, deep and long was music to his ears.

"Look at me, Josephine,"

Eyes filled with passion need and love devoured his.

He started to pull out, ever so slow, shaking with control. "You are the most beautiful thing that has ever happened in my life." Lifting one boot clad leg over his shoulder, he ran his hand down the inside of her inner thigh to where their bodies joined. Rolling his thumb around her clitoris, he slowly entered again, doing the same rocking up and down, this time in sync with the movement of his thumb as it played with hardened nub nestled within the moist folds. Transfixed he watched her twist and turn, fists clenched as she demanded more speed and pressure.

Complying, he moved out and in a little quicker, thrusting harder each time he was deep inside, keeping up the movement of his thumb and reaching out with his other hand to tweak at straining nipples. A sweet 'yes' answered his thrust. Again, he went out and in, and again, each time getting slightly faster and harder.

Head thrown back and eyes open to the twinkling of stars, her face shone with rhapsody. The music faded and a new song began, and the melody resonated, weaving the web of love tighter around them in the moonlight.

Hips straining and clenching tight around him, he felt the power of Jo's inner muscles urge him on. She squeezed and pulled, leading him to new heights, until he was lost in a tempo of their making. He thrust and thrust again, holding her firm against him, plunging deeper and deeper taking them both to the brink of the precipice. Head thrown back, his cry joined hers as he tipped them over the edge and into a sky of breathtaking sensation, two hearts flying to the heavens above, as the glorious fulfilment of love washed over them.

Axel lifted Jo into his arms and held on tight, as if he never wanted to let her go. For a while neither of them spoke, as they drifted slowly back to earth, for the first time blended as one in true harmony. The only sounds that could be heard other than the heaviness of their breathing, were the rustle of the leaves in the nearby trees and the chirping of crickets overriding the fading notes of the music.

"Wow. You are incredible." Emotion flooded his words as he smoothed the damp strands of hair away from her face.

Jo nodded her head against his chest, when she was finally able to talk she pulled back and looked up at him, "Axel Stone, you can do that to me any time," and gave him the sweetest, softest of kisses, that engulfed him with sensation.

He growled his pleasure, kissing her back with a passion that left them wanting to start all over again. A little breathless he pulled back. "Tempting as that is, I think we should get dressed," placing a gentle kiss on the tip of her nose.

Dusting off her discarded clothes, he held them out, helping her dress and enjoying playing cheekily, hindering rather helping, as she did up the buttons to her shirt before he threw on his own jeans.

The moon well in the sky, cast a silvery glow over the ledge. Axel leaned against the rock and pulled Jo in front of him, wrapping his arms loosely around her waist.

"Josephine, you are the most beautiful sexiest woman I have ever met. I didn't plan on that tonight." He hesitated, feeling a little awkward as he rubbed his fingers over her chin. "Sorry, I didn't use a condom last night either. I don't have any, believe it or not. It has been a long time since I slept with a woman"

She reached for his hand and bought it to her lips and snuggled in close as if she couldn't get enough of him. "I am on the pill."

He raised his eyes in surprise at her frank open manner.

"For pimples, not sex. It balances my hormones. Face is a mine field without it. Mind you, for some strange reason I haven't taken it these last few days."

He hadn't yet put on his shirt and she reached out with her free hand to touch his small tattoo. ""Is this heart for Brodie?"

He accepted the subject change, but not the subject. Not sure he was ready to confront his past. Remaining silent for a while lost in thought, he jumped when she questioned.

"Are you ok?"

"Sure." He grabbed her around the waist and sat her on the ledge. He threw on his shirt and jacket and jumped up next to her. Hell, he wasn't ok. Brodie had tried hard to be a good kid; the tattoo was a silent reminder of a young boy he failed to protect. Ben. Dead. It was why he had run away. He shoved the thoughts aside. That was done and past, he refused to think of it. His priority now was to keep those who were dependant on him this time safe.

Axel reach out and grabbed the beers, popped the tops, offering the other to Jo, with a relaxed smile.

"Thanks."

He took a swig. The beer tasted good. Wet and cool with an after tang of bitterness he found refreshing. Jo took a few sips of hers then leaned her head against his shoulder and they sat in comfortable silence for a while

"I hear bikes?" Jo sat up and cocked her head to one side

Axel listened. "Could be Jeckle and Feral coming back up to the house, sounds like more though? What's the time?"

Jo checked his phone. "twenty sixteen."

He chuckled at her use of the military twenty-four-hour clock.

"Well its better than saying sixteen minutes past eight. A lot more efficient with words."

"What about eight sixteen?"

"Could be morning or night."

He chuckled again, glad to be away from his dark thoughts. He clinked his beer against hers. "How long shall we stay waiting for Willows call? I think we need to go back and see who has turned up on the bikes."

"Why not go back now. Check it out. We can put the phone back up on the ledge. If the service is still no good, maybe we or just you can slip out a bit later."

"Sounds like a plan." He finished his beer and jumped off the ledge, turning to help her down, pleased she graciously accepted his help.

"Whatever happens remember I care about you very much, Josephine Brennan, I just want to keep you safe."

"I know and straight back at you, Axel Stone."

The track wasn't wide enough to walk side by side and he was conscious of Jo following close behind, wondering how he was going to get her to say up at the plateau.

They were almost back at the house when he held up his hand indicating to stand still and quiet his mouth close to her ear. "It's visitors?"

Cautiously they crept forward to the corner of the house. "Damn, they're on the veranda." He pulled her to him, gave her a quick kiss and asked, "You up to this? We'll get to my room as quick as we can, but it might take a while."

"Sure." She took a mouthful of the now warm beer, handed the bottle to him, undid the top two buttons to her shirt, roughed up her hair a bit more, took her beer back and said, "Who are they?"

"Hell Raisers. I recognise one of the voices." He did one button back up pulling her flush with his body. "Stick close to me, follow my lead, these guys play rough."

"Yo, Phantom!" A solid ape of a man called out as soon as they started up the steps. "Where the fuck you been?"

"What's it to you, Mad Dog?" His cold formidable voice of the Phantom questioned. "And what the fuck are you doing here, you scraggly haired mutt?" he said, plonking his empty beer bottle on the veranda railing.

Mad Dog eyed Phantom warily. "Got a problem?" He took a step closer, flicking his eyes to Jo and back again.

Phantom's answer was stiff and chilling. "Nope, you?"

Axel, the taller of the two, although they were both just as buff, faced off against each other. At the same time, they laughed and punched fists together, obviously completing a familiar ritual.

"Who's the little filly?" Mad Dog stepped closer to Jo reaching out to touch her face, Axel relaxed his grip slightly on Jo's shoulder and she took the cue, slapping his arm away green eyes flashing.

Phantom's laugh was so cold he felt Jo shiver. "Mad Dog, meet Wildcat." He sobered quick smart. "Lay one finger on her and I'll smash ya fucking head in."

Mad Dog stared at her, then commanded, "Oi, Wildcat. Go get me and Phantom a beer."

Jo looked at Phantom as if for confirmation. Axel clasped two hands around her butt and nestled tight against her, planting a rough kiss on her lips, then nibbled near her ear, whispering, "Trust your instincts. Something's not right." before slapping her butt as she walked away.

CHAPTER 38

Kevin's head felt a heck of a lot better. Hardly able to stand on his knee he knew it needed medical attention. If he sat for too long it would seize up, it wasn't broken, probably a torn ligament, and something with his knee cap. He constantly got up and hobbled around the room, giving it gentle stretches. Mouse made a coffee and a sandwich giving it to him in her own head bowed shy manner.

After using the basic bathroom and almost falling asleep on the bed, the child's soft cries brought him back into the land of the waking. He watched as Mouse changed the nappy and redressed what he guessed to be a four month old child. It was obvious Ruby was very comfortable with the woman, she gurgled happily reaching up to grab at her hair.

Mouse was a very apt name; she wore her timid nature on her sleeve for all to see and he wondered what she was doing with this gang. Her grey blonde hair hung constantly in her eyes and over her face and with her head down, hunched over appearance it was hard to guess her height, maybe five foot four, one hundred and sixty odd centimetres. Slim build, but strong, he had felt that when she had helped Axel get him to the bed. Most of all he remembered her eyes, a most unusual shade of grey. Soft, intelligent, and inquisitive, glimpses of at least, she barely held eye contact, always lowered them, like now, looking in short little darts in his direction.

Without the eye contact it was no use even trying to talk to her. Besides she seemed skittish, and he didn't want to scare her any more than necessary.

Mouse could feel him watching her. A quick glance confirmed the sensation. He was sitting on the bed, awake now. Even though they were puffed up, his dark eyes followed her every move. She concentrated on the little girl. Once the nappy was changed and the jumpsuit was on, she cuddled her for a while, anything so she didn't have to look at him. She didn't want to think about him, his eyes held too many questions.

Spontaneity was not her thing. Change messed with your thoughts. Structure and order were best. Now, with her freedom so close, she didn't know how to deal with the added burden. *Freedom what would it be like?* she thought, *what would it bring? This was the only life she could remember. What if something went wrong? What if Jeckle caught her?* She started to shake.

Giving herself a mental kick, she went over positive affirmations she had learnt. Paddy had taught her how to do it. Her life had got better once he joined the gang. He had shown her so many things, shown her on his phone what the outside world was like. It excited her and scared her at the same time, never had she been away from the gangs' house, wherever it was, and there had been a few places, but she was always confined to the property. Sadness overcame her. It had been summer when he didn't come back. Phantom said he died. She missed him but trusted Paddy's friend Phantom, he was helping her. He would save both her and Ruby and now this man too.

Kevin got up and hobbled around a bit, wondering what the time was and hoped Jo was ok. He felt useless. If it came to a fight, he would be no help at all, he could barely even stand on his feet. He was just about to sit back down on the bed when Mouse put the baby down and waved her hands frantically in his direction to get his attention.

Moving towards her he stopped when she held up a hand before squatting on the floor like she had done before, feeling the ground with her fingers. Her eyes wide with fright locked on his. For a moment she was like a doe caught in high beam, unable to think or move. She shuddered, breathing erratically, held up two fingers, and then frantically pointed to where he had been tied up on the floor before. His hair shook from side to side as he said no with his head. If he got back down on the floor again, he knew he would never get back up.

The bikes must have free wheeled down from the direction of the upper house and the whoosh of spinning tires as they slid into the compound spurred him into action. There was no time to appreciate Mouse's ability to feel vibrations, as he grabbed the gun Axel had given him from the bed side table, raising it above his head only just managing to get in position behind the door when it flung open.

Kevin smashed the butt of the gun into the skull of the first man through the door. With a loud crack he staggered forward falling to the floor. He swung at the second man catching him a glancing blow across the side of his face. The man grunted, staggered and dropped to his knees.

Pain ripped deep inside Kevin's knee from the sharp movement and he cried out as it gave way beneath him, the gun flying from his hand as he lost balance and fell. Scrambling unsuccessfully to reach the gun, he saw movement out of the corner of his eye, trying to twist at the last minute to face the man. All he could do was lift his arms in defence as he saw the man stand, thunder in his eyes, as he drew back his booted foot.

Braced for the kick, Kevin watched in astonishment as the man's eyes rolled back inside his head, before crumpling like a building being detonated. Mouse stood behind him, a cast iron frying pan in hand and a fierce look on her face. She dropped to her knees, putting the pan on the floor and began to undo the belt of the unconscious man. Quick nimble fingers pulled it free and she started to bind his feet, looping it around to slide through the buckle and pulling it tight.

A smart move to secure the feet first, Kevin was impressed with her quick thinking and started to do the same with the other man. By the time he was finished Mouse handed him some torn up bed linen and they bound the men's arms and placed gags in their mouths. Together they propped one up where Kevin had been tied before and placed the sack over his head, so that with a quick glance it looked like him. The other they left slumped behind the door.

Grinning, he went to high five Mouse, only to see she was shaking from head to foot and had gone a deathly shade of pale. Hand over her mouth she ran to the toilet and was sick. Kevin could hear her dry reaching long after there was nothing left in her stomach. Not knowing what to do he left her so she had some privacy and put the jug on made to make her a cup of tea, thinking about what would be their next move.

He looked over at the two unconscious men. They couldn't stay here, that was evident. He rubbed at his throbbing knee; they couldn't go far either.

CHAPTER 39

J o felt Mad Dog's eyes follow her every move, and as she came back through the door, he saw him give a slight nod to her right. A firm arm shoved across the door frame effectively blocked her way. The man pushed off from his casual stance and stood threatening in front of her.

"Stay put, sweet cheeks. You an' me got some business together." There was nothing sweet about the way he said it, nor by the way his palm rubbed over his groin.

With exaggerated care, Jo placed the beers on the floor out of harm's way. She glanced at Axel who continued to look relaxed. She knew better. His slight wink let her know he was paying attention and had her back.

The man's disappointment rang loud and clear as she seductively reached up and placed her hands on his shoulders. "Thought you was meant to be feisty."

Nervous, but knowing exactly how she wanted to play this. Her heart was racing as she looked at his face with what she hoped was a sexy smile.

Eyes a little too small, made them look beady as they scanned her body.

"A bit old. Still, a fuck is a... FUCK!" he shouted, as he doubled over clutching his groin.

"You're not man enough." Tossing her hair over her shoulder she walked past him. It wasn't a hard blow by her standard. She wanted him to come at her again. Judging the moment out of the corner of her eye she tucked her right elbow close to her body, clenched her fist into a tight ball. Placing her left hand, palm over the flat bridge between the knuckles, she spun, digging her elbow deep into his solar plexus. The added pressure of her other hand pushed the pain home.

The moment she felt him buckle, she dropped to one knee as she simultaneously reached with two hands behind her, using his own momentum to throw him over her hunched shoulder. He landed with a heavy thud in front of her. He wasn't out cold, but he wouldn't be getting up for a while.

Retrieving the beers, she side stepped the gasping man on the floor. She stuck her head inside the lounge door, primarily to check out what numbers they might be up against. "Hey Spike, Jeckle," Jo called out a cheery greeting. Even though there was no love lost between them, the look on Spike's face told her something wasn't right.

Jeckle had stepped close to the door, smirking at the man rolling round on the floor. Spike who was sitting on the couch, Vipers head in her lap, took the opportunity of Jeckle's back to her to lift her hands to show they were bound. She tucked them quickly under Vipers body when Jeckle turned back around.

∽

Axel knew they were in trouble. Mad Dog told him plans had been changed. Someone higher had decided to move things forward. Change the format. Instead of Riding the Range they were just going to take the child out in a van. It was risky and that was something this gang didn't do.

There were reasons they rode the range. First and foremost, they couldn't be seen, and what you couldn't see, you couldn't trace. Second, the seven-kilometre road in and out of the valley was the only road. Trackers or trappers, police or rival gangs could be hidden anywhere, and prying eyes watched what you were doing. In the valley they knew of two houses that had video surveillance, catching every vehicle that passed.

With what they were doing now all he could think of was they must be dismantling the whole system, moving on with MICO being so close.

"Here's your beers, boys."

Axel took a swig then reached out and pulled Jo possessively towards him, turning so his body was in-between hers and Mad Dog's. He made his kiss as cold as a dead fish to grab her attention. He ran his hand up her leg and under her skirt, dropping something, small cool and metallic down her panties. Just as abruptly as he grabbed her, he released her, giving her a small shove in the direction of his bedroom. "Go get that pussy ready." He waited until she was through the door before he turned on Mad Dog.

"What the fuck was that about?" Axel decided attack was the best form of defence.

"A little spitfire your Wildcat, just wanted to see what she was made of," Mad Dog countered.

Axel relaxed his Phantom persona a little. "Ex-lover had a black belt in karate, flexible as shit mate." He called out to the man who had risen to his feet, puffing and wheezing. "Hey Thumper, don't mess with my Wildcat man."

Thumper didn't smile.

Mad Dog spoke. "It's not like you, Phantom, hope she hasn't got ya by the balls?"

"Like I told Viper, I would have waited, but..." He left the sentence hang, shrugging it off with, "she's mine, I'll keep her in line, so what's the new plan?"

Axel was having a mammoth time keeping up the Phantom's cold resolve. He struggled, working hard at remaining detached. Kevin, Mouse and the baby, were in grave danger. What about the lower house kids? Mad Dog and his minions had to have come to the house first. Then there was Jo, she handled herself like the professional she was, but now they knew. Next time they would be ready. She would have a tough fight on her hands, and they wouldn't play fair. A cold shaft of fear for her pierced his heart.

"But for the record, I trust you with my life." Jo's words from earlier had constantly played over in his mind and guilt began to gnaw at this conscience. *Ben, his small stepbrother had trusted him, look where that had gotten him, beaten by an abusive step-father into an early grave by the time he was seven. It wouldn't happen this time. He would keep her safe, them all safe, or die trying.*

"You paying attention man?" Mad Dog's expression oozed suspicion. "I'm telling you straight. We got an undercover pig at the compound. Not taking any chances. Ricko and Spud are taking care of him. His sister, the fuckin' undercover slut, is right there in your bedroom. Their agency is coming in." he looked at his watch. "Four am, that's roughly five hours from now. We'll be long gone, just waiting for the boys to come back." Mad Dog emptied his beer, belching loudly as he threw the bottle over the railing and into the forest where it clinked and smashed against a tree trunk.

Axel looked towards his bedroom door and back to the man before him. This was worse than he originally thought. "Fuck." He let his body speak the most important words by slumping a little, clenching his hands into fists and releasing them a few times while letting off a steady stream of profanities.

Mad Dog's body language screamed danger. His solid footed stance had his feet pointing right at him, the unwavering stare and the way his arms were tense and ready to fight. Axel could tell he was judging his reaction and trying to work out what to do when back up arrived. They obviously didn't want to raise attention with gun fire, otherwise they would be dead by now.

He let his own rage build and show throughout his whole body. "You better not be fucking with me?" The veins on the side of his neck bulged.

He seemed to relax a little. "No way, bro." He held out his fist for Axel to punch. "Just looking out for you. Don't kill the bitch, we have plans for her." He pointed some rope on a chair against the wall, "Tie her up, bro, she's your responsibility. We gotta get out of here."

Phantom picked up the bundle, slapping it angrily against his leg as he walked towards the bedroom, realising Mad Dog was up to his old tricks of letting others do his dirty work. Once he had Jo restrained, and the others came back, he had no doubt he would be fighting for his own life.

CHAPTER 40

O nce Jo closed the bedroom door, she didn't waste a moment. First, she retrieved the key from her knickers, unlocked the wardrobe, loaded two combat pistols, left one in the wardrobe and kept the other with her. Stripping off her clothes she redressed in what she had laid out previously.

Engaging the safety, she shoved the pistol down the back of her jeans. Quickly plaiting her hair she went back to the wardrobe, shoving anything they may need into Axel's backpack. First aid kit, ammo, flares, and... she spun as the door opened, grenade in her hand and the gun in the other. Relaxing when she saw Axel. He locked the door behind him, took the grenade from her and added it to the backpack along with a few more.

"You have an arsenal in here," she exclaimed.

"I was a boy scout so am always prepared, and hey, you did great out there." He sobered. "But we're in deep trouble and there's no time to explain. This is what I want you to do, we don't have much time and I have got to get us out of here." As he spoke, he grappled around under the wardrobe shelf, bringing out an allen key and ran over to the bathroom window. "Start yelling and screaming as if I have just found out who you really are, throw around the furniture, make noise, but remember," he kissed her cheekily. "I win and tie you up." He tossed her the rope. "May as well put it in the backpack as well."

Jo sprung into life and put on a noisy convincing act, smiling as she heard Axel chuckle softly at her antics.

It didn't take him long to undo the bolts that held the metal grate in place. Jo had quietened down now and was watching him with interest. Cocking her head and raising her eyebrows as the grate came off in his hand.

"Something else I learned as a boy, always have a back door." He climbed on the toilet seat, looked out the gap and squeezed himself through. Jo followed easily, passing him the backpack before jumping to land lightly next to him. Looking forward to the time when they could just sit and talk finding out everything about each other, there was so much in his past that seem to haunt him.

Jo kept her voice low. "Spike's tied up and Viper doesn't look well at all. Jeckle is watching them. I have no idea where Beth is."

Slinging the pack onto his back he nodded, signalling for her to follow. There were no doors on this side of the house. Light spilled onto the narrow decking from windows thrown wide open to catch the cooling night breeze. Stopping at the living room a quick peek showed, Jeckle standing in the doorway his back to them looking towards Axel's room. Spike's shotgun was resting against the cabinet by the far wall.

Jo pointed to the gun and raised her eyes in question. Axel shook his head and whispered in her ear. "It's too close to Jeckle. Although it would be handy, a gunshot will raise immediate attention. Can't do that until everyone is safe. Otherwise they might go on a killing spree."

Jeckle moved onto the veranda talking to Mad Dog.

Using one of the knives from his boot Axle ran the sharp point along the screen part of the window. The plastic mesh was cheap and soft, giving away easily. He passed the knife to Jo. She appreciated the fact he already saw them as a team by accepting she would be more agile and quieter going through the window. She gave him a thumbs up letting him know she trusted him to be back up, confident he would have his other knife ready to throw if she got into any trouble.

Placing her foot in his cupped hands he hoisted her easily into position to climb through the gap. Crouching low she moved behind the couch and ducked down behind it. Axel signalled it was still all clear. Jo stood, leaned over the back rest and whispered in Spikes ear. "Hold up your hands."

Spike moved fast. Once she was free, she was out the window as quick as a flash, relief evident in her face.

Jo felt Vipers pulse, looked at Axel and shook her head. Checking the door Jeckle had gone through she cautiously retrieved the shotgun, returned to the window and passed it to Spike, so Axel could help her out.

Axel leaned close and whispered, "Where's Beth?"

"She fucked off before they could grab her. Kicked Thumper in the shins." She gave Jo a light punch on the arm and grinned. "Nice moves. You should have heard him once he could talk. I wouldn't like to be in your shoes if he gets hold of you."

"Let's go and keep your eyes open for Beth." Axel signalled them to follow. Then paused at the end of the decking, listening to make sure all was clear, before going up the path a short way and into the forest opposite the house.

Once in the forest Spike grabbed Jo shoulder and signalled for her to stop. Jo let out a short soft whistle, Axel turned and waited. Spike leant close to Jo, whispered, then disappeared deeper into the forest, going up rather than down like them. Axel raised his brows at Jo who shrugged. Said she owes us one.

"Let's go we have more urgent things to do than worry about what Spike is going to do."

"What's first?" Jo questioned.

"The compound, Kevin, Mouse and Ruby are in danger and have priority."

CHAPTER 41

J o and Axel surveyed the compound from just outside the entrance. Two motor bikes were just visible in the moonlight, the dull dirty chrome almost blending into the background. The hut sat in complete darkness. Staying just outside the entrance they listened for any noise coming from within.

A faint muffled bumping mingled with the sounds of the night. They listened for a while to the irregular thumps before Axel signalled for Jo to stay where she was. He slipped into the dark shadows between the compound wall and the hut with the stealth of a panther on the hunt.

The only way into the hut was via the door and there were no windows to peep through. The irregular thumping was louder but seemed weaker. Axel knew the layout of the hut and formulated an entry plan. He looked to where he hoped Jo had stayed. It took a while, she blended in so well with her black beanie and dark clothes. They had streaked their faces as well. She moved, his eyes narrowed in on the gesture and she moved her hand again to signify she was ready and had his back.

Knife in hand he heaved his shoulder against the door and commando rolled inside, coming to his feet in a low crouch, before reaching up and flicking on the switch, moving instantaneously away putting his back to the strong light.

Axel removed the sack off the head of the man on the floor, relieved it wasn't Kevin.

Jo was only a few steps behind him, gun in hand. She reset the safety and tucked it in the back of her jeans as she surveyed the two tied up men on the floor. They must be Ricko and Spud. A quick surveillance of the hut confirmed Kevin, Mouse and the child must have made good their escape.

One of the men was still out cold, the other looked relieved to see Axel, then let out angry muffled yells and struggled hard against his bonds as he realised Axel was only checking them, making sure they remained tight. Kevin had done a great job; the men weren't going anywhere in a hurry. Not wasting any time, they plunged the hut back into darkness, making their way to the deepest shadows on the compound to regroup.

"Maybe they have gone to the plateau?" Axel questioned. Then he remembered Kevin's injury. He wouldn't make it that far.

Jo shook her head and put a finger to her lips. Poised, she let out a rolling 'kwook-a-woo' noise, changed direction, re-cupped her mouth and did it again. After the third try she had an answer, somewhere in the forest above them and to the left of the track. The call came back to them again, twice in quick secession. Jo whispered, "That's Kevin, he's coming to us."

Axel gave her a questioning look. "It's the call of a day active bird, the Bar-shouldered Dove," she explained. "The sound carries well and it's unobtrusive, we used it in our night training. Now we wait." Jo hunched down and watched from the direction the call had come.

Axel squatted besides her, in awe of the way she was handling the situation, nothing had fazed her. Not this, although he would have preferred if she stayed hidden and protected. She backed him up to perfection, being captured by Feral, not even when she had been confined by him. Cool headed she attempted to escape and ended up trusting her judgement and in the process trusting him. He had total admiration for her cool calm precision, realising for the first time she was a damn good undercover agent and the whole situation fitted her like a glove. She was alive and in her element.

It felt like a sucker punch to the gut as it dawned on him that they were from totally different worlds and what would happen when this was over. Arrest. Jail. Investigations into his past juvenile crime, the death of his stepbrother who had taken a beating meant for him.

He had stayed on the right side of the law until the involvement with the other gang. The last year he had struggled watching a lot of drugs and guns smuggled through the range. Sure, there would be a little leniency for his help now, but he wasn't stupid, there would have to be some atonement for his sins. The thought of prison had terrified him as a fifteen year old runaway. Digging deep now, he realised nothing had changed, he would run again rather than be locked up. There was no way he wanted to saddle Jo with his past. Maybe, in the long run, she would be better off without him.

Jo reached out and took his hand giving it a gentle squeeze as if sensing his withdrawal. She squeezed his hand tighter and he was relieved when she spoke, it was mundane. He was in no mood for personal talk.

"It's obvious where most of the members get their gang name from, but why Thumper?"

Jo's whispered breath in his ear did nothing to ease how hot she made him feel just by being close. "Are you sure you want to know?"

"Oh, like that is it?"

Axel continued anyway, "If he is not sleeping with someone 'male or female' he thumps himself and doesn't care who knows or sees it."

"That's disgusting."

"Yea, can't say I have ever hung around." He fell silent wishing he hadn't said anything and thought again how different their lives were. Some of the things he had seen, done himself and put up with would make her more than disgusted, she would probably hate him.

They both became alert at the sound of something jumping off the wall, it sent all the hairs on the back of their necks leaping to attention. Jo was closer and she was just about to leap on the appearing shadow when Axel pulled her back with a sharp, "It's Mouse."

Mouses' internal scream splintered her thoughts as she almost fell to the ground when the figure leapt up at her from the darkness. It had taken a lot of persuasion by the man who was hurt, to come back down the track to the hut, now she knew why. He had been using signs she was not familiar with and did them way too fast. Finally, the moon had come out enough for her to lip read and he made her understand, 'a woman' was down at the hut and he wanted her to bring her here. He said a word, but not knowing what it was she couldn't work it out, so he said another word, but she still didn't know, and he showed no patience. Cranky man.

Then he mouthed to go quietly. Stupid man, how would she know if she made a noise or not? She looked up in relief to see Phantom as well as the woman and immediately felt guilty about the man with the hurt leg. He was also a kind man, with gentle eyes. Smiling eyes.

She pointed to the hut and held up two fingers. Phantom signalled he knew, and then questioned where she had come from. Mouse was relieved. Phantom knew how to talk to her, she felt safe with him. He had promised to help her and Ruby get away, she believed him, trusted him. Leading the way to where she had come over the wall, she put her feet in what looked like weather worn cracks and scrambled up and over. Once the others were next to her she led the way up her secret track, smiling at his surprised look and treasured the pride in his face when he saw where she had hidden Kevin and Ruby. Phantom wasn't the only one who could make secret places. She'd stolen the idea from him once he had shown her the plateau cave and with so many spare hours at the hut it hadn't been hard to find a suitable Strangler Fig tree close by to hide inside.

∽

Mouse took the sleeping baby out of Kevin's arms while Jo rushed to his side, running anxious hands over his bruised and swollen face.

"It's not as bad as it looks, sis. Mainly the leg, the rest will fade in no time at all."

His words were laced with pain. She emptied the backpack and took out the first aid kit and put a couple of Panadol in his hand. "That will have to do we don't have much else."

"I thought it would be ok. My knee locked; flat ground is do-able but it won't take the hill."

Axel let Jo have a few private moments with her brother while he thought about what they still had to do. What he had to do. Mad Dog would be missing them by now and any minute he expected to hear bikes roaring down the hill. As if reading his thoughts, Mouse clutched onto his arm, then turned to the other two almost jumping in-between them. Holding her finger to her lips she placed her hand on the ground. They weren't that far from the track and Axel almost missed the hiss of the bike freewheeling.

Mouse held up her finger indicating there was only one and for a few drawn out seconds they stayed as still as the trees around them. Once he deemed it was safe, Axel moved first, swiftly repacked the bag, leaving out a few items for himself and Kevin. He slung the pack over Jo's shoulder, letting her adjust it to the right fit and signalled for them to huddle in close to Kevin.

"Right, this is the plan." His hushed tone still held a strength that offered no defiance. "Kevin, you have no choice but to stay here, we'll leave you with one of the guns, some ammo, a couple of grenades and a flare. Tuck in tight to the tree and stay hidden until help arrives." He turned to Jo and Mouse, giving them each a Traverser. "Jo, you'll have to walk with Mouse to the Plateau, we can't risk the bikes. It should take a couple of hours or so. It's past midnight, go as fast as you can. Take the phone, there might be a message from Willow. If there is no chopper wait in the cave until someone comes. Eventually they will, Willow has the coordinates."

"Mouse knows where to go, doesn't she?"

It wasn't only evident in her voice, Axel could see it in the restless twitching of her body, Jo did not want to be left out of the action. She shrugged off his hands when he placed them on her shoulders, so he leant close and said with soft resolve, "I am relying on you to keep them safe, to make sure they get to the plateau. Both Mouse and Ruby need protection."

He could see she was torn between what was right and what she wanted and knew there was nothing she desired more than to stay here with Kevin and Axel. The moon light wasn't very co-operative, and he struggled to see the expression in her eyes and sighed with relief when she accepted his plan.

With a brief nod she set the coordinates into her Traverser and squatted to talk to Kevin. "Keep your head down, I'll come back as soon as I can."

"Believe me, if it wasn't for this knee, I'd be right with you."

She could hear the frustration in his words and it snapped her out of her own self-pity and she smiled at him. "I wish you could too."

"The way I see it," Kevin continued, "Mouse and the baby couldn't be in better hands, if that chopper comes in, go with them Jo. Please. Go with them all the way, make sure they are ok. It will all be over here if you came back down anyway."

Jo held his hand briefly, a little teary eyed at his faith in her. She wasn't used to it and it felt good. Wanting to leave him with a happy thought she said, "Before I go here's a bit of news to keep that brain of yours ticking over. Promise not to tell the rest of the family, not just yet, until we are sure."

She waited till he said their childhood oath. There was nothing stronger. "Patrick's alive, at least we are pretty sure he is. He's deep undercover and Willow's his contact." The ecstatic look on his face was everything she could have hoped for. His grin nearly reached his ears, and for a moment the moonlight glinted off the tears in his eyes before his hand wiped them away.

Axel tapped Jo's shoulder and when she looked up, he indicated the light just visible through the trees. Someone had put the compound lights on. Any minute now Axel knew he would hear the shouts and sounds of the men once they were freed. The odds against them were rising. Three at the upper house, the two now being released and then there was Feral and whoever else was at the lower house. It was more important than ever to get the baby away and safe. It sparked an urgency to get moving.

Mouse, her pack already on her back, was busy securing Ruby in a homemade sling across the front of her chest. Once the baby was snug and in place, Mouse gave her a few more drops from a bottle.

Jo raised her eyes at Axel as she readjusted her backpack making it a little tighter.

He whispered close to her ear, "Herbal drops. When she first came to us, she was heavily sedated, we changed that. Mouse is giving her enough to keep her quiet and drowsy and only when necessary. She has to, if Ruby cries at the wrong time..."

The statement was left open as he pulled her into his arms for what could be the last time.

"I have to do what I can to help the Babs and gang." His lips moved urgently over hers, as if he was pouring out all that he felt. Love, regret, need, hope, anguish and then back to love before it turned into a reluctant kiss of goodbye. It almost broke her heart.

"Keep your head down and stay safe," he said as he pulled away. Her words about trust from earlier came back to haunt him again. *It's about letting a person make their own choices, life or death. It is their life. A person must follow their own code of ethics and morals, without that we are not the people we proclaim to be.* And he knew, if the opportunity arose, she would be back down here in the thick of things.

Turning away he bent down to Kevin. "Use the gun only if you have to. I want to make sure the others are safe." He clapped him on the shoulder and with a quick backward glance at Jo he disappeared down the path and into the shadows.

Forcing one foot forward after another was one of the hardest things he had ever done, each step took him further from the woman he wanted to protect. He almost faulted as he admitted to himself, 'the woman he loved,' he wanted to turn back and tell her, declare it to the world. He loved her and the warmth of that knowledge filled his body with a fierce determination to see this through to the end and do everything in his power to make sure she was safe. Not just tonight, but from him and his past as well.

CHAPTER 42

S he felt as though she was Queen of the mountains. Spread out before her lay the valley in all its moonlit glory. Placing her shotgun on the rocks she tilted her head and reached with outstretched arms for the heavens. Here out in the open, at the top of the largest of the horseshoe of hills that surrounded the valley, she had left behind the damp and musky odour of leaves rotting on the forest floor. Crisp and clear the air carried the blended scent of rainforest trees fresh and alive. It matched her mood perfectly. She had done it, freedom, and with one point two million in her pocket from tonight, pocket money when she add that to her offshore account stash, she could do what she damn well pleased.

She found a flat surface and sat on the rocky outcrop. Her chest pounded a wild beat, and her leg muscles were burning, but the fast, steep climb was worth the pain. The fresh air frolicked around her sweat drenched body, cooling her with its playful embrace. She lay back on the boulder listening to the monotonous drone of cicadas and grinned at the star strewn sky, revelling in the fact she was finally free. The moon was in a downward climb and most of the clouds had vanished as if they never existed and she let her mind drift.

Viper was dead, let them think Mad Dog did it. When the Hell Raisers surprised her with their arrival, she had just given him a lethal dose of heroine, ready to set her own plan in motion. Now, she had another score to settle, she didn't like being double crossed. Thumper's words ate at her soul. *"'The man' don't need you anymore',"* he had gloated when he tied her hands tight, looping the rope around Vipers inert body so she had no chance to get up and escape. *"He said to tell you thanks for all your work over the years, and he hopes you like your new role in life."* When she spat at him, he laughed. Saying she would bring a good price on *'The Market.'* She knew what that meant, and it would be over her dead body. Well not now, she had the last laugh.

Nothing about tonight remotely resembled the plans that were meant to take place. The arrival of the Hell Raisers destroyed her hope of freedom. Jo and Phantom had given it back. It was a debt that would never be forgotten. Elation flooded Spike's body. She could hardly believe it, and for the first time since she was fourteen years old, she was free.

The sharp shrill of her phone shattered the tranquillity. She muttered a curse that she hadn't thought to get rid of it. Bouncing to her feet she fumbled in her pocket. Only one person knew this number. Raising her arm to throw the phone as far away as she could, she checked herself just in time. No doubt he had found out about the money. Unable to resist the urge to have a final gloat she answered it.

"So, what are you going to buy with your dollar?" That was all she had left in the account. She would have done anything to see his face.

His unexpected reply instilled a grain of fear. "Money means nothing slut, what you were paid is a drop in the ocean compared to what I have. I would be more concerned about living long enough to spend it."

Cursing her automatic reaction to look fearfully around, she pulled herself together. He had no idea where she was and with her escape plan, she should feel secure. Confidence oozed as she spoke, "You'll never find me, not in a month of Sundays. Maybe I will come after you...Mantis."

"My code name won't get you anywhere, you fucking whore."

"Sticks and stones."

"I gave you life, I can take it away. Those burns and cuts on your sagging tits are nothing compared to what I will do when I get my hands on you."

Spike put the phone on speaker so his constant hawking cough didn't burst her ear drums and retaliated, "Keep smokin' and I won't have to do a fuckin' thing, by the sounds of it you are puttin' nails in your coffin every day."

Surprisingly he chuckled. "Just for you, I will give them up. I don't want to miss Thumper shaving the skin from your body, strip by strip."

Spike was shocked, not so much by this threat, even though it had been said with malicious venom, but by the name. "Thumper?"

"Got him on it already. A one-man killing machine. He's a sick crazy bastard. Already eliminated one loose end and hot on the trail of the second, in fact I wouldn't be surprised if Mouse is dead already."

"You're the sick bastard."

"That's only the half of it. He gets a bonus for every extra he kills, and Thumper's a greedy man. Goodbye Range Riders. When he is done, he will be coming for you, but he won't kill you princess, I want you alive."

"You had better hope I don't take him out first and make him talk, then I'll be coming for you." Her words were strong, but she had gone cold all over. The way he called her princess took her back to her young teenage years. She started to shake, recalling his phrase from earlier, 'those burns and cuts on your sagging tits'.

She let him keep talking.

"I'm not stupid. I will just cut my losses and walk away. It's such a small part of the business. Thumper has no idea who I am, just like you, phone contact only. No one has anything on me."

She disconnected the call in the middle of his nerve grating laugh not trusting her voice to conceal what she realised. She threw the phone as far as she could into the trees.

A chill rippled through her body, there was nothing she could do to help those below. She needed, for the first time in her life, to think of herself. She was free and that overpowered everything. A smile spread across her face as the fresh wind pushed at her back, telling her it was time to move.

She had a reasonable idea of the direction to head. If she went down the other side at a forty-five degree angle, she should end up close to the Cathedral, a local swimming hole named for the gigantic trees that held together the riverbank. The branches criss-crossed high above mid-stream, intertwining with vines allowing dabbled sunlight to imitate stained glass windows, reflecting like sparkling diamonds on the water below. She would miss it; it had been one of her favourite places to swim.

Standing tall and aiming her shotgun in the air, she fired once, re-cocked, fired again and then for a third time. The blasts echoed around the valley and she added her voice in a triumphant "WooHoo!"

She wouldn't be heard by anyone, but it gave her a sense of release along with the satisfaction the gunshots would be heard across the valley. With a bit of luck the cops would be called, that was the least she could do for kids left in the lower house. With a bit more luck, it would fuck Mantis big time, spoil his plans, maybe they would catch Thumper.

Smashing the gun on the rocks, regretting having to destroy it, but wanting nothing that would tie her to the gang, she was off and over the other side, with one thing on her mind, working towards revenge. Not only was Mantis the man who pulled her up out of the gutter, he was the man who put her there. She rubbed her hand over her the scars on her chest, to know they were there, he had to have done it. She didn't have a name, but she had a mental picture of him burned into her brain. She would find Mantis, the bastard who had thrown her into hell, even if it took the rest of her life.

CHAPTER 43

The echo of the gunshots caused Jo stop in her tracks. They were almost at the Plateau. Mouse, who had confidentially taken the lead as soon after they began, had pushed on relentlessly. If Axel thought she couldn't look after herself he was sadly mistaken. She was a single-minded power horse and Jo was working hard to keep up. They navigated an extremely slight track, one Mouse was obviously familiar with, and it was evident she had done this before. Not once did she look at the Traverser to confirm the way. A few times Jo had wanted to turn back, feeling rather obsolete.

Naturally Mouse didn't hear the shots and Jo jogged a few paces to catch up, placing a hand on her shoulder and when she turned, put a finger to her own lips. Mouse complied immediately, her hands and arms automatically forming a protective cover over the sleeping baby.

In the dim light, Jo signed gunfire.

Mouse shook her head indicating she didn't understand the sign.

Jo tried more basic moves, making a gun with her hand and pretending to shoot, three times then spread her hands wide apart mouthing loud. Mouse nodded her understanding, watching Jo intently for what to do next. Jo waited, ears straining. A Boobook Owl called in the distance and a few moments later one answered a little closer to them. Crickets started chirping again and fruit bats could be heard squawking and squabbling over some prize treats high in the treetops. No more shots were fired, and everything seemed normal.

Jo shook her head and shrugged her shoulders, trying hard to keep her face free from the rising panic she felt inside. The urge to run back to see if Axel and Kevin were ok was overwhelming. Mouse looked at her for guidance with anxious questioning eyes, and Jo realised Mouse did need her. She might be strong and confident within certain boundaries, but she needed someone to be her ears, to have her back in case anything went wrong. Jo knew this was where she was meant to be right now and with a new resolve, she indicated for Mouse to continue and lead the way.

For a while, as they trudged along, Jo became lost in her thoughts about Axel and what might be happening below She pushed the thoughts aside, keeping her ears tuned for any further shots or sounds of a fight, relieved when they made it to the base of the plateau without further incident.

Mouse felt terrified. Not at what she was doing, but that she wouldn't succeed. The thought of being back in the clutches of Jeckle made her feel sick to the core, death a preferable option. She had waited so long to escape. Paddy promised to help her; Phantom gave his word too. So, when Phantom's lady; she didn't know her name, no one had bothered to tell her; when she pulled her back as she started to climb the rocks and pointed in another direction, in fear and frustration she lost her temper.

A deaf person can't yell and for the first time in her life she put everything she had into the movement. Phantom had insisted she climb the rocks, not use the quick way, so that she had a back door to escape if she was followed. And climb the rocks she would. She glared at Phantom's lady who stepped back looking at her strangely

before signing okay and indicating with a sweep of her hand for her
to continue the climb.

What Jo had seen of Mouse so far was very typical to her name.
But the woman on the trail tonight was a totally different person.
Mouse might be deaf, but her actions screamed louder than any
words possibly could. Strong, focused and determined. Just now,
she had pulled herself up tall, stuck her index finger out at her,
bringing down the clenched fist of her other hand in a sharp flick
against it, and she did it with attitude. A very effective NO!

Jo began to follow her, maybe this was the only way she knew.
Regardless they needed to get to the safety of the cave. And even
though Mouse carried the added burden of Ruby and a backpack
she was ploughing ahead as if the devil chased her tail.

Once at the top Mouse still didn't stop. With single minded
purpose, she rushed across the plateau, ripping off the backpack
and pulling it behind her as she squeezed through the gap in the
rocks at the far end.

While the Plateau glowed with moonlight, the path and the cave
were shrouded in darkness and Jo had to hold her hand against the
rock wall as she walked, bumping into Mouse as they reached the
cave, steadying them both by placing a hand on her shoulder. Now
the destination was reached Jo felt Mouse visibly collapse, all the
strength seemed to evaporate from her body as she slumped. Her
limbs started to shake as she clutched Ruby to her chest and Jo
helped her sit on the cave floor before she buckled. Immediately
Mouse began a rocking motion as she made soft sobbing sounds.

Jo's heart filled with compassion. Sitting beside the distressed
woman she wrapped an arm around her shoulder and pulled
her close, rocking with her, thankful when the heart wrenching
weeping ceased.

It was too dark to see any signs, so Jo took Mouse's hand and held it to her face, letting her feel the comforting smile, relieved when she was rewarded with a strong hand squeeze.

The importance of seeing if there was a message from Willow sat at the top of Jo thoughts. How to tell Mouse she needed to go back to the Plateau for reception was another. Retrieving the phone from her pocket she turned it on. Shadows danced around the cave as their eyes squinted against the light. Mouse jumped, fear ripe on her face as she tried to cover the brightness with her hands. Jo huddled closer and typed a message. *"Have to go up, need reception to see if help is coming."*

Mouse studied the words for a long while, twice Jo had to refresh the screen as it blanked out, finally she nodded reluctantly and cuddled the baby closer to her.

Jo hoped there was some communication from Willow. There had been no chance until now to check. She wondered what her brothers and father were doing. Were they on their way to rescue them? She hoped so, Axel and the gunshots were on her mind and she had to override a panic of her own not to rush to his aid. What if he was shot or injured? What if he needed her help? What if he was dead?

Gritting her teeth, she pinched her arm hard, the sharp pain helped her draw on an inner patience she didn't realise she possessed. She formulated a plan. Check for contact, if a chopper was coming in. Get Mouse and the baby on board and on their way to safety, then she could go and help Axel. If there was no rescue by air, she would just have to wait it out, she didn't think Mouse would be able to handle staying here on her own. She prayed for a chopper.

With a reassuring pat on Mouse's shoulder she made her way back to the plateau, hugging close to the rock wall well aware of the dramatic drop off to her right. The closer she got to the crack in the rocks the lighter it was and once through, the moonlight added welcome warmth to her vision. She looked at the phone, it was searching for service

Her mind wandered momentarily, to another rock in the moonlight and she smiled softly as she remembered his hands and mouth on her body. It was beautiful out on the plateau and if she could wish upon a star, she would wish him right by her side.

Stone kicking stone sent a bolt of cold terror rushing throughout her body. Her hair literally stood up on end as the unmistakable stench of Feral's unwashed body assaulted her senses.

CHAPTER 44

Axel manoeuvred closer to the compound. The light still blared so he avoided the fingers of brightness invading the forest by hugging close to the outside of the wall, working his way around until he came to the entrance. He didn't need to go back in there, the younger members of the gang were his priority, but he did want to see what was going on. The quiet was uncanny, he thought he would at least hear them talking. Peering around the corner, Axel flattened himself back against the wall as Thumper kicked his bike into life, shattering the silence as he sped through the entrance so close to him, they could almost have touched.

Axel expected to hear Ricko and Spud follow close behind, but all remained quiet and when he peeked around the corner their bikes still stood as silent sentinels. He had to assume they were still inside the hut, or taken off on foot after Jo and Mouse. Stilling his fear, he took off at a jog the way the bike went, using its noise to cover any sound he might be making. Pleased with the distance he travelled by the time the bike pulled in at the lower house, he found a suitable spot to go off the track and take a short cut down the hillside.

Once in the forest he took care where he placed his feet, from tree to tree he made his way downward. A startled owl spiked his adrenalin and he automatically ducked as the whoosh of wings dipped close to his head, then it was gone flapping and gliding noiselessly between the trees looking for a less disturbing place to hunt. All the night creatures shied from his invasion; a bandicoot let off a high pitched distress squeak as it ran-hopped away from the human intruder. Worse were the green ants that clung tenaciously to the exposed skin on his neck and hands as they nipped and squirted acid, and other insects that seemed to come rather than flee. For the one hundredth time he flicked at a bug as it crawled up the side of his face.

He didn't linger in his current position next to the mango tree close to the lower house. Above him the bats were having a feast on the ripe fruit; their squabbles and chatter had drowned out any sound his approach would have made. The ripe smell of bat droppings and the fresh ones raining down around him encouraged him to press on.

The lower house shone like a beacon in the night. It was close to one am and the lights in every room stopped him from coming any closer in case he was seen. So far, he had only observed Thumper, but from what he understood there were other Hell Raisers and Feral in the house with the younger members.

Preparing to move closer, he dived behind a Hibiscus bush as three shotgun blasts reverberated around the hills. The bats took to the air screeching in protest, flying in wild circles before settling back down to squabble and feast. Axel immediately thought of Jo, the shots came from high and he battled the urge to abandon his task and rush to her aid. A vision of her popped into his head and he remembered how fearless and smart she could be, and there was no more time for thought as he flattened against the damp grass.

Thumper came running around the corner of the house, stopped on the edge of the lawn, looking up at the darkened forest. Axel held his breath; he could hear him muttering and swearing as he rummaged around in the small garden shed. Then he was gone back around the side of the house.

Standing, Axel took one of the knives from his boot and balanced it in his hand.

Petrol fumes, sharp and astringent assailed his nose and a scream from inside spurred him into immediate action. Everything happened so fast he reacted on pure instinct. The night became alive with flickering firelight.

Axel felt as though he was moving in slow motion as he reached the back of the house. Thumper didn't see him as he whizzed by in a flash of noise and speed roaring back up the hill. Screams ripped through his head as he kicked open the back door.

Torn between trying to put the fire out and finding his young friends, he stood for what felt like an eternity, in reality it was but a fraction of a second. The fire, only just beginning to take hold, still packed a heated punch as he dashed from room to room following the screams. He found the gang tied together on the floor of one of the bedrooms. Billows of smoke thickened the air attacking his chest. Coughing deeply, he pulled his t-shirt over his nose and began cutting the ropes.

Al was the first to be freed. Axel passed him his second knife. "Help me free the others." He worked on Stretch's bonds next. Once free the lanky youth stood paralysed, fear wide in his eyes.

"Stretch," Axel commanded. "Wet some towels, cloths, sheets anything and pass them out. Help him," he said to Babs once her ropes dropped to the floor.

The fire began to feast, the roar and crackle sounded like a thousand hail stones pelting against a tin roof and the smoke thickened reaching out to smother their eyes and noses.

"Crawl...back door," Axel yelled, between bouts of coughing.

Single file they crouched low covered in damp material making a mad dash for the open back door. This part of the house was the least engulfed and they were spurred along by the crescendo of crackle and hiss that grew behind them.

Axel, bringing up the rear, took a side turn to the living area where the fire had a deeper hold, wondering where Feral and the others were. He put his hands up in front of his face to shield his eyes from the heat. Flames licked the ceiling as they devoured the curtains and began feasting on the walls. The sight sickened him to the core. Deep slashes across the throats of the two Hell Raisers yawned like frothing red gaping smiles and a bloody mess splattered all over the furniture and flooded the floor in large red pools. The raw metallic smell mixed with smoke as the couch burst into flames jumping onto the clothes of one of the bodies.

An arm grabbed him. "Come on man," Al, coughed into his hand which held a damp towel over his nose. "Aint nothing we can do 'ere," he yelled, pulled Axel towards the door. They kept moving until they reached the others who had gathered well up the track away from the inferno.

Fresh air flooded his lungs setting off a fresh bout of violent coughing. "Feral? Beth?" Axel questioned

"Not in the house. Feral left soon after the others came, haven't seen Beth," someone answered.

"Is everyone here? Anyone missing?" He scanned the shocked and scared faces. This was the closest he had to a family and he was almost overwhelmed with emotion, what was he going to do without them? He looked back as the fire consumed their home, apprehensive about what was going to happen to them and him?

The noise wasn't quite as loud as it had been inside, but the house was well ablaze now. A loud crash as part of the roof collapsed jolted him into action. There was a gas bottle for the kitchen. He didn't know how full it was but didn't want to hang around to find out. "Right, let's go, Al take the rear, we are going to have to go around before we can go down. Stick together now."

Axel kept them moving fast, they were away from the heat, but could still hear the crackle and hiss as the fire consumed the house, the flames leaping high above the treetops.

The group picked up the track below the house and were almost at the creek when a commanding voice yelled 'freeze' and blinding lights had them bumping into each other as they threw their arms across their faces in protection, except for Axel. He stood firm and strong as he surrendered his hands in the air, averting his eyes downward away from the light.

"Copy me," Axel said in a loud confident voice, praying this was back-up.

"Down on the ground... put hands behind your heads...NOW!"

Axel smiled. Yep, this was typical cop/military talk. He complied, putting his hands on his head then purposely sat instead of lying on the dirt. "Are you MICO?"

"Who's asking?" came back the reply.

"Axel Stone, working with Jo Brennan. These kids are innocent. Can you take them to safety?"

The light stopped shining in their faces. Instead it illuminated the ground around them, causing tall intimidating figures to appear as threatening shadows on the road in front of them.

Axel stood, indicating for the others to stay put and took a step forward, his hands still in the air.

"Stay where you are," came the sharp commanded. "The road has been trip wired. You guys are damned lucky to have had a clear run. Who's with you? Are Jo or Kevin there?"

"No, but I know where they are."

The leader stepped forward and indicated Axel do the same, holding up a hand when they were about three feet apart. Axel could see the dozens of thin wires now. He was shocked they would have walked straight into them.

"This is the second lot, working on dismantling it, or we would have been here sooner," he said.

Now the gang were in the grasp of safety, Axel desperately wanted to get back to Jo. He talked fast and precise. "Kevin is injured, can't walk but he's safe, hiding near the compound." He gave him the coordinates. "There could be two men inside the hut so take precautions. Jo should be at the Plateau with one other and a baby called Ruby."

He paused for a breath, repeating the coordinates for both places. Fists clenching and unclenching, impatient to be off to find Jo, but knowing he must impart as much information as he could.

"At least six Hell Raisers turn up out of the blue, the two at the lower house are dead, killed by a man named Thumper, real name is Ed...something? He also set fire to the house. One of the kids told me he was cursing as he tied them up, saying, 'The whole operation was busted and all he had to do now was get the hell out of here.' The way he took off I imagine he will Ride the Range and be long gone."

A loud explosion caused them all to flinch and look toward the direction of the house. Black smoke and a thousand flickering sparks flew up into the night sky. They were far enough away for it not to have an impact, although Babs started to cry.

"That's our home," she sobbed. "Where we gunna go now?"

"Gas bottle," supplied Axel with a lump in his throat. There wasn't going to be much left of the house, the closest part forest would burn but not too much. Rainforest didn't burn that easily and around the house had been cleared. He turned to Babs and the others. "It's going to be a rough few weeks, but I promise I will find a place for us. For now, you just have to do what the authorities say. Trust me" Axel had never been clearer about what he wanted to do with his life, and he hoped Josephine would embrace the idea with an open heart, doing it on his own wouldn't be the same. He was done with running.

Axel addressed his friends. "I have to go. Stay with these men, I promise I will be back." He turned the man in charge. "Can't wait. I need to get to Josephine." With that he took off at a full speed run back up the hill, his desire to find and protect the woman he loved overriding all else.

CHAPTER 45

Feral's high pitched crazy laugh grated worse than fingernails on a blackboard, setting Jo's terror filled body even more on edge. Fighting him now scared the shit out of her. Drained of energy both emotionally and physically she didn't know if she could find the strength. She instinctively stepped away from the direction of the sound trying to put some distance between them.

He appeared out from the shadows to her right, a gun pointed at her chest. "You won't get away from me this time. Move again and I'll put bullets in both ya kneecaps." He lowered the gun to match his words. "Then I'll find Mouse and make her squeal before I finish you off."

Jo stopped moving.

Feral giggled, stepping further into the moonlight. "I knew Mouse would come here tonight. Bad things happening with the Raisers coming." He giggled again stepping closer. "Where is the stupid bitch?" As he spoke, he didn't take is his eyes of Jo, his stare full of bitter hatred.

"How did you know she would come?" Stepping backward as he moved along the rocks, Jo tried to keep him talking as she inched steady fingers towards the gun tucked in the back of her jeans.

"Drop your phone and kick it over here and put ya hands where I can see em."

Jo moved them slightly away, her brain thinking a mile a minute about how to get them all out of this mess.

"Do it now!"

Reluctantly she complied, kicking the phone slightly away from him hoping to distract him long enough to make a grab for her gun.

"Hands on your head. D'ya think I'm stupid?"

His manic giggle made Jo realise how unstable he was. She didn't know what to do. Maybe if she got closer, she could jump him. The gun he held was wavering a bit. If she timed it right...

He inched over to the phone, kicking it over the edge of the rocks, not taking his eyes off her for a second. "I followed her before a few times, heee heeee hee. I even yelled at her when she was sitting on the rocks. Deaf bitch never knew. I thought she'd come here, bad things happening tonight."

Jo moved a few steps closer as she spoke. "Yes, bad things. Why don't you just take off, the whole place will be crawling with Special Forces any minute now." Another step. "Forget Mouse, save yourself."

"Quit movin'." Feral raised the gun at her chest. "Heeeheee...Don't give a fuck about Mouse, I want the kid." He almost sang the words. "Money, money, the kid is money."

Jo could see his tension building. He was going to pull the trigger. She was too far away to stop him.

Feral's grin went utterly insane, "I'm done fucking round."

As he said the words, Jo sprang into action, dropping to the ground and rolling sideways, ignoring the sharp pain in her shoulder as it hit uneven rock. The loud explosion rang in her ears and for a split second Jo filled with dread waiting for the impact of the bullet to slam into her flesh.

It didn't come, but she lost her momentum and knew Feral would follow any second with a repeat performance. She rolled again, coming up into a crouch reaching for the gun tucked into her jeans, knowing she would be too late.

On the edge of her vision she saw a black shape fly out of the shadows, and crash into Feral's back, sending him spiralling towards the cliff's edge. The momentum of the shove proved to be so strong his flailing arms could not stop his forward projection as he tumbled over the precipice with a strangled cry of astonishment and fear. His body crashed through trees getting fainter and fainter until nothing else could be heard.

Jo bounced to her feet facing her rescuer with open mouthed astonishment.

Mouse looked furious. Like a lioness protecting her cub, the strangled cry she omitted was like nothing else Jo had ever heard on earth. Shaking all over she flung herself into Jo's arms, hugging her as if she would never let her go. Her guttural distorted 'bad man' repeated over and over until Jo's rocking her back and forth settled her distress.

Jo wiped away tears of her own. This remarkable woman had been through so much in her short life. Axel said he thought she was nineteen, hells bells, she could even be younger. Jo decided right then and there she would stick by the young woman's side until she knew she was completely safe, in fact Jo had more than enough room in her apartment for Mouse to find her feet in a pressure free, secure environment. While it didn't ease her worry about Axel or lesson the urge to go and help him, it felt right.

Jo grinned at Mouse, knowing in her heart she wanted to help more women like her. Now the door had been opened ideas came flooding in and she had to force herself to put a cap on them until she could talk them over with Axel, hoping he was as receptive she was.

Mouse indicated her intention see to the child left tucked just inside the crevice in the rocks. Jo turned her attention outwards; manmade sounds were coming from every direction.

Walking out to the middle of the plateau she concentrated, smelling a slight tinge of smoke on the breeze and way down behind low lying hills and trees there was a red glow. Frustration and worry grew. What was happening down there? With no phone there was nothing she could do but wait it out.

In the extreme distance, every so often she could hear the muffled sound of a trail bike, but it was way off deep in the hills to her left and moving away. Her attention was brought back to the direction of the fire. Although it was faint, she could hear the high-pitched wail of sirens getting closer and closer and thought it must be the rural fire brigade.

Worry and fear battled just below the surface and she forced herself to be calm and patient. Then relief washed over her in waves, if she wasn't mistaken, she could just make out the distinctive deep throbbing beat of a helicopter.

The sound lifted her spirits and spurred her into action. She made her way back to the cave and found her backpack and bought it with her to where Mouse sat with Ruby just inside the crevice. She felt confident they were safe now. If anyone had been working with Feral they would have made their move as soon as he let off the shot. Besides, she grinned, her big brother was coming.

Jo's excitement proved contagious. As she rummaged through the backpack and located the emergency glow sticks, Mouse, grinning like a Cheshire cat, tied Ruby back around her chest and retrieved her own pack, zipping it up tight and clutching onto to it as if it were her lifeline to safety.

When they were ready, Jo gave Mouse a high five, this was it. For Mouse a brand-new beginning and for Ruby a safe return to her family. For her she finally knew what to do with her future and she prayed yet again that Axel was alive and would still want to be with her when this was all over. It was undeniable they formed a strong connection, but he was fighting his own demons and his last kiss felt like a final parting. Remembering it now almost broke her heart and she desperately wanted to see him, tell him nothing mattered except what they felt for each other.

Indicating that Mouse should stay just behind the crevice, Jo cautiously slipped through the crack, taking her time to check the shadows before stepping out into the middle of the plateau, snapping the sticks as she went so they produced a brilliant florescent green glow. After placing them in a large triangle on the flattest part of the rocky surface, she moved back against the wall. Facing the plateau she wedged herself half way through the gap. Stretching out her hand behind her, searching for Mouse's hand, squeezing it with tight reassurance when she made contact. The steady thump, thump, thump, of the chopper came closer.

CHAPTER 46

A xel needed a bike. He would never get to the plateau on time on foot. Closest was the compound and it was just as he had left it. Lights blaring, bikes standing sentinel and no sign of life. Time ticked away, with a boldness born out of desperation he sprinted across the bare dirt, checked the bikes, no keys.

He flung open the hut door almost falling over his own feet in the effort to avoid stepping in a lake of putrid blood. The coppery tang mixed with the stench of urine and faeces from the lifeless bodies, smacked him in the face filling his mouth with a foul taste. Flies rose and buzzed angrily before returning to settling on the corpses of the two men, turning them back into moving black canvases.

Sickened, Axel slammed the door behind him, hand over mouth fighting the urge to vomit. There was nothing he could do for them. Thumper hadn't even given them a chance, they were still bound and gagged when he slit their throats. The keys to the bikes were not in the ignitions and there was no way he was going to wade through all the blood to look in the dead men's pockets trying to find them. Thumper had probably thrown them into the forest anyway.

His powerful legs did not slacken in pace as he raced out of the compound along the tracks then up the hill to the main house, small puffs of dirt exploding around his feet at every step.

Muscles burning and struggling to regain his breath, a similar scene greeted him, except the bodies were not tied up, showing Axel that Thumper was sadistically efficient at what he did. Mad Dog lay on the veranda face down, indicating his throat had been slit from behind. Jeckle's body was in the middle of the living room, same scenario face down, but the unnecessary slash across Vipers throat revolted him the most. Viper had already been dead, so it served no purpose.

Fear for Josephine flooded his mind, he grabbed his keys from the kitchen bench where he had tossed them what felt like years ago. Flinging open the fridge door and grabbing a bottle of water, he didn't bother to stop to close it as he raced outside. Taking a huge gulp and swishing the cold liquid around his mouth before spitting it into the garden had little effect in removing the taste of death from his taste buds.

Standing by his bike he took a precious moment to listen to his surroundings. The distant tinny whine of a bike going flat chat away from the plateau, into the hills, that he had heard as he jogged to the upper circle house was long gone. Sirens, probably fire brigade along with the police, were getting louder with every rise of the wail.

A rustle off to right had him in a crouch, his knife in his hand and ready to throw,

Beth screamed and put her hands over her face.

Axel put his knife away and rushed over to her side. She was unhurt, but traumatised.

"What's happening, The Hell Raisers came, started hitting Viper. I jumped over the end of the veranda; don't think they saw me. I saw Thumper come out covered in blood, but he didn't see me either. I am too scared to go inside, and I don't know what to do, I am worried about Babs and Freckles"

"It's going to be ok, Beth." He hugged the woman close; he could see she was coming down off a high. She was older than the rest and had a mean streak in her when she was on ice but seeing her like this made him realise a lot of people needed help. Society label people, slotting them into preconceived moulds, he knew her abusive family background. Made a few bad choices along the way, given half the chance to work towards a better life and she would take it. The thought hit home. He was not a bad person either.

"Don't go in there." He had to tell it blunt. "They are all dead, except Spike. She went bush."

Fresh tears filled her eyes.

"Sorry, Beth. You will be ok, but I have to go and save Jo and Mouse."

"What will I do?" she looked up at him with fearful eyes.

"Stay here, hide back in the bush if you feel better. Thumper has long gone, and a government rescue squad is on its way. You will be safe with them."

"Will they arrest me?"

"We are both at crossroads, Beth. It is up to you to choose. You can go bush or you can stay and face what you have done, the choice is yours."

"What about you?"

"Once I have seen that Jo and Mouse are ok, I'll be back to face the music, I know the path I want to tread."

She gave him a brief hug. "I'll sit here and think about it. Thanks Phantom."

Axel was desperate to be off. He felt like time was running out. Nodding to Beth he kicked his bike into gear at and took off at neck breaking speed.

The wind from the rotor blades flicked Jo's hair into a frenzy. Bits of dust and small rocks flew into the air and were tossed about as if in a cyclone and she threw her arms in front of her face for protection. Squinting against the swirling debris, Jo watched the chopper settle with grace and ease between the glowing green beacons and slow the rotor speed.

Robert Jnr and four men jumped lightly to the ground and made their way over to the far side. Jo launched herself into her brother's arms and gave him the biggest bear hug she could muster. Ever the emotionless leader and so typically like their father, he disengaged her arms from around his neck, but not before he gave her a quick tight hug in return.

Mouse came out from her hiding spot and stood uncertain with one arm protecting the baby, the other clutching her backpack tight in her fist. Robert signalled one of the men to help get her settled in the chopper, then turned back and surprised his baby sister by giving her an extra hug.

"What news do you have for me? There's a heck of a fire burning near the bottom of the hill." He pulled her further away from the noise of the chopper so they could talk without yelling.

"I think it's the bikies lower house," supplied Jo, worry evident on her face about the occupants.

"Looks like it. I spoke to Steven, the ground force, squad were just about to go in. They are on radio silence. I received a green buzz a short while ago so things are fine with them for now. As soon as he can he will contact us with what's going down. Meanwhile the boys and I will go down, link up with Kevin and wrap things up."

The glow-sticks mixed with the clear moonlight gave an eerie glow to the whole plateau, almost like dawn on a tropical stormy morning. Robert put his hand reassuringly on her shoulder. "We were worried when Kevin rang through you were missing, any idea where he will be." Jo handed him the traverser, "He is at these co-ordinates, injured but safe and ok tucked inside a large strangler fig tree."

Robert reached up to the fading purple mark on her cheek, his touch remarkably gentle for such a large man.

"What happened to you? Axel Stone, Phantom, he's not the one who hit you is he?"

"No, he would never do that, and for the record, look out for him. I trust him with my life." Her voice was filled with passion and truth.

"Good enough for me." He looked over to where his men were waiting. "I would stay Jo, but I've got a job to do. My orders are to put you on the chopper." He looked as if he expected resistance, raising his eyes in surprise when she just nodded.

She knew they must to keep the momentum going even though there was so much she wanted to talk about, she desperately wanted to tell him about Axel, about Patrick, find out more about Willow and share what she and Kevin had been through. She could see Robert had already switched to the task ahead. He spoke again.

"The chopper is going straight to Cairns Base Hospital, so the child can get the proper care and be reunited with her mother. A second chopper is on standby, with another squad so we can use that for Kevin and anyone else that may need it. Stephen has an office already set up in Cairns from the case he is working on with Matthew. He will meet and debrief you there."

Jo knew she had changed. In the past if one of her brothers had given orders, she would raise her hackles quick smart. There was nothing she would rather do than stay in the action and find Axel, but she knew she must see her part of the job through. She looked at the chopper, Mouse and the baby were snug inside, and the pilot had been keeping the machine just on the ground, ready for a quick take off. Robert had been leaning in close to make himself heard over the methodical thumping of the rotors.

"I'll bring them back," he promised.

Jo nodded her understanding, trusting her brother to do just that. *Them*. With such a simple word he had included Axel as an important part of the rescue. She gave a salute of good luck, climbing quickly into the chopper before he saw the tears forming in her eyes.

As the rotors picked up speed for take-off, she watched Robert and his men scale over the plateau edge and realised too late, she could have told them about the short cut through the crevice and about Feral who had gone over the edge. Nothing could be done about that now. She reached across and squeezed Mouse's hand as the chopper began to lift off into the dawning sky.

CHAPTER 47

A xel knew he was too late. After hearing the single gunshot and realising it came from the plateau, he had ridden with reckless abandon and ended up stacking his bike. With cuts and bruises, he continued relentlessly on foot, tapping into stamina he never knew he had. When he heard the chopper come into land, he pushed himself to the absolute limit, making it as far the bottom of the path to the cave before he heard it pick up speed and take off.

He sat on the ground in defeat, stifling his ragged breath so he could hear any possible sounds of life. A small stone tinkled over the rocks to his left and he was instantly alert. Blending into the background he shifted slightly so he was protected by a boulder.

A few short moments later, five silent figures materialised at the bottom of the escarpment, continuing stealthily, until the forest swallowed them as if they had never existed. They had to be the rescue squad. For a slight happy moment, he thought maybe Jo had geared up, but logic clicked in and he realised they were all far too tall. He stayed still and quiet letting them pass. It dawned on him then, that they should have come down the path from the cave, Jo would have told them it was by far the quicker way.

Dread filled his thoughts. The gun shot. Jo. Feral, the only one unaccounted for, Mouse. Ruby. Wild scenarios running rampant became almost unbearable. He fought for control, pushing away the 'what ifs' that threatened to engulf him. Needing to move, he rose to his feet, deciding to go up onto the plateau. Once there, he could see if there was any evidence of what had happened, then he could sit quietly and work out what he was going to do.

His foot nudged Jo's backpack which was just inside the crevice. Why hadn't she taken it with her? Fear resurfaced. He pushed it back beneath his subconscious. Death was not an option. He squeezed through the crack in the rocks.

Cool refreshing air licked at his face as he observed the glowing green beacons pushed out of formation by the down draft of air. The chopper's beat faded away into the distance. Maybe it would come back, perhaps with Jo in it, once Mouse and the baby were safely settled somewhere.

Disappointment and uncertainty took hold. It was only now he realised how much he had been banking on finding Jo still on the plateau waiting for him. Standing at the edge of the rocks looking out over the hills and valley below, he watched the blink of the chopper's lights slowly being swallowed by the dawning sky until they winked out of existence. He was not going to let that happen to his love for Josephine.

Jo thought about Mouse's last sign movements. That woman proved to be so much more than what she seemed on the surface. Her deep insight, a smooth intuition and a hidden strength was all concealed by her shy exterior. With confident movements she had told and shown Jo what to do in a short, clear and precise way.

With a sweep of her hand, and then the curling of her index fingers and pointing them down, Mouse had signed 'you stay,' followed with a 'we safe.' Mouse smiled big and wide as she did a sideways thumbs up and rotated it in a circle for 'okay.' With that said she had reached over and placed a hand on the pilots' shoulder, indicating for him to wait. She practically shoved Jo out of the door as the chopper dropped back to hover inches above the ground. Her final smile and wave as the chopper took off sent Jo crying anew.

From her shadowed perch, where Jo had sat to gather her thoughts and dry her tears, she watched the man walk out onto the plateau. She immediately knew who he was. His sexy rolling gait, broad shoulders and wild dark hair sang to her in a way she couldn't explain. After savouring a few stolen moments to admire the man she loved, Jo slid off the rock and stepped out into the light, softly calling his name.

He turned at the sound. Surprise, disbelief, and then undeniable joy radiated from his soul.

She ran towards him, saw him do the same and then she was in his arms as he twirled her around and around before lowering her to the ground, keeping his hands firmly around her waist. She clung on tightly around his neck never wanting to let him go.

They went to speak at the same time, stopped, then went to start again. Laughing they hugged each other tight and when he smiled it was the warmest, sexiest thing she had ever seen. Vibrant blue connected with glistening green, and all the things not yet said became irrelevant as they instinctively knew there was nothing they couldn't accomplish together.

Standing silhouetted by the rising sun, his mouth met hers in a kiss of infinite tenderness, a warm discovery of truth and trust. It was a kiss of everlasting love.

Also By

A **Hostage To Love**
Book 2 in the romantic suspense series – *All Roads Lead to Love* by Brenda May – set in the tropics of Northern of Australia.

#Rule number two for an undercover... *Never* get too close to the hostage.

Undercover agent Matt Brennan is committed to doing almost anything to infiltrate the highest levels of the crime syndicate responsible for his brother's death, and if that means pulling off a jewellery heist, then that's what he'll do. When an off-duty Amazon gets tangled up in his plans, he has no choice but to protect her the best way he can. One look into her obstinate hazel eyes and his perfect scheme begins to unravel as he starts to think about more than her safety...

Kellee McGlover is a police officer on forced leave after being shot in the back by a traitor to her department, her lover. She's sworn off bad boys for life, but her vacation hits a hurdle when she's kidnapped by a charismatic thief and carried off for leverage. When the next step in their criminal plans involves her being auctioned on the black market, she is faced with a dilemma, can she give her trust to a stranger with a cheeky, lopsided grin and keep her heart out of it?

About Author

B renda May worked and lived on a tropical island and in remote Cape York Wilderness areas, before settling down in Far North Queensland with her partner to raise their two daughters. After successfully running a wildlife tour business for twenty years, she now lives in Innisfail caring for her daughter's two adorable Papillons, who may just appear in one of her books. Her passion is writing and interweaving it with her love and knowledge of the flora and fauna of the Australian landscape.

You can find out more about the author and her books from her website brendamaywriter.com

From there you can sign up to her newsletter, check out her social media and keep up to date with new releases.

I hope you enjoyed the first book in the series of All Roads Lead to Love and leave it a great review.

ACKNOWLEDGMENTS

First and foremost, to my writers' group, Licualawinq. Licuala Writers in North Queensland. A wonderfully eclectic bunch of inspiration and encouragement. Thank you one and all for your ongoing support. A special thanks to Margaret Saunders for dotting my I's and crossing my T's.

To Jacque Duffy, who took my dust gathering manuscript out of the bottom of my wardrobe and encouraged me to breath it back to life. I am eternally grateful. My gosh, it was embarrassingly raw and only half the size then, but your input and enthusiasm helped create the novel it is today.

Where would this book have been without my Beta readers, with special thanks to Jordan Harley, your cinematic approach is perfect to see how a story flows and Kellee Sloan, you're a star, in fact I named the main character in my next book after you.

To the wonderfully intelligent Sue Chapman, who taught me more about the English language than school ever could. I thank you.

I am in debt to my structural editor Deonie Fiford, for your advice and encouraging kind words that lifted my novel to another level.

And last but never least, to fellow author K.A.Allen. Ken, words are not enough to express my gratitude for lifting this old fossil into the modern world of self-belief and publishing. Your patience and dedication have been greatly appreciated. This book would not have made its debut if not for you. You have my humble thanks.

www.ingramcontent.com/pod-product-compliance
Lightning Source LLC
Chambersburg PA
CBHW020347120726
47904CB00002B/484